HERE COMES CHAOS

A SLEIGHVILLE NOVEL

BOOK 2

AMANDA SIEGRIST

McCord Family Novel

Protecting You

Trust in Love

Deserving You

Always Kind of Love

Finding You

Dare You to Love

Mona & Mason

The Paranormal Chronicles, Volume I

Perfect For You Novel

The Wrong Brother

The Right Time

The Easy Part

The Hard Choice

Psychic Love Novel

Exploding Love

Captured Love

Slaying Love Novel

Won't Let You Go

Doomed Love

Deadly Crazy

Evidence of Sin

Finding Redemption

Obsessed Hope

Short Stories

Paint By Murder

Follow Me, Sweet Darling

Sleighville Novel

Dashing Through the Fear

Here Comes Chaos

The Last Noel

Standalone Novel

The Danger with Love

Conquering Fear Novel

Co-written with Jane Blythe

Drowning in You

Out of the Darkness

Closing In

1

THE LINES BEFORE HIM BLURRED. Everything went out of focus. He didn't want to do anything but crawl underneath his desk and hide from the world.

A loud beep had him jumping in his seat.

Bryce hit the intercom button that would patch him through to his secretary, Rebecca—a godsend that he wouldn't be able to live without. Right now, he wished nothing existed, even her and her coordinated and organized ways.

"Yes, Becca." He made sure to add in the cheeriness. If she knew he had too many troubles on his mind, she'd force him to spill them all. She could bulldoze through any problem. Most times, it was a brilliant thing to witness. But this latest problem...

Well, no one could save his marriage. Not even him.

"She's here."

Oh damn.

The very person he'd been trying to avoid all week had decided she'd had enough of his absence.

"Ms. Lila Hansley."

So not his wife.

A glance at his open planner lying on his desk told him exactly who she was and why he shouldn't be surprised. It'd been jotted down there for the past week.

"Yes, of course. Thank you, Becca. I'll be right out." Well, as soon as he composed himself and looked like the professional he was.

The damn mayor of Sleighville.

His office was the largest on the floor. Not that he had demanded any such thing when he took office. It had always been that way. The building was built in the early 1900s, many positions shuffling around the building. At one time, over fifty years ago, the head judge had occupied the room. The whole floor had been designated for the judges and lawyers, until one mayor had decided they didn't like being cooped up in a tiny room on the first floor as if insignificant. The two departments swapped floors and it'd been like that ever since.

It was an honor to hold the position, and it wasn't one he took lightly either.

He checked himself in the mirror, even though he knew not even a strand of hair would be out of place. A nasty habit he'd developed because every time he was around Denise, she nitpicked every part of him. Your tie is crooked. Your hair is flat. Your shirt needs to be tucked in better. Why is there a scuff mark on your shoe? To avoid those remarks, he always double-checked—hell, triple and quadruple checked—his appearance.

He couldn't even remember when the snide remarks started in the marriage. But he knew he would've never married her if she'd displayed that dark part of her before they tied the knot.

Just as he took his job seriously, his marriage was no

different. He might be the unhappiest he'd ever been in life, but he'd never ask for a divorce.

She took the option out of his hands, demanding one.

He let out a small breath before walking out of his office with the friendly mayoral smile he wore around town.

"Ms. Hansley. Welcome to Sleighville. I hope your travels were pleasant." He walked up to the woman seated in one of the chairs against the wall and held out his hand.

She stood and shook hands. Though she wore a smile, he swore it was as fake as his own.

"Roads were a bit rough, but I made it in one piece so I can't complain."

She rubbed her hand on her thigh. He couldn't be sure if it was a nervous gesture or her trying to rub his germs off. Was his hand sweaty? Was the turmoil he'd been suffering in his office sticking with him? He could normally shake that off with a flick of his wrist.

"Let's chat in my office. Becca, if it's not too much trouble, could you get us some hot chocolate?"

"Of course."

"Oh, it's not necessary."

Becca and Ms. Hansley stared at each other after speaking at the same time. Becca wasn't one to lose a battle, if a person wanted to consider the simple request one. But she knew how important this meeting was. How vital it was to their little town for everything to work out.

"After such a long, dreary drive, hot chocolate is the perfect thing for you. No one does it better than Sleighville." Becca widened her cheery smile with a hint of determination and walked away before Ms. Hansley could argue.

As a general rule, he didn't ask Becca to run and get him any kind of drink. As his secretary, she had a tremendous amount of work to do, and adding on a task he was quite capable of handling on his own wasn't fair—not in his eyes. But he wasn't sure if he was up to the task. His nerves still hadn't settled after reading the document he had—for the billionth time. The last thing he wanted to do was spill hot chocolate all over himself and their guest.

He gestured toward the chair in front of his desk, then rounded it and sat down, scooping up the papers and shoving them into the top drawer. He'd worry about all those troubles later.

"My apologies, Ms. Hansley. I forgot to introduce myself. I'm Bryce Stuart, the mayor of Sleighville."

Which, of course, she knew. That had been her destination from the beginning. But as a professional, it should've been the first thing he had done. Introduce himself.

"You can call me Lila."

He leaned back in his chair, though not too loose as to imply he didn't have good posture or anything, but he wanted her to feel at ease. If using their first names also helped, then he was all for it. Not that he was big on people calling him Mr. Mayor or anything. He tended to be a pretty informal guy. He wanted to feel approachable and liked.

"I insist you call me Bryce. I want everything to go smoothly between us."

She smiled, yet said nothing else.

Another fake smile, if he had to guess.

He shouldn't be surprised by her lack of enthusiasm. The task before her would be enormous. Not many wanted to take it on. *He* didn't even want to deal with it.

The past summer had not been kind to their small town. Finding out one of its trusted members was a disgusting pervert had been hard to swallow. A man who had been involved in things like the Fourth of July festival, the Labor Day parade, and Thanksgiving events. Not to mention all the festivities when the actual Christmas holiday rolled around.

As a town that celebrated Christmas every day of the year, it had to keep up its appearance and feel welcoming and safe.

Mark Wilson had had access to all the places in town for rent, considering his sister was the realtor who dealt with it all. With that privilege, he'd turned it into a nightmare. He'd installed cameras in all the properties, spying on people, ruining their privacy. Making them feel wholly violated.

Since he'd been caught, the newspapers hadn't been kind. The media tore their town apart and painted it as the worst place to visit.

It killed them the last few months. Even in December, two months ago, when the real Christmas arrived, tourism had plummeted to the point most places struggled to stay open. For a town that lived off the festive holiday, it was unacceptable. Bryce had been forced to hire a public relations company to turn their image around. To get people to love Sleighville again.

Here sat the answer to all his problems—well, the town's problems—right in front of him. Lila Hansley would be their savior.

Hopefully.

It had taken contacting five PR companies before one accepted the job. Since he started with the best first, he hoped he hadn't gotten the rotten of the pile.

The woman herself was put together. She sat poised with a determined look on her face. The weather wasn't great, and for February, not a surprise. He didn't expect all women to wear skirts or anything, even if that was a fashion statement his wife thought was a must. Lila wore black slacks with a white blouse and a sharp-looking blazer over it. Black, sensible high heels. Nothing too pointy and diffi-cult to walk in, but not plain either. Another thing Denise would've snickered at. She thought all women should wear shoes that killed their feet—even themselves—or why bother leaving the house.

Her blonde hair was down, not pulled into a fancy chignon Denise loved to wear. Soft waves that he wasn't sure if they were natural or if she put the effort into it and curled it. When Juliet, his sister, had a special event or a date, she curled her hair, otherwise she liked to throw it in a messy ponytail and out of her face.

And why was he focusing on the woman's hair? He had more important things to attend to.

"What did you think of the town as you drove in?"

First impressions were everything. Some tourists became regular visitors when they happened to drive through without realizing it was a town that celebrated Christmas year-round.

"Well—" She paused when Becca strolled back into the office.

"Hot, steaming cup of hot chocolate. I promise you, the best you've ever had."

Becca set a cup in front of him and the other near Lila. She departed before Lila had a chance to pick it up and take a sip. She wasn't one to hover. At least, she picked and chose when to do so. Becca knew now was not the time to get into Lila's face. That was his job.

He grabbed his mug, a white cup with Santa and his eight reindeer wrapped around the ceramic piece. Lila's had a bunch of elves dancing.

"Cheers. Here's to Christmas."

He held out his mug, hoping his cheeriness was just

right. His smile just as perfect. The inflection in his tone showing none of the tension he'd been drowning in earlier.

A TINY, invisible breath released before she picked up her mug. At least, she hoped it hadn't been witnessed. She didn't need this man to know she was in way over her head with this project.

She liked to think all the many jobs she had over the years prepared her for anything. Like now. Being a world-class actress. She'd been an extra in two movies a few years ago. They were B flicks and never even made it to the theater, but still. She also hadn't had any lines, more like a silhouette in the background. But again, still. She'd been an actress once. She could pretend right now.

"Cheers." With a light clink, she met his mug with her own. Though her hand shook, and she was grateful she didn't spill a drop of the hot drink. No need to embarrass herself—yet.

"Well?"

His smile didn't ease any of the discomfort swimming through her veins. What was he expecting from her? That the hot chocolate was as divine as Becca had promised.

"It's delicious." She squinted, taking another sip and swirling it in her mouth. "Do I detect a bit of Baileys in it?"

The mayor, for the first time, showed his own discomfort, and it helped to reduce a teeny portion of hers.

"I cannot confirm nor deny that. I don't prepare the hot chocolates around here. I only drink them."

She giggled, then snorted. Her eyes widened at the faux pas, mortified she let that slip out. But when she found something hilarious, she couldn't help herself. It went from an innocent giggle to a snort in the blink of an eye.

He leaned forward and his smile brightened even more, and this time she sensed it wasn't as fake as all the other ones had been. Not the smarmy politician smile that thought it would convince anyone to do anything.

"I also taste some peppermint. The ton of mini marshmallows add a special touch. And the cinnamon on top is delicious." When one wanted to avoid further embarrassment, pretend it never happened. At least, that was her motto in life.

Whether he wanted to avoid the truth, she knew better. There was no doubt in her mind Becca had added a splash of Baileys in the hot chocolate. She would know. She'd bartended for five months. It'd been an intense five months behind the bar, learning drink after drink, and because she couldn't help herself, taste testing lots of liquor. Her partner in crime at the time, Manny, insisted that a bartender shouldn't merely know how to make a drink, they needed to know how it should taste to perfection. She could make a mean chocolate martini, and one of the key ingredients was Baileys.

"I'm glad you like it. A touch of Christmas here and there is what we're known for."

A touch of Christmas?

More like Christmas threw up everywhere.

He relaxed back in his chair again. "I'd love to know your thoughts about the drive into town."

Horrifying!

"It felt...welcoming."

The first large sign she had seen, she cringed. *Welcome to Sleighville. Where you are sure to have a holly, jolly time.*

Honestly, there was nothing to change there because she

knew it was a slogan meant to instill the holiday spirit. At this point in time, changing the town name itself was out of the question. But Sleighville? Maybe it was the horror fan inside her, but her mind went dark hearing the name. Like a slasher film about to come alive.

Bryce's smile died and a slight huff escaped. She imagined he hadn't meant to reveal that when he straightened his body as if that would erase the sound he'd emitted.

"What didn't you like?"

Well, the town name didn't help its case. The sign itself was decent. Then driving down Main Street and seeing the Christmas lights strung up in all the window shops. Santa and his reindeer hanging out in the middle of the square. A large Christmas tree near them lit up in its glory. Some shops had Valentine's decorations mixed in as well, and it all looked...odd.

Where did she begin?

Not with the truth.

Because the truth was she didn't like Christmas.

She wouldn't go as far as hate because, well, that was a strong word and she rarely used it unless necessary. But when the holiday rolled around, she didn't get into all the hoopla surrounding it. She bought presents, but only when it was mandatory. Like the secret Santa exchange her work insisted on this past year. Of course, for her family as well because she wasn't a complete Scrooge.

"I can't say anything I didn't particularly like. It all screams Christmas when you drive through town. If it weren't February, I'd think the holiday was approaching for real. That's a good start to a great image. That's what you want to portray."

She said it so professionally and like she knew what the hell she was talking about. Yay her!

"Okay, that's good. You had me worried for a second."

She waved her hand in the air as if telling him not to worry at all. Everything would work out splendidly.

"The problem is, you need more merriness." If a bathroom were nearby, she would've rushed out and puked after saying that. Lying never felt right to her, but in this job, she'd learned that telling the truth put you in the hot seat.

Case in point—stuck on a mission to turn a Christmas town into the merriest place in the world when she disliked the holiday and screwed up her last PR campaign.

Her boss literally hated her.

His brilliant smile reappeared. "That's why we hired you."

She took another sip of her hot chocolate to stop from blurting out anything inappropriate. Like why in the hell he'd work with the shit company she continued to let boss her around.

"I'd love to know some of the ideas you have." He leaned forward again as if excited about the prospect of inserting more cheeriness into the town. "You do have some ideas, right?"

She might not care for the holiday, and she despised her boss when he inflicted this assignment on her, but she was a professional. At all times. No matter the job she held at the moment.

Bending down to the ground where she set her bag, she then pulled out a manila folder. "I put together a few things I thought we could start with. This will not be a quick task. I read what happened and…" She couldn't help but wince. "It is disturbing to think about. Especially for anyone wanting to even rent a place here. Is his sister still employed at the realtor's office?"

Bryce shook his head. "She moved out of town after it all

happened. The rental properties have suffered around town. It was a big part of revenue for quite a few residents. The city itself owns a few properties, and they haven't been rented in at least three months. Big losses everywhere.

"My sister-in-law is Eve Carrington. She owns Carrington Hotels, a big chain down in Florida. She has a great idea to build small cottages around town. You know, really give that magical Christmas experience, though she has hit a snag with the board of directors. They want a hotel, and she wants cottages. They are at a stalemate right now."

Most of what he said was good to know. She wasn't quite sure why he mentioned his sister-in-law other than to brag. Because if the cottages weren't even built, she didn't care. There was nothing she could do with that. So she decided to ignore that piece of information.

"I would like to meet the new realtor. That is one place to start building a better image."

"Of course." Bryce pressed a button on the phone. "Becca, please set up a meeting with Joy. Lila would like to meet her."

"I'm on it."

Lila appreciated Becca's confident response. She had no doubt that if Bryce asked for something—even something unattainable—Becca would make it happen. She had that poise about her.

"Her name is Joy?" She could feel another giggle rising to the surface, which meant a horrid snort would follow. She had to push it deep down so it wouldn't escape.

"It wasn't planned." Bryce's lips twisted into a short wince.

"It's perfect. I love her name. We are going to roll with that."

That confidence she recognized in Becca sprouted in Bryce. She liked the look on him as well.

A quick knock sounded on the doorframe. She twisted around to see a man dressed in uniform and it had her heart pumping in an instant. Why were the cops here?

"I don't mean to interrupt."

Bryce looked braced for the worst. "What happened?"

"The cafe's on fire."

Bryce jerked from his seat, shoving his chair back so hard it hit the wall behind him. "Juliet? Eve?"

"Both fine. Everyone got out, but the kitchen is in flames. I don't know what went wrong yet." The man looked at her. "Thank god you're here. You can start with this debacle."

A fire wasn't her forte. If it started in the kitchen, then it sounded like an accident. It would make her job worse if it turned out *not* to be an accident.

By the grim looks on both their faces, she had a feeling she was stepping into chaos.

2

He didn't say a word when Lila followed him and his brother, Griffin—also the chief of police—out of the office. They dashed out of the building and down the sidewalk a short distance before crossing the road toward the cafe.

The traffic had stopped. A big fire truck in the middle of the road would do that. People were milling around outside, but the police department was handling crowd control. Griffin and his team were nothing but efficient.

Lila stood by him not saying a word, though her eyes cased the area like a hard-nosed detective arriving on the scene. Griffin stood on the other side, then shot off like a rocket when he saw Eve standing in front of Tidings and Joy Apparel, Shannon's clothing store, next to Juliet.

"Come on. You can meet my sister." He and Lila made their way in the same direction.

Despite the commotion, he made quick introductions with everyone, then it turned silent. It felt like ages as the fire crew tackled the flaming beast. In reality, no more than twenty minutes had gone by. The entire time, everyone remained quiet.

Fire Chief Noah Brach approached them in his turnout gear. Like his brother, being in charge didn't mean he didn't get his hands dirty like his crew.

"The kitchen is torched. We managed to save the front, but..." He looked chagrined. "There's a bit of water damage. Sorry about that."

Juliet shook her head. "You have nothing to be sorry about. Thank you for your quick response."

"What happened?" Griffin asked, demanding the question he'd been thinking since Griffin stormed into his office.

Juliet shrugged. "I don't know. I was in the front with Eve and Tabitha. Breakfast rush, you know. Chip was making his bread. So delicious." Juliet's smile, though weak, brought out more smiles around her, which had been her goal, he knew. "He popped out to say he was using the bathroom. I didn't think anything of it. Nothing was in the oven yet. A minute later, smoke started billowing out from under the door. I rushed over there—"

"Seriously, Jules!"

Her lips twisted with malice as if she couldn't believe he'd interrupt her. But what the hell was his sister thinking? When smoke appeared, a person should run and call the fire department, not go and check it out.

"As I was saying, I rushed over there and peeked inside. The flames were everywhere." She gave him a dead-eye stare. "So I called the fire department."

He pressed his lips into a tight line to keep a retort in. The last thing he wanted to do was get into an argument with his sister, but her recklessness bothered him.

"Any issues with the equipment? The oven? The fridge? Anything electrical?" Chief Brach asked.

"No. Everything is up to code. I have no idea what could've gone wrong."

Griffin sighed. "And no one was in the kitchen to see what happened. Was the back door locked?" This time Griffin looked at her with a scolding expression as he had done. "Or was it propped open like you do sometimes? Something I've told you not to do."

Juliet crossed her arms. "I prop it open when there's a delivery. It's easier that way. And no, it wasn't at that time because I had no deliveries!"

Chief Brach chuckled under his breath, not fazed by their sibling squabbling. They were known for it, but also known to be very close. They might argue and fight, but they never held grudges against each other.

With the past violent history Juliet had to endure from her ex-husband, Bryce worried about his sister. Especially when she kept the abuse from them for as long as she had. So, if she had any other issues going on, she might not tell them right away.

"We'll investigate and we'll let you know what we find. For right now, nobody goes inside there."

Juliet nodded, her eyes welling up with tears. "How long do you think it'll be before we can start cleaning up?"

"I'll be as quick as I can. But thorough." Chief Brach walked away.

Bryce decoded that as, it would be a few days. Juliet wasn't one to sit around and wait. She'd always been a go-getter. This would kill her.

"There's nothing we can do right now. Why don't I drive you home, Juliet?" Eve suggested, putting a comforting arm around her.

Juliet looked ready to argue, but nodded. Eve kissed Griffin, then the two ladies went on their way.

"What do you think?" he asked Griffin, knowing his

brother had an inkling. He always did about things. That's what made him such a good cop.

Griffin looked at Lila, who had remained quiet the entire time. She hadn't even offered different expressions at all the commotion to suggest what she was thinking. But her eyes had been hard as stone. She might not have been giving away her suspicions on the matter, but she was watching everything like a hawk. Griffin met his gaze. "I think we should reconvene in your office and let Ms. Hansley finish her hot chocolate."

"Lila is fine."

Griffin offered a short smile at her suggestion, then waved a hand for her to lead the way. It didn't take long to make it back to his office. Maybe it was his closed-off expression or Griffin's determined one, but no one stopped them to ask any questions. They knew when they didn't want to be disturbed. Even Becca didn't inquire about what happened. Though he knew Becca had been right in the fold, getting all the information she needed. Because that's what she did. She helped him stay ahead of the game as mayor.

Lila sat down first and picked up her mug, taking a sip. It had to be chilled by now, but she said nothing, taking another sip.

He took a seat as well, while Griffin took a spot by the wall, leaning against it with his arms crossed.

"I'm going to be candid." Griffin looked at Lila. "Is it okay if I'm candid here, Lila?"

"Of course."

His brother made eye contact with him, silent for a long moment. He heard the unasked question. Can we trust her? Should we trust her? His leveled stare answered it. Yes. Because they had no choice. She had to save the town from any pandemonium.

"How bad will it be if the fire was deliberate?"

Her brows puckered, contemplating Griffin's question. "Well, it's certainly not going to help the problem already present. A pervert, and now an arsonist. Do *you* even feel safe knowing someone intentionally could've done that?"

A sharp nod by Griffin was all that was needed. He agreed. To think someone would have deliberately set the cafe on fire frightened him. Why? Why the cafe? Why now? So many why's.

"How do we handle this?" Griffin asked, as if she had all the magical answers. Bryce sure in the hell hoped she did.

She glanced from him to his brother, then back to him. "We don't until we know for sure what happened. Speculating does no good for anyone."

"I should make a statement." Because that's what he did. He calmed the town down. That was easy enough. He could do that in his sleep. What he struggled with was bringing in new town members and tourists.

"And say what?" she asked with a sharpness in her tone. For the very first time. "You know nothing. It's easy to see there was a fire. For now, we wait on the fire chief to do his job and report back to us."

"I always make a statement." Because that was his job!

A crooked smile emerged along with a devilish glint in her eyes. "Do you always do as you should?"

Was this a trick question? It felt like one.

"Yes."

She giggled with a tiny snort escaping. She looked mortified for a hot second, then masked it as if it never happened.

"It's what makes him an annoyingly good mayor. Always making statements."

Bryce crossed his arms, frowning. "I like to keep the citizens of this town informed. An informed citizen is not a frightened one."

Lila clapped her hands, then picked up her folder she had left on his desk before they rushed to the fire. She opened it and laid the top sheet over on his side.

"Let's make a statement. Super brief. Like yes, there was a fire, it's being handled. After that, we move on to something fun and exciting."

Bryce picked up the piece of paper and read the contents, then he set it down.

"You want to have a carnival in the dead of winter?"

She crossed her arms, as if mimicking him from moments before. "You have a snowman building contest in the dead of summer. Should we argue which one is more odd?"

That sharp tone again. With a slash of her tongue.

He liked her forthrightness. Not too mean in her words, but firm to get her point across. He was being ridiculous questioning her ideas. She was the PR expert. Not him.

"Well, it's good we have the chief of police with us. We can talk about logistics and crowd control and such."

Griffin mock laughed. "If there's a crowd."

"Oh, there will be a crowd. But you need the right incentive to reel them in."

Bryce loved her optimism. The worry he'd had since deciding they needed to do something drastic to save their town started to dissipate. She would save them all.

"What kind of incentive?"

She smiled wide as she rubbed her hands in glee. "A big one."

"You didn't have to follow me here." Though Lila appreciated his kindness. The roads were bad, and he didn't want to see her get hurt. He had even offered to drive her to where she'd be staying for the foreseeable future. But she didn't want to be without a car, so she declined.

"I didn't mind. Come on. I'll show you around."

Lila followed Bryce up the surprisingly shoveled short pathway. The snow had returned and wasn't being kind at all. At least four inches had to have accumulated since she sat strategizing with the mayor and the chief of police. Of course, if this was the service the town provided, it would be a good thing to add when advertising rental properties.

Bryce unlocked the cottage door and deactivated the security system, then stood back to let her enter. She wiped her shoes on the festive rug decorated with candy canes and Christmas ornaments, then slid them off and dropped her bags to the floor. Bryce followed suit, wiping his feet and removing his shoes.

"It's small, but secure. New locks on all doors. A security system that will have you sleeping peacefully, and we stocked the pantry and fridge before your arrival."

Thoughtful. Another thing she appreciated about him. She hadn't thought of food, and she had no desire to leave the house again tonight.

"You didn't have to, but thank you."

He smiled. Not the smarmy politician smile she had received when she first met him, but a genuine, kindhearted smile. She preferred this one over the other one. It brightened his features and made him more handsome. Not that the man wasn't already handsome.

Dark brown hair that wasn't too long or too short. He had it styled to perfection with products she assumed to hold it in place, though it didn't look greasy or anything. His eyes were also brown with a friendliness in the depths she'd come to see more and more as the day drew on.

Her first impression had been a man with a chip on his shoulder, especially name-dropping his sister-in-law. That opinion had evaporated as the day wore along. And she always loved a man with a bit of facial hair. He had a goatee with a little fuzz around his jawline. Enough to make a woman want to swoon.

Which she didn't, of course. Because he was a married man. She'd look and appreciate the fine specimen, but she would never act on any attraction. Not to mention, she needed her job. Fooling around was a sure way to get fired.

Bryce showed her how to operate the security system and gave her a tour of the cottage. He hadn't fibbed when he said it was small. She'd describe it more like tiny. Super tiny. The living room connected with the kitchen. A short hallway brought her to the bathroom and the lone bedroom. That was it. No basement or any other rooms to be found. It had a small backyard that looked out into the woods. It was pretty watching the snow fall. She'd do that later—watch it—when she was alone.

"My brother, Griffin, lives right next door. He owns the cottage. If you need anything, don't hesitate to knock on his door." Bryce pointed toward the wall where, if it didn't exist, she'd see the house he was referring to. "And please, call me if you need anything. Anything at all."

She worked at a fancy restaurant for a short period. About three months. The manager had been a nice-looking man in his thirties. Dressed professionally. Clean-cut appearance all around. Not a strand of hair out of place, smooth cheeks. He was the epitome of a gentleman. Until he wasn't.

She'd heard that line before. *Call me for anything.* And

she had when she had trouble setting the alarm one night when she closed. Turned out nothing had been wrong with the alarm. The manager had created the problem to get her to call him and then he tried to get in her pants. The year of karate she'd taken had helped her in that situation. She never worked at a restaurant again or at a job that required her to close up by herself.

"Did I say something wrong?" Bryce's brows pleated as he stared at her with a bit of panic in his eyes.

She liked to think she had a good sense of reading people. Most of the time, anyway. She didn't sense a bad vibe from Bryce, but she also couldn't let her guard down. Not with anyone. Not in this day and age.

A weak smile appeared as she tried to wipe out any lingering memories of times best forgotten. "No, of course not. It's been a long day, and my thoughts are wandering right now. Thank you for all your kindness today. I appreciate it all."

That sweet smile reappeared. "Okay, good. Would you like to join us for supper tonight?" He pointed toward his brother's house again. "We'd love to have you."

"Thank you, but no. Another time."

He nodded and bid his good night.

She locked the door and set the alarm after he left. She put her bags in the bedroom, removing her PJs. First a shower, then scrounge for food.

By the time she had a full belly and clean skin, she felt more like herself. Traveling always wiped her out, and putting on a fake persona drained her. She'd flown in the day before, stayed the night in Minneapolis, and then driven to Sleighville early this morning. It'd been a very long two days of travel and work. She wanted to crash.

She grabbed her phone, dialing her sister, Zinnia.

"What's up, Lil? Did you make it okay?"

"I did. It's snowing right now. Already four inches."

"Eww."

Yeah, she had to agree. None of them were used to snow. Growing up on the west coast near the water made snow a very foreign thing to them. That's why she enjoyed staring outside watching it fall down so gracefully. It was another reason she appreciated Bryce offering to drive her home, since she wasn't used to driving in the nasty weather. But if she was going to be here for a while, she had to figure it out herself, which was also why she declined his offer.

"So, what's the town like?"

"Like Christmas puked everywhere."

They giggled together. Lila couldn't resist snorting as well.

Lila told her everything that happened, including the fire and her idea about the carnival.

"Well, what's the big draw to get people to come?"

She sighed at the simple question. "I didn't get that far in my bright idea. Though I think I have the mayor's approval. I just have to think of someone great." She rolled her eyes as she stood up from the dining room chair. "It's not like I know any celebrities."

"Call Aster. He could hook you up."

Yeah, her brother no doubt could. His band toured all around California, and while they weren't huge where the whole country knew their name, they had connections in the music industry.

"Maybe. I won't keep you. I called to check in. That's all."

"I love you, sis. Don't let this job scare you. You got this. Show that asshole what you're made of."

She promised she would and hung up. Though she didn't feel the strength in her promise as she said it.

Her last PR job working with a dog food company had blown up in her face. She thought she'd been doing all the right things, helping create a wonderful image when all she'd been doing was covering up the fact the company sold shit food. When more dogs started getting sick after using the food from that despicable company, instead of the fault landing on them, for some reason it landed on her. She'd been the villain for hyping up a company that essentially poisoned animals. How it'd been her fault, she still couldn't figure it out, but someone had to be the fall person, and they'd chosen her.

When the mayor of a small Christmas town called requesting their services, her boss threw her the case knowing she'd fail again and he could fire her ass for being incompetent. Because he figured this was a losing battle, turning this town around to something positive again. When it couldn't be done, it'd be so easy to lay the blame on her once again.

Well, she wasn't going to let that happen.

She'd make this the holliest, jolliest town there ever was.

Or die trying.

3

HE WIPED his face with the napkin, then tossed it on the plate. His gaze glided to the sliding glass door and the winter wonderland going on outside. Bryce wasn't looking forward to driving in the snow, but he wasn't going to shy away from Denise, even if she thought he would. Like he was some pansy or something. She might think he was, but he'd never drop to that level.

"Okay, what's going on with you?" Griffin asked as he stood up to put his dish in the sink.

Eve's graceful smile toward him made him nervous. She brushed his shoulder as if offering support and walked out of the room.

Damn it. He was being ambushed. He didn't like it.

Bryce leaned back in his chair, weighing his options. Keep ignoring the problem or let it all out?

Well, his brother wasn't one to back down, so it wasn't worth it to keep it in.

"Denise served me divorce papers."

Griffin slumped against the counter, crossing his arms. "I'm sorry, Bryce."

"Are you?" Because he knew Griffin and Juliet didn't like Denise. Even Eve, who got along with everyone, kept her distance from Denise.

Of course, in the beginning of their relationship, Griffin and Juliet had liked Denise. But as time went on, they noticed the change in her behavior, even if he tried to hide how she treated him. They'd told him a few times to let her go. To be the first one to leave. But he wasn't a quitter. He wasn't one to walk away without trying to fix the problem first.

Turned out, Denise thought *he* was the problem.

"I'm going to pretend you didn't say that to me." Griffin narrowed his eyes. "Because no matter my thoughts on that woman, I would never want you to be hurt. So yeah, I'm sorry she's doing this to you. That she continues to hurt you. I know how much you wanted to work through the issues between you two."

"I shouldn't be surprised. We haven't had sex in over six months. She hasn't smiled at me like she used to in..." He shook his head, trying to remember. "I don't even know. I don't know where it all went wrong."

Griffin shrugged. "I wish I knew the answer to that."

He bowed his head, blowing out a breath. "I need a lawyer. I'll call Darcy tomorrow. I don't want it to be a nasty divorce, but I'm not going to let her railroad me either." He looked at his brother. "I think she's having an affair."

Griffin nodded as if he knew the whole time, but Bryce knew that wasn't the case. If his brother had known something of that nature, he would've told him.

"Who?"

"I don't know, but I sense it. She works late. She doesn't touch me anymore. I swear I've smelled aftershave on her that isn't mine. I think she thinks I'm an idiot, that I wouldn't notice."

"Well, in addition to a lawyer, let's hire a PI as well."

Bryce stood up, cleaning up his plate. "I'm sure the news will get out soon enough, but I'd appreciate it if we didn't talk about it outside of this house for right now."

"I have your back, Bryce. Always."

He said good night to Eve, gave Walter, Griffin's old-soul cat, a few rubs, then made his way home. He took the roads with care, though still got home at a decent time. No surprise when he entered a darkened house. Denise was gone as usual and wouldn't return until very late. No doubt would claim she had to work late. Nothing but lies. He saw that now. Something he should've seen months ago.

Boxes of Christmas decorations were sitting in the living room and the tree was in the corner, though nothing was on it yet. He wondered why the hell she had pulled out the decorations. It was one thing to doll up the house on the outside with festive cheer. The tourists loved to see that kind of thing while driving around town. But it was another thing to do it inside. Most folks around town didn't do that. A person could only take the holiday paraphernalia so much.

What was Denise trying to do?

Make him go insane with the decorations blasted in his face. He wasn't about to start a war over something so ridiculous. He'd let her put up the tree and decorate it to her heart's content.

He still didn't see her the next morning, wondering where she'd spent the night. Amazing how she'd served him divorce papers and didn't even pretend anymore she wasn't having an affair. Being so blatant about it. What a bitch!

He felt bad after that thought rolled through his mind. He had loved her at one time. Now that love was hard to conjure, but it didn't mean he should resort to thinking such horrible things about her.

Becca greeted him with the cheerful smile she always wore and as if she knew nothing about his troubles. Perhaps she didn't, but he doubted that. Becca was always one step ahead of the game. By eight thirty he was ready for his third cup of coffee. To his pleasant surprise, Lila had brought him one.

"Sorry I'm late. I'm not used to driving in the snow," she said as she set a cup in front of him and took a seat.

"We didn't set a time to meet yesterday, so I wouldn't say you're late." He picked up the cup, smiling. "This is much appreciated. I was craving another cup."

"And what number are you on?"

"This is the third."

She eyed him for a while, before losing her smile. "When I drink copious amounts of coffee, it means I'm stressed. This cup is my fourth. What has you stressed, Mr. Mayor?"

He set his cup down, gauging whether to be brutally honest or go for the joking manner to blow off the truth. In a split second, he decided. "My wife served me divorce papers. Also, I insist you call me Bryce. What has you stressed?"

"This job."

He couldn't argue with that. He felt the weight on his shoulders about that issue as well. Surprise filtered in that she didn't comment about his divorce. Most people would've jumped on that piece of news right away—then answer the question.

"It is a large task ahead of you. I'm sorry."

Her mouth curved into a beautiful smile as she waved her hand frivolously in the air. "Not your fault, so please don't apologize for anything. I'm sorry about your wife."

Finally a comment about it, but nothing too invasive. He appreciated her approach on the subject, since it wasn't something he wanted to talk about, even though he'd been the one to mention it.

He mimicked her gesture while offering the same sweet grin. "Unfortunately, I should've seen it coming. It hasn't been a happy marriage in a long time. So please don't apologize for that." He picked up his cup, clearing his throat. "Well, now that we have that out of the way. Where are we starting today?"

Lila set the same folder she'd had with her yesterday on the desk and opened it. She also pulled a notebook out of her bag, perching it on her lap with a pencil ready in her hand. "The carnival. I do have to make some calls about operating rides and such in this kind of weather and see if it's even plausible. The games aspect should not be a problem, but to get the full effect, I want the rides too."

"The funhouse is my favorite."

She giggle-snorted. He found the sound rather adorable and couldn't hide his smile.

"And what's funny about that?"

She covered her mouth as if that would hide her infectious grin. "I don't know why I giggled. I guess I didn't expect that to be your favorite."

Hmm. What had she expected?

"And what's yours?"

"The zipper. I love the thrill of it."

"Well, that's why I love the funhouse."

They stared at each other for the longest time before she broke the gaze first. From there, they talked about logistics. She mentioned she was working on finding the star of the carnival to reel in the spectators. Though she didn't mention who that'd be yet. Bryce had full confidence that she'd pull it off.

He looked at the time and shuffled the papers they'd been working with back into her folder. "We have to go. Becca made an appointment with Joy for ten o'clock, and if we don't leave now, we'll be late."

"Of course."

They left his office and walked to his car where he drove to the realtor's office. Joy wasn't as peppy as Mindy had been, and considering her name, one would think she'd be a bit more cheerful. But one didn't choose their name as a baby, so he couldn't fault her for it.

He made introductions as they took a seat at a table. He sat by Lila while Joy sat on the other side.

"How can I help you, Ms. Hansley?" Joy asked with the right amount of professionalism. Her smile was simple and not too bright but not too dull.

"Please, call me Lila." She held her stare for a beat before speaking again. "Do you like your name?"

Joy jerked as if surprised by the question. "Why do you ask?"

"Well, when I heard your name I pictured this bubbly, happy person who exudes...well, joy."

A tiny, mirthful laugh echoed out of Joy's mouth. "And what do you actually see?"

"A well-put-together woman who doesn't have a high-pitched voice that I judgmentally pictured. A pleasant smile. An air of confidence. I love a confident woman."

"I'd have to agree," Joy replied with a sparkle in her eye that told Bryce she thought the same of Lila.

"You might not have lived up to what was in my head, but when people hear your name, that's what they're going to see. When they meet you, they'll be even more pleased to see a professional, confident woman. One who puts the joy in living."

Joy chuckled. "Is that the start of a slogan?"

Lila wiggled her hand in the air in a so-so gesture as a short giggle-snort escaped. "I'll work on it, but yeah."

"I do enjoy my job. I work hard at everything I do."

"I believe that. Now we need everyone else to believe that as well. I noticed around town and even as I drove closer to the town, there were no billboards with your name or face."

Joy averted her gaze as a hint of red dusted her cheeks. "I'm not very photogenic."

"You're gorgeous and the camera will love you. Right, Bryce?"

The plea in Lila's eyes, in addition to the encouraging smile, told him he was supposed to seal the deal in whatever plan she had brewing in that beautiful mind of hers.

Nothing he would say would be a lie either. Joy was gorgeous. Long blonde hair. Blue eyes. Flawless skin. A figure most men would find pleasing. She dressed to accentuate her body. She would be very pleasing to the camera.

"I can already picture your confident smile and ready to do business glee in your eyes on every billboard leading to town," he said with a flare of conviction. "I don't know why we didn't think of this sooner."

"I've never been very fond of pictures in that sense."

"Well, we don't have to..." Lila drawled, then she struck like a scorpion out of nowhere. "Business is down. You live to find that perfect place for someone. I can sense it. I feel it oozing out of you, that drive for success. We need to encourage people a little more. Get you that attention you deserve. A few simple billboards are a good start. Don't you agree?"

Bryce thought she was asking him again, but her focus was set intently on Joy, so he remained silent.

"You're right. A picture won't hurt." A crafty smile emerged on Joy's face. "With a catchy slogan."

"I know with a bit of brainstorming we can come out with the best one."

After an hour of finagling back and forth, they did. By the time they left, Joy was merrier than when they arrived, and his spirits about everything inched further up as well.

"You have a way about inspiring confidence in people when they didn't realize they even lacked it," he commented as soon as they were snuggled in the cold car, the heater on blast.

"Thank you?" Lila looked puzzled, as if she weren't sure about his sincere compliment.

"You're welcome. Now how about lunch?"

"Show me the best place in town. I need more places of ammunition to bring life back to this town."

His merry mood fell.

Her hand touched his shoulder before letting it fall to her lap. "What did I say?"

"My sister's cafe is the best place in town and we can't eat there."

He put the car in drive. "But I know the next best place."

LILA'S BELLY was stuffed to the brim. She couldn't wait for the cafe to open again to compare it to Vinnie's Diner Bryce took her to eat at. The food had been divine. The house special had been meatloaf, and she wasn't a hardcore fan of that meal, but being the house special, she had to try it. She couldn't have been happier. The flavors. The decent-sized portion. The pretty presentation of the food itself. It had all been perfect. Another place she jotted down on her list to advertise more heavily. Something she also relayed to Bryce. He had smiled, but it wasn't a full smile he'd used before. She knew it was because he wanted his sister's cafe to be advertised in greater detail, not the diner. But she had to roll with what was available. He had to understand that.

The only thing she didn't like about the place was the name wasn't very Christmassy. Vinnie's Diner? Like, come on. Something more along the lines of Chestnut Diner would be better. Not that she was brave enough to point that out. At least, not yet.

After lunch, they reconvened in Bryce's office to talk more about the carnival but couldn't devise a plan for long since he'd set up a town meeting for that afternoon.

The place was packed when they entered the assembly hall. Bryce ventured to the podium while she hung back. She'd let the residents of the town take a seat.

A light hand tapped her shoulder. She twisted to see Juliet standing next to Eve.

"How's it going?"

She nodded at Juliet, not sure how to respond to that. It was going, but she wouldn't say well. It wasn't as if she had done anything yet. Only planning had occurred so far.

"Fine. Making headway." Though she could bullshit her way through most things.

That brightened Juliet's smile, and Lila hated it. She hated all the weight everyone in this town was putting on her. It confirmed that she couldn't fail.

"We're going to stand up front. Come on." Juliet waved for her to follow.

Lila didn't want to be rude, so she trailed behind them, standing by Eve with Juliet on Eve's other side. The woman was quieter than Juliet. Besides a cordial smile, she didn't say much. Right now, that's what she preferred. Eve didn't act like a woman who owned a multi-million dollar hotel empire.

She'd looked a few people up on the internet last night. Got the lay of the land, so to speak. Not much but town festivities popped up about Griffin and Bryce. A few articles about Griffin as the chief of police and dealing with criminal cases, nothing too nefarious in nature. Juliet had a few news articles about her abusive husband and how he went to prison for ten years for his crimes against her. And Eve had also endured abuse, but by the hands of her own brother. The story had been riveting how she'd run from him to this small town, finding a safe haven. How he tried to kill her and she beat the bastard at his game. Now she ran the company from here and did what she loved more than the hospitality world—baking sweet treats at Noel's Cafe.

It wasn't hard to see why Juliet and Eve got along so well. They shared a lot in common. Things they enjoyed, but traumatic pasts as well.

She felt out of place standing next to them. Because she didn't have much in common at all. Nothing abusive in her background—thank goodness—and she wasn't a huge baker or chef. She liked takeout more often than not. It was easier.

Not long after they took position near the stage, Bryce started speaking.

"I want to thank all of you for coming today. I know the fire yesterday at Noel's Cafe has concerned everyone. Fire Chief Brach is looking into the matter, and we should know something soon. Please do not speculate about the cause or worry about it. I can assure you it was an isolated matter."

Lila appreciated his confidence in that sentence, and she

hoped it was true. Because if it wasn't it would make her job harder. And make the mayor a liar. She imagined he wouldn't like that outcome either. She'd despise doing it, but she'd have to tell him not to say things like that again.

"When we know more about the incident, we'll update everyone. On to the next matter, we have hired a PR company to help the image of our town."

Whoa!

She did not expect that. The mayor went down a notch in her book. If he called her up to the podium, she might murder him later. Or right in front of everyone. Where it happened wasn't as important as the deed itself. The least he could've done was give her a warning he'd be bringing this up. She thought this impromptu town meeting was going to focus on the fire and to mention the carnival. He didn't have to add she was the one organizing it.

He'd just added more weight to her shoulders. The entire town's approval of her work.

"I know most of us have struggled with the decline of tourists coming into our wonderful town. All because of one man that did despicable things." Bryce paused, as if giving everyone a moment of silence. To say prayers. Or to curse the man for his devious ways. "We've tried our hardest to climb out of that turmoil. This is another step to climb even further out. I'm working closely with Ms. Hansley to get this town up and running to the beautiful place it is."

Bryce glanced at her with his smarmy politician smile. She had no choice but to display one in return. Though the man was smart enough not to wave her up to the stage. He must've seen the murderous rage in her eyes.

"So please welcome her with open arms. Give her the undivided attention she deserves and let's make Sleighville the merriest, happiest place we all know it is. We are currently working on having a carnival. If any of you have an idea you'd like to contribute to this event, please let us know. We welcome all creativity to make this the best event Sleighville has had in a long time."

Lila wanted to gag at his positivity and calculated words. The man knew how to speak to a crowd and gain their attention.

Another thousand pounds of weight slumped onto her back.

She drowned out the rest of his words, backing up a little farther from the stage. She didn't want to be called up there or eyes on her from the crowd. The farther away she was from everyone, the better.

Bryce ended with offering the crowd to ask questions. He dutifully answered in that perfected way he displayed. Soon after, the meeting ended. Bryce mingled with some people who had rushed the stage to ask more questions. Juliet and Eve either sensed her stay-away vibes or didn't notice she'd slunk away, but they conversed with Griffin and two other people she hadn't met yet. While she knew she should mingle as well, she stayed in her corner far away from everyone.

"So you're sleeping with my husband."

The voice coming close from her right startled her. Lila looked at the woman, wondering who the hell she was and why she'd accused her of such a thing. She hadn't even been in town that long.

The woman had long black hair swooped up into a fancy hairdo with bright-red lipstick. She wore a red dress to go along with it and vivid red heels that told Lila she was trying too hard to stick out. The woman was asking for attention. More like begging.

"Excuse me?"

The woman smirked. "You heard me."

Lila frowned. "Yeah, and I have no idea what or who you're talking about."

"Bryce Stuart. The mayor you're working *so closely* with." The woman emphasized the phrase Bryce had used when introducing her.

"Oh, so you're the wife. The one who asked for a divorce." Lila winced, then chuckled, a snort escaping. She didn't even care the embarrassing trait slipped out. She wasn't here to impress this disgusting woman. "When one acts the way you do, they're deflecting from their own indiscretions. I'm not sleeping with your husband, nor have any intention of doing so. But if I was you, if you're looking to make out big in the divorce, I'd stop screwing whoever you're sleeping with."

The woman inched closer, scowling. "You better watch yourself, bitch."

Lila didn't let anyone speak to her that way. Especially not a stuck-up, cheating slimeball like this woman. She closed the distance between them, either frightening or surprising the woman, making her flinch and back up a step. The woman must be used to people cowering from her. Well, she picked the wrong person to mess with.

"You don't know who you're messing with. So I suggest you walk away before I show you who you are messing with. And if you mention that disgusting lie ever again, you'll be sorry."

The woman huffed and stalked away.

Lila let out a heavy breath, grateful that didn't turn into anything else. She would've hated to get into a fistfight on the second day of her job.

"What was that about?"

She was startled once again. This time by Bryce who had

crept up to her on her left side. Why was everyone trying to scare her?

"I just had the pleasure to meet your wife. Though she forgot to tell me her name."

Bryce's brows pleated together a few short seconds before responding. "It's Denise. It looked like you two were arguing."

"Seems she has a jealous streak. She mistook your words earlier on the stage to mean we're sleeping together. I informed her she was wrong."

Bryce looked at the floor, groaning. When he lifted his head, his cheeks were dotted with a red tint. "I am so sorry. I can't believe she would do that. That will never happen again."

"I can handle her. Don't worry about it. Some women are..." Lila almost said bitches but managed to stop herself. Bryce wasn't the one who filed for divorce, so he still cared about her. For reasons unknown because he deserved much better than that viper. "Like that. They can't help themselves when...they're hurting."

Lila doubted Denise had a good bone in her body, but she wasn't going to badmouth the woman. Not when Bryce was already struggling about his failed marriage.

He eyed her far longer than she liked before offering his grimy politician smile. "Why don't we head back to my office and chat more about the carnival. Some of the townsfolk offered some wonderful ideas."

And like that, the issue was swept under the rug. Not that Lila had wanted a different outcome. She said her peace, he said his. Conversation over. But she didn't like how he abruptly displayed his fake persona. That smile grated on her nerves, and she wanted to wipe it off his face.

"Of course. I'm ready to get to work."

And flee this town.

4

HE SLAMMED THE DOOR, letting Denise know he'd arrived home. Why pretend anymore? His marriage was kaput, and he was done being a doormat. Bryce found her in the kitchen. Not cooking, because she never made supper. But drinking a bottle of wine, half of it gone.

"What is wrong with you?"

She lifted her wine glass with a cheeky smile. "Whatever do you mean?"

"Ms. Hansley is here to help our town. Are you trying to jeopardize that?"

"Maybe if you kept it in your pants, there wouldn't be a problem."

So she decided to accuse him to his face. Her audacity knew no bounds.

"I've been faithful in this marriage since the day we spoke our vows. Since the day we started dating. What happened to you? Why have you changed to this woman who acts like she doesn't care about anything?"

"Oh, I care, Bryce. I care about a lot of things. I care that you're a damn pansy. That you let this town fall apart. That you don't aspire to be more than a small-town mayor. You could be the governor of the damn state! But no, you want to be a little pissant in a dumb small town. I'm sick and tired of pretending like I enjoy standing by your side. I don't. It physically makes me sick. And now, on top of all that, I have to endure the knowledge you can't even be faithful."

His wife had turned delusional. Not only was she a world-class stuck-up bitch, she wanted to twist the narrative and make him the bad guy in the marriage. No doubt to screw him over in the divorce. He'd always known she wanted more in life. That she wanted him to climb the political ladder. His continued refusal finally got to her. He was happy here. He liked his dumb small town as she put it.

"Well, Denise, I hope you covered your tracks. Because when I find the proof you've been cheating on me, I won't hesitate to use it against you. I'm done playing the nice guy."

"You're pathetic. That's what you are."

He couldn't disagree. That he lived this long in an emotionally abusive marriage *was* pathetic.

"I want you to get out."

She laughed, the maniacal sound bouncing off the walls. "No. You get out."

"I will not live under the same roof as you any longer. You wanted a divorce. Fine. It's happening, but you can leave. Not me. This house was bought with my money. Not yours."

"The only way you're getting me out of this house is in a body bag. We both know you don't have the guts to kill me."

Before he did something he'd regret—like commit the deed she didn't think he was capable of—he decided to walk away from the fight. Denise never backed down. Her wicked laughter as he walked away proved once again who had the power in the marriage. Her. Always her.

He was more than pathetic. He was a poor excuse for a man.

He didn't want his siblings to see how much of a failure he was, so instead of running to one of them with his tail between his legs, he went to the bar. Frost's Pub and Grill.

For a Tuesday evening, the place was empty. It didn't help they hardly had any tourists in residence as well. Bryce took a seat at the bar and ordered a beer.

Anson delivered his beer but must've sensed his mood so he didn't attempt to start a conversation. Bryce appreciated his perception. And Anson could be a chatty guy when he wanted to be.

The first beer disappeared with speed. Anson set another one in front of him without him asking. He took another large swallow, then set it down, pushing it away. If he kept the current pace, he'd be drunk before long and he'd be forced to call Griffin or Juliet. The last thing he needed was a DUI for drinking and driving. He wasn't that dumb. Only heartbroken. And he wouldn't allow Denise to control any more of his life. He should stop wallowing in his sorrows.

"Hey, stranger."

Bryce twisted his gaze to his right, nodding at Melody, one of the last people he wanted to see. She was best friends with Denise. For the longest time, Denise had tried to hook Melody and Griffin up, something his brother had detested.

"Hi." While he didn't want any company, he couldn't be rude either.

"What's wrong?"

Did she honestly not know or was she playing dumb? She and Denise talked about everything. He assumed they talked about him as well.

"Why would something be wrong?"

A merciful laugh escaped. "Because you're sitting in a bar alone. You never come to the bar like this."

"Did Denise call you?"

"No. Why?"

Bryce frowned, not wanting to play games with her. Word had gotten out Denise filed for divorce, so why was Melody pretending she didn't know?

"She filed for divorce. You had to have known. We argued tonight. She accused me of cheating."

Melody leaned closer, whispering, "I know you'd never cheat on her. You're one of the good ones, and she's an idiot for not seeing that. I know who she's been sleeping with."

He had his suspicions, but for Melody to confirm them hurt more than he thought it would. "And why are you wanting to impart with this information now? You could've let me know a long time ago if you cared, Melody."

She flinched, her eyes shattering with hurt.

Nope. She was not the injured party here. He was! How dare she try to put on a show as if he'd hurt her feelings. There was a reason she and Denise were such good friends. They were alike in too many ways.

"I would never hurt you, Bryce." She rested her hand on his shoulder, caressing down his arm in a way that disgusted him. "I care about you. I always have."

He shook off her hand. "I'd like to be alone, Melody."

For a brief moment, a flash of fire lit her eyes. The hurt turned to rage. Then it was gone as if it never occurred, her pain renewed as if he'd fall for her trap. She was trying to play around with his emotions. Hitting on him as if he'd fall into bed with her or something. Either it was a power play move designed by Denise, or Melody was trying to strike while he was vulnerable.

"I'm here for you if you need me. For anything."

Her words didn't ring with sincerity, and if he did need something, he'd never go to Melody for it.

"Would you like to know who Denise has been having an affair with?"

Griffin had hired a PI to look into everything, to find even a small crumb of evidence to use against Denise in the divorce. He had no worries about what they'd uncover.

"I think it's best you stay out of my marriage problems. Have a good night, Melody."

"She hurt you more than I realized. I'm so sorry." She stood up from the stool and left.

Bryce finished off his beer, threw some cash on the bar, and left.

He sat in his car debating where to go. He'd had two beers, not too much where he couldn't drive, but to be safe, he lingered in his car longer than he normally would've. The decision where to go hadn't been made either. Going home was not an option. Enduring any more of Denise's spiteful hate wasn't going to help his depressing mood.

That left Griffin or Juliet's house to crash for the night. He was leaning toward Juliet's since she lived alone, whereas Griffin had Eve. He didn't want to bother them.

His phone rang before he could make a decision either way.

"Lila, hi. How are you?"

Like a light switch, he put on his professional tone to hide the actual turmoil he was going through.

"Well, I hate to bother you so late, but could you come over? I think someone is outside. Or they were. I don't know." She let out a breath, then a giggle. But she didn't snort after it like she did so often while working, so he knew she was putting on a show. She was scared. Her real laughter produced the most adorable snort he'd ever heard. "I'm so sorry to bother you. I'm sure it was nothing."

"No. I'll be right there."

He hung up before she could argue with him. He would not discredit anything she said. After what Mark had done last year, he couldn't be lax about anything. He'd check it out and make her feel better. Himself as well.

It gave him more time to decide where he'd spend the night.

LILA FELT silly for calling the mayor with her overactive imagination, but the town had problems in the past with this issue and she didn't want to take a chance. Of course, after she started speaking about it, she felt even more ridiculous, which was why she'd tried to blow it off as nothing. Nevertheless, she was glad he'd decided to come.

Less than ten minutes later, a knock sounded on her door. She checked the peephole before disarming the alarm and letting Bryce in.

He wiped his shoes on the rug in front of the door, but didn't take them off.

"You okay?"

She nodded, producing a smile she didn't feel. "I'm sure it was nothing."

"Tell me what happened."

She pointed toward the kitchen. "I was making supper and I thought I saw someone walking in the backyard. When I switched on the outside light, I didn't see anything. I heard noise by my bedroom window, so I went to look and again, I didn't see anyone. I don't know. It weirded me out, and now I feel foolish I called you. It had to be an animal or something. I mean, there's woods behind the cottage, maybe it was a deer."

Bryce nodded as if he agreed. "I'll go look around outside. I'll be right back."

She smiled again as if she could fool him, then closed the door behind him and locked it for extra measure.

Ugh. Ridiculous. She didn't need to lock it. She flipped the lock back to its other position.

She wrapped her large, cozy sweater tighter around her and thought about pacing the living room floor waiting for him to come back. He returned in short order, and she felt a small dose of fear leave her body. She felt so much better with him in the house.

"Well?" she inquired when he didn't say anything at first.

"There were footprints outside. In the backyard and near your bedroom window."

She shivered at the implications. She hadn't been imagining anything. Why the hell was someone walking around her place so late at night?

"Griffin doesn't seem to be home, but I will talk to him about this. You should have his number. I realize now that you couldn't have walked across the yard to him with someone prowling outside. I'm glad you didn't do that."

It hadn't crossed her mind to go to Griffin's house. Her first thought had been to call Bryce. Griffin would've been the smarter option as he was the chief of police.

"Thank you. I don't understand. Why was someone outside trying to scare me?"

Bryce blew out a breath, shrugging. "I don't know. I can't imagine anyone is against the thought of turning the town's image around, but I could be wrong. I'm so sorry this happened."

"Mr. Mayor, it is not your fault. So please don't apologize. Would you like a drink? I think I need a drink."

He hesitated, his brows pleating as if waging a war of decisions in his head. She shook her hand frivolously in the air, chuckling to reduce the sudden tension she felt floating between them.

"It's late. You didn't come over—"

"I'd love a drink. And it's Bryce. You have to call me Bryce."

His earlier hesitation was gone and that true, handsome smile she adored lit up his face.

"Can you make it a strong one?"

"The best I can do is wine."

"Fill it to the top." Another delectable smile brightened his face.

He slipped off his shoes and followed her to the kitchen. They took a seat at her table after she poured them both a glass to the tippy-top.

"Is this how it was last year when...Mark was around?"

Bryce fiddled with the bottom of his wineglass before meeting her gaze. "For most of the residents, no. He watched them from the cameras he set up. Now Eve, he did come around here and break in, moving things around. He's in prison though. He's awaiting trial, and I don't foresee him getting out anytime soon. It's not him."

Ugh. Poor Eve. Dealing with her brother, escaping his rage, then finding herself in another frightening position. Lila didn't know how she survived it all. And she would never ask. That would be too intrusive.

"The one person I seemed to have offended since I arrived is..." Ugh. Mentioning his wife didn't seem wise, but that was the one person to enter her mind as the culprit.

Bryce took a large gulp of wine. "Denise." A strangled

laugh echoed out of his mouth. "She'd hire someone to frighten you before she'd ever stomp around outside in the snow herself. Something like that would be beneath her."

"So not her?"

"The footprints seemed to have come from the woods. Someone could've been out there walking around or something and exited the woods via your backyard. It could be nothing nefarious."

She hoped that was the case.

"I hope this doesn't scare you away from the town." He leaned forward, an earnest expression on his face. "We need you."

Umm...that was debatable. She was not the best person for the job, but she didn't want to dash his hopes either.

"I don't scare easily. I still feel like a ninny that I called you about this."

He reached forward, placing his hand over hers resting on the table. "Never hesitate to call me. About anything."

They stared at each other, the energy in the room electrifying for a brief moment before he realized he still had his hand over hers and disengaged.

"Make sure you keep the alarm set at all times. I'll even have Griffin look at the security cameras positioned in the backyard. I know he has them for the front too."

"I'd appreciate that."

From there, the conversation moved to idle chitchat. He asked questions about where she lived in California and her life in general. She lived on the coast, loved going to the beach and bingeing on reality TV shows. She returned the same questions. He'd never been to the coast before—east or west. He loved going to the lake, especially fishing, and he was more into crime shows than anything else.

Laughter filled the space along with more wine being

poured. After two full glasses of wine and opening another bottle, she knew she was sporting a good buzz, if not nearing drunkenness. Nothing good ever happened when she drank too much. She wasn't a novice to a one-night stand. And the last thing she needed to do was sleep with, essentially, her boss—and a married man. Because the charged glances they gave each other now and again said it wasn't out of the realm of possibilities to take this mini party to the bedroom.

"It's getting late," she said with a giggle then her signature snort. "That is such a bad habit. I have to stop that." She giggle-snorted again, louder.

He joined in the laughter as he stood up, following her actions. "I find it rather adorable."

The heated glance he sent her way radiated tingles of pleasure through her body. He stepped closer to her, his gaze intense and unyielding. "It's very, very adorable. I know it's an honest laugh."

"You shouldn't drive home tonight." And that was *not* what she meant to say. Though it was true. He had drunk way too much to get behind the wheel of a car.

He licked his lips as he leaned a bit closer. "I know. I had way too much to drink." He snapped out of whatever pleasured haze he'd been in and backed away. "I'll crash at my brother's. Set the alarm behind me."

He was gone before she could protest. Though that would've been the dumbest move in the history of the planet.

When the alcohol cleared away, she knew she wouldn't even have these kinds of thoughts about him.

Thank goodness one of them had been in the right mind. Sleeping with her boss—and a married man— would've sent her career crashing into the ground.

5

THE HOT LIQUID slid down his throat, soothing his rattled
nerves. It was his second cup, and he knew he'd need a third
to get his bearings back. It had been a week of hell. He'd
vacated his residence to avoid Denise at all costs. Juliet had
graciously let him crash at her place in the spare room, but
he knew he couldn't do that for the duration of the divorce.
It could take a while.

Their lawyers had already chatted, and she was still
claiming he had slept with Lila. Though no proof. The PI
Griffin hired had already procured the proof he needed for
her infidelity. She was sleeping with Judge Riner's son, Eric.
The man himself was a lawyer and no doubt thought it
would make it easier to skate the truth.

They were both denying it despite the photo evidence.

One week and she was already pounding him into the
ground. Never in anyone's presence did she show how cruel
and horrid she could be. But as soon as they all disappeared,
she did what she did best: broke the man inside.

His only bright spot was Lila.

She kept him sane and the light burning inside him. She

made him laugh and feel good about himself. And she kept everything professional between them. Denise might claim he'd slept with her, which he hadn't, but it didn't mean he didn't want to.

For the first time in a very, very long time, he wanted another woman. He'd been faithful to his wife, never letting his gaze linger too long on another woman. Now he couldn't keep his eyes off one. He shouldn't feel guilty about it because his marriage was over, but he did. Every time he had a lustful thought about Lila, the guilt attacked him, making him feel worse inside.

He wanted the divorce to be finalized. But he knew with Denise running the show, she'd drag it on until there was nothing left but a shell of a man.

Besides Lila, the other bright spot was news of the fire in the cafe. An electrical issue with one of Juliet's new fridges had gone haywire, causing the fire. Juliet was in the process of fixing the damage to reopen. She was also arguing with the company where she bought the fridge to handle the expenses for delivering a faulty item. Nothing nefarious to the fire. Thank goodness for that.

Lila had no other problems outside her cottage. Good news on that front as well. One of the neighbors had been walking in the woods and used her yard to cut through to his own. Griffin had procured that information after chatting with a few neighbors, trying to get an inkling if they had seen anything odd. The backyard camera also confirmed the same thing.

All in all, his only issue was his soon-to-be ex-wife.

Even the carnival they were planning was coming together without any hitches. They'd decided renting any rides would bring liability they didn't want, much to Lila's disappointment. He secretly vowed he'd have a summer carnival, invite her, and make sure she had the best time. Not because he liked her more than he should but because she was helping their town come back to life. She deserved the recognition for a job well done.

Instead, they would be having an ice sculpture festival, fireworks, and all the fun carnival games that people loved. It would be the best winter festival their town ever put on. He swore he'd make it happen. Lila said she was still working on getting the best entertainer to draw the crowds in.

"Sorry I'm late. I hate driving in the snow," Lila said as she rushed through his office doorway, setting his much-needed third cup of coffee in front of him. Bryce grabbed the coffee cup. "I nearly ran into the ditch."

He burned his throat, gulping too much at her words. "Are you okay?"

A gentle smile graced her beautiful face as she took a seat. His worried expression must've been way too obvious because she reached forward to brush his hand, but stopped herself at the last second.

"I'm okay. I said I nearly ran into it, not that I did. Driving with snow on the road is not something you can get used to. At least not for me."

He let out a silent breath, forcing a smile out. Taming his racing heart was a different matter altogether.

"If it ever gets to be too much, I can pick you up."

"Bryce, you already do enough for me. Stop worrying I'm going to pick up and leave town. I'm good. I like it here."

Yeah, but not enough to stay.

That thought rolled through his mind, surprising him. He didn't want her to stay forever. Of course not. Only until the town was back to normal and bringing the festive cheer to everyone visiting.

And he had reason to worry. Denise wasn't being silent about her accusations. He knew Lila received looks from people, wondering if she had slept with him. Though, most knew it to be the lie it was. They'd seen Denise's viciousness before he ever had. How had he been so blind for so long? Well, not necessarily blind. He'd wanted to save his marriage, not admit defeat.

"So, good news, last night I found a band to come play at the festival."

They'd started calling it a festival rather than a carnival once they'd nixed the idea of rides. Winter festival sounded better.

"That's wonderful. Who?" he asked as he took a tentative sip of the coffee this time.

"Well, so, they're not super famous around the entire country, but," she drawled with a hopeful smile, "they are pretty big in the area I'm from in California. They will draw in people from there. Which is what we want! New people coming to town."

Her enthusiasm didn't hide her worry. He could sense her underlying concern about the entire event.

"Okay. I trust you. Who is it?"

"They have a unique band name. Don't be concerned about it. People love it. Because it's unique."

Bryce nodded, hoping that would encourage her to spill it. He didn't like to be held in suspense, at least not about something this important.

"They're The Cackling Bellies, and they play the best rock music I've ever heard."

"The Cackling Bellies?" She had to be joking. They couldn't advertise that kind of band name with a town that celebrated Christmas year-round.

"Look." She leaned forward again, desperation now

displayed. "I'm going to be honest. I've had trouble finding someone. The ones I tried to reel in wouldn't do it. This is my brother's band and they're good. Like, really good. They've headlined for some big stars, so it's not like they're some nobodies. They will bring in a crowd. I promise you. I even told him to start practicing some Christmas songs."

He couldn't afford to be picky. This was her job and he had to have faith in her.

"If you're not worried, then I'm not."

"Okay, great. Perfect." She rested back, grinning from ear-to-ear. "They will be here tomorrow to mingle with everyone and to set up. This should draw some people in advance for next week's festival."

"I will call Joy to have a place ready for them."

She waved him off. "I already did. They have a cottage all booked. I will have ads going with their name plastered everywhere. They've even announced on their website they'll be playing here next week. He did that last night, and Joy told me she already reserved two places for a week stay. So it's already working!"

Now her enthusiasm seemed real, and it worked to rub off on him. He wanted to stand up and hug her. Despite his urge to do so, his butt remained in his seat because he knew that hug could easily turn into a kiss. He wanted to kiss her so badly the ache inside made his gut hurt.

"That is wonderful news. We better get busy on all the other aspects of the festival."

She waved her folder and notebook she brought everywhere. "I'm ready. Let's dive in."

They got to work, and Bryce tried his hardest, as usual, not to stare at her. The way she smiled. The way she laughed, then snorted in her adorable way. The way her excitement filled the room.

Yes, the faster they got this town up and running, the better he'd sleep at night. Because having temptation across from him was too much to bear. The last thing he needed was to give Denise real ammunition in the divorce. Turn her lie into reality.

"LOOK, I asked for a castle ice sculpture, and that's what I expect to get. I even paid for it already. So stop bullshitting me and have it delivered by Sunday because the event starts Monday. Okay, cool, thanks."

Lila ended the call, wanting to slap her phone to the table, but instead set it down without making a sound. It wasn't her phone's fault the ice sculpture company they'd picked wanted to give her problems. They ordered several large sculptures to make it an amazing event, one where people could ooh and aah as they walked around a winter wonderland. Not to mention, the town was paying a pretty penny to get these sculptures. The last thing she needed was a delay in any aspect. Things needed to go off without a hitch.

"I wish I had something stronger for you, but this is all I have," Juliet said as she set the steaming cup of coffee in front of her.

"Thank you, you beautiful goddess. This is just what I needed."

Juliet laughed, the exuberant sound filling her heart with glee as she took a seat across from her. She and Bryce had decided to break for lunch. He had a few things he needed to take care of not related to the festival, so they went their separate ways.

She decided to grab a bite to eat at the cafe. It wasn't

fully operational, but Juliet opened it this morning offering light sandwiches, coffee or tea, and certain sweet treats. The back end of the building needed repair, but most of the items she served could be prepared in the front or were delivered by the food company she ordered from for supplies.

"Please, call me a goddess again. I do like the sound of that."

"Hey, I call it like I see it. Your coffee is divine. Best in town."

"Stop." Juliet waved her off as if she didn't care, but her smile said to keep going.

Lila liked Juliet. And Eve, though they didn't chat as much as her and Juliet. But they were both very welcoming and easy to talk to. Since Juliet was Bryce's sister, she saw her more than she figured she would've otherwise.

"You okay?" Juliet asked.

Bummer. Juliet had decided she wanted to broach the subject of the call she overheard.

"Nothing I can't handle. I chatted with Joy a little bit ago. Two more places booked for three days next week. Things are looking up. I'm not about to let anything mess it up."

"If anyone is a goddess here, it's you." Juliet pointed at her, her appreciation spread across her face. "I had to make a run out of town yesterday and the drive back in...girl, those billboards you had put up for Joy are amazing."

Lila winced, then smiled behind her mug before taking a sip. "The slogan isn't too silly?"

Because Joy had her reservations when Lila suggested, "Let us bring the JOY to your next home." They'd taken several different photos of Joy as well in front of different houses and used each one on a different billboard. Her face was plastered everywhere. Her smile alone would reel people in. She had a way of smiling in a confident, I-have-your-best-interests-at-heart smile.

"Nope. It was great. She's so photogenic too."

"Right!" Lila's heart filled with elation. "I couldn't agree more."

"Well, I won't keep you too long. I know you have to get back to work. Enjoy your sandwich and coffee."

Juliet left her to finish her meal, and she missed the company. It was hard being away from home and family and friends. Here she felt isolated and alone. Except when she had mini pockets of happiness with one of the few people she'd connected with. While she knew this was a job, she wanted to be liked. With Denise spreading her nasty rumors, not everyone liked her.

Bryce told her not to worry about it, but it wasn't that simple. She couldn't turn her emotions off like a switch. Not like he seemed to do. Not that the subject came up too often about his wife, but he seemed so unaffected by what was happening between them. The only time she noticed it bothering him was when she knew he didn't know she was looking at him. He could pretend all he wanted that Denise's actions didn't affect him, but she knew better.

The day went by in a blur. More things accomplished concerning the festival. They'd added the event to the town's website. She even had the woman, Harper, who ran the site, add a few more things to highlight the best parts of the town. Like Vinnie's Diner and their daily specials "sure to make your mouth water for more." Or Shannon's clothing store, Tidings and Joy, that had the funniest and most stylish clothing around town. Little things that would appeal to someone browsing the website.

She had a glass of wine with her simple meal before resting in bed with a book that had her falling asleep faster than she wanted. Of course, that's what hard work did to her. Exhausted her to the point of going to bed at eight o'clock. No more calling herself a night owl.

She woke up feeling refreshed and ready for a new day. As usual, she picked up a coffee for her and Bryce from Mocha's Merriment and met him in his office. They proceeded to do what they did every day: work well with each other. They separated again at lunch, then reconvened in the afternoon. Another positive day in getting the festival ready for Monday.

By five o'clock, she was ready to go home, shower, eat, and go to bed again right away. Of course, she couldn't do the last part until she knew her brother had arrived safely. A light sprinkling of snow was coming down, and according to the weather app, it wouldn't accumulate too much. Thank goodness since her brother and his bandmates weren't used to the snow like her.

She was packing her bag to leave when Bryce cleared his throat. She looked up to see the fake smile he wore when he wanted something. She hated that smile.

"What's on your mind?" No sense beating around the bush. If he wanted something, he should say it.

"I know your brother and his friends are arriving tonight. Griffin thought a nice welcome supper at his house would be nice. What do you think?"

That would require mingling with everyone, which wasn't a bad thing. She liked Griffin as well. The Stuarts were a very open and welcoming family. But she'd also have to make sure her brother got settled into his cottage, and it could turn into a long night.

But she also didn't want to offend the Stuarts.

"That sounds wonderful. He texted me a little bit ago. He's about forty minutes away. I'll let him know."

"Good. I'll meet you at Griffin's in an hour."

She smiled, though had to force it, then bid goodbye. Her brother didn't mind the change of plans. Not surprising. He had always been a go-with-the-flow kind of guy. Sometimes, it irked her. She liked to know plans ahead of time and got frustrated when they got changed at the last minute.

Taking a shower would have to wait along with her early bedtime, but she refreshed herself before waiting for her brother to arrive. When he texted they got delayed behind a snowplow, she told him to take his time driving and to meet her at Griffin's. She had to be around people while she waited for him, otherwise she'd go out of her mind with worry.

When she stepped outside to walk across the lawn to Griffin's house, the snow was coming down heavier. So much for the weather app telling the truth. It had lied! No wonder why the snowplows were out.

She knocked on the door and tried not to pretend she was worried when it swung open. Eve answered it.

A quick glance behind her told Eve that she was alone. Her brother hadn't arrived yet.

"They're stuck behind a snowplow. They'll be here soon."

"Come on in. Do you want a drink?"

Bless this woman for knowing what she needed to calm her nerves. She nodded and a wineglass was in her hand before she could even worry a second about her brother.

Griffin and Eve took a seat on the couch, while Juliet stood near the fireplace, warming up from the burning blaze. Bryce sat on the loveseat. She had no other option but to sit by him or take a stance by Juliet. She chose to sit by Bryce but not close enough to touch.

"Thank you so much for having us over. They'll be here soon. Stuck behind a snowplow."

"We want them to feel welcome. Of course, say thank you for doing this for our town," Griffin replied.

Small chitchat commenced while they waited until the doorbell rang. Lila shot up from her seat, then froze.

"Not my house. I guess I should let one of you get it."

Eve laughed and waved her hand toward the door. "Go ahead."

She set her wineglass on the coffee table between the two couches and answered the door.

"We made it!" Aster said in the loud, boisterous way he always spoke. He stepped inside, picked her up, and twirled her in a big circle as he hugged her.

"You had me worried," she whispered in his ear.

"That's because you worry about everything. I'm the big brother. You're the little sister. I'm supposed to worry, not you," he whispered in return.

He let go so his other bandmates, Toby, Stan, and Carson, could say hi and get their hugs as well. Even though they lived in the same town, she rarely saw all of them. They were all good guys. They'd be there for her in the blink of an eye if she asked.

They all removed their shoes and entered the living room. Lila made quick introductions and the nerves she'd had since the snow started dissipating. Her brother had made it safe and sound.

"Thank you for inviting us. We love playing in different venues, and this will be fun."

Bryce had stood up to greet them, beaming his smarmy politician's smile. Lila figured he couldn't help it when he went into work mode. "We also thank you for coming. I'm sure playing in a Christmas town is not your usual forte."

"Na, but that's what makes it fun. Changing it up a bit," Aster said, then swung an arm around her and pulled her closer. "And it's hard to say no to Lilac."

Juliet giggled, still standing near the fireplace. "Lilac?"

Aster's grin widened. "Come on, sis. You didn't tell them your full name."

She shoved off his arm playfully, hoping she didn't look as red in the cheeks as she felt. "Our parents are huge anthophiles. We were each named after a flower. Aster, Poppy, Zinnia, and me—Lilac. I go by Lila most of the time."

"Girl," Juliet started, "I love your name. It's so pretty and unique."

"I love her," Aster said, pointing at Juliet with a smile that said he was going to flirt with her. "She's amazing."

Lila forgot how much her brother could annoy her with his carefree attitude and flirtatious manner.

"Aww, Lilac," he said, chuckling, and grabbed her again by the shoulder, pulling her closer. He decided to embarrass her even further by giving her a noogie. "I missed you, sis."

If she could crawl in a hole and die, she would've picked that moment to do it. She decided the best course of action for the rest of the night would be to avoid eye contact with everyone.

6

BRYCE HAD FELT the shift in their relationship the moment Lila entered his office. She seemed more distant than usual. The night before had been different. Bryce wasn't sure what he expected her brother to be like, but it hadn't been what he'd witnessed. The man was loud, but kind. He loved to talk and be the center of attention. And the flirting with Juliet had been noticeable. Though he didn't say a word to Juliet because she had outrageously flirted back. It wasn't his place to say anything about her relationships. He couldn't even manage his own without failing. Plus, she was single and was free to date whomever she pleased. Though Aster wouldn't be his first pick...or his last.

Throughout the evening, Lila had been quiet. She smiled when she should've, spoke when spoken to, but otherwise remained silent.

This morning wasn't any different.

He didn't know what had gone wrong for her to change her demeanor, and like he feared way too much—her leaving—he didn't broach the subject. By lunchtime, he decided whatever issue needed his attention would have to wait. He'd be dining with Lila today. She seemed surprised but didn't argue.

They decided to go to Vinnie's and saw her brother and his friends. Aster waved them over to their table. Another table was attached to theirs and he took a seat across from Lila.

"So, how's the party planning going?" her brother asked as if they weren't putting on a huge festival, but more like a simple party with friends and family.

"Real well. I need all of you to be at the stage in Yuletide Park by three. Do not be late."

The way Lila emphasized the last part, Bryce knew her brother had a tendency to not be on time.

"Are we playing outdoors the entire time?" Carson asked, shivering as if he were outside at that very moment.

Lila's lips curved into that delectable smile that had Bryce doing anything she asked. "Yes, and you'll do it with a smile on your face."

Aster slapped Carson on the back, laughing. "Dude, you did that polar plunge thingy in Minnesota one time. You can handle this."

"That wasn't hours on end. This will be. I hate the cold." He shivered again, biting into his hamburger.

Conversation continued around the table while he and Lila waited for their food to arrive. It didn't take long, and they were able to eat and chat like the rest of them.

The lunch passed in a blur, and he wasn't sure whether he was happy to go back to the office alone with Lila or not. The opportunity to speak with her about her quietness wasn't going to happen. Not with her brother and his bandmates in the vicinity. Before leaving, he excused himself to use the bathroom.

When he stepped out of the stall, he flinched. Aster

stood by the sinks, leaning against one of them with his arms and feet crossed. He looked relaxed, but the alertness in his eyes said he would be ready to pounce if need be.

Bryce decided to wash his hands two sinks away from him. He washed them as thoroughly as he always did, then grabbed two paper towels to dry them off. The wet towels went in the trash bin. One minute, maybe, had gone by. Aster still rested against the sink not saying a word.

"Was there something you wanted to talk about?" The man was unnerving him, and it wasn't a feeling Bryce felt very often. He could admit he felt confident in most situations—well, at least when it didn't deal with his wife.

"I've been in town less than a day, Mr. Mayor. The things I've heard about my sister do not make me happy."

The horrible rumors that they were sleeping together. Just. Great.

The man he'd met last night, the man he dined with, had disappeared. The hard glint in Aster's eyes said he could get down and dirty if need be. Apparently, he thought that's what was needed.

Honesty had always been his best policy. It would continue until the day he died. He never thought lying got a person very far.

"I apologize for those nasty rumors. I can assure you I have been nothing but a professional with your sister and haven't touched her in the slightest." He let out a ragged breath. "Unfortunately, I am going through a divorce. My wife isn't playing nice. She's the one cheating on me, and she must think deflecting that fact will help her in the divorce. It won't, but it doesn't stop her."

Aster stood to his full height, letting his arms drop to his sides. "I hear what you're saying. I believe what you're saying." He took two quick steps toward him, which gave him no time to react. If Aster had wanted to punch him square in the face, he wouldn't have been able to duck. "But what your lips don't tell me, your eyes do. I see the way you look at my sister. So I suggest you stop doing that."

Bryce swallowed hard and gave a tight nod. He wouldn't fib and say he had no idea what he was talking about. Because if Aster saw the desire in his eyes, then he wasn't doing a good job of hiding it. That begged the question, who else saw it?

Like a light switch, Aster produced a big grin and slapped him hard on the shoulder. "Now let's talk Christmas songs. What is your favorite one? I feel like as mayor of the town, our band should play it."

Like that, the conversation—more like threat—was finished. They walked out of the bathroom talking music, joining the rest by the door. Lila looked at them funny. Aster still had his hand on him, as if reminding him the entire way he had the upper hand. That he would show Bryce never-ending pain if he hurt Lila in any way.

They parted ways outside the diner. Aster and his crew hopped into their rental car while he and Lila walked back toward City Hall.

"What did he say to you?" Lila asked halfway back to their destination.

The whole not lying to people raced through his mind. But this situation felt like he needed to skirt the truth.

"We were talking about Christmas music. I don't have a favorite song. Maybe because I've been desensitized to the holiday. I hear the music so much it's hard to pick which one I love the most."

Lila stopped walking. They were near the big Christmas tree that was displayed in the center of the town. No one was in earshot, so the conversation was as private as it could be.

"I know my brother. The person I don't know well is you. In the short time I've gotten to know you, I sense you don't lie. Yet, that's what you're doing right now. My brother didn't go into that bathroom to talk about Christmas music."

This was not a discussion he wanted to have in the middle of town, even if no one was around. It appeared as if Lila wasn't giving him a choice. Just as Aster had dominated the situation, Lila had the upper hand as well. He felt trapped once again.

"Okay. I'll tell you what we chatted about if you answer one thing for me."

She eyed him with a narrow gaze, then crossed her arms as her brother had done. "No. You'll tell me regardless of whether or not I answer any question you may have."

Unlike Denise, when she demanded something of him, he didn't feel threatened. He didn't feel like the scum of the earth. A nobody that no one cared about. She was simply not being coerced into anything. Not that he was trying to coerce her or be difficult. His question had nothing to do with the attraction he felt, but why she pulled away from him and everyone else last night.

"He's heard the rumors around town. He doesn't like it." Bryce shoved a finger into his chest. "I don't like it. So I get why it upsets him. It upsets me too, and I wish I could make it stop. Damn my ex-wife!"

Lila uncrossed her arms, letting them fall to her sides as a gentle smile graced her lips. He liked that look more than the stern, I'm-ready-to-drop-you-on-your-ass expression she had moments before.

"You know that's the first time you referred to her as your ex-wife."

Well, it was happening. He didn't even want to stop the process. He stayed in a loveless marriage way too long. It was time to end it. Why not start changing the language now?

"It's what she's going to be when it's final. I haven't even been staying in our house. It pisses me off I'm the one kicked out when I didn't even do anything wrong. All I did was try to love her."

"Aster can get..." She pursed her lips, as if trying to find the right word. "Ridiculously overprotective. I'm sorry for that."

"Don't be. I'm the same way with Juliet. When the time is needed. I don't fault your brother for confronting me. It is my fault some people are treating you with disrespect."

She waved the comment off as she resumed walking. He followed suit, grateful the conversation was over. He didn't have to tell her the last thing they had chatted about. She didn't need to know he was attracted to her. That, for the first time in a very long time, he wanted to kiss another woman.

"It's nothing I can't handle. Don't worry about it. So what was your question?"

Now that the moment was upon him, he wasn't sure how to ask her why she'd pulled away. Because the last few minutes had been like they usually acted—direct and open and like no awkwardness stood between them.

———

"Bryce? It's your turn. You were honest about my brother, which I appreciate, so go ahead and ask me your question."

Because now she had to know what it was. It would bother her if he didn't.

But she wasn't a woman who was railroaded by anyone. She didn't do bartering, not when it came to her family.

And the amount of times Aster had stepped into her business was too high to count. She hated when he did that, and he'd be getting an earful later. Were the rumors annoying? Yes. Could she handle it? Also, yes. She wasn't a meek and mild woman who ran away with her tail between her legs. If she was, she would've quit her job after the dog food failure.

"You were quiet last night after your brother arrived. This morning as well. I was wondering why?" He frowned and she wanted to smooth the wrinkles out of his forehead and make it disappear. "Did I do something wrong?"

This man and his worry that he always created the problems. His ex-wife was to blame for that. She could only imagine how she tore him down in ways he'd never confess.

Spoiled, entitled bitch. She wished she could inflict some pain on Denise, but she didn't know what kind. Something to knock her down a peg or two.

"You did nothing wrong. I'm sorry I acted that way. My brother..." She paused again, hating to talk bad about him. Aster did the things he did out of love. It didn't mean she always enjoyed his behavior. "Can drive me up the wall sometimes. I didn't want to call him for this festival, but I had no choice. I couldn't find anyone else, and I knew he wouldn't say no. But his carefree attitude and his over-protectiveness can get on my nerves. Not to mention he has no qualms about embarrassing me. That's the first thing he did when he got here."

Bryce opened the door to City Hall, letting her enter first. He didn't respond until they entered the elevator.

"You're talking about revealing your full first name?"

She nodded once, not wanting to talk about it. She wouldn't say she hated her name, but some kids weren't kind when she was growing up. Those hurtful words stuck with a person. It was hard to erase some memories from her mind.

"I think Lilac is a very beautiful name. Please don't feel embarrassed. Of course, I'll continue to call you Lila. It doesn't have to be a thing."

The elevator doors swung open and they stepped out. She stood still as the elevator doors shut.

She loved how he cut right to the heart of the matter. A lot of the times when someone found out her real name, it did become a thing.

"Thank you, Bryce. I'm sorry I—"

"No. You're not apologizing. Because you did nothing wrong." He gestured down the hallway toward his office. "Let's get back to the festival and move on from any negative vibes."

"I can do that."

The sappy smile that hit her face didn't dissipate for the longest time.

The remainder of the day went much better than the morning had. She was glad Bryce had called her out on her moodiness. She hadn't needed to make it a big deal and she knew that now.

She swore when they parted ways at the end of the day, Bryce's gaze lingered longer than normal. Because she had a hard time looking away as well when she bid him goodbye.

The drive to her cottage didn't take long. She sent a text to her brother, took a quick shower, and was dressed and ready for him by the time he rang the doorbell. She opened the door, her mouth salivating at the pizza in his hand.

She told him two things in the text: Bring food and your apologies.

They dug into the pizza right away, even forgoing grabbing plates.

After eating three slices each, Aster spoke first.

"So what am I supposed to be sorry about?"

"Oh, I don't know. Maybe the part where you cornered the mayor and embarrassed me. Again!" She leaned back in her chair, trying to remain calm, but she wanted to get into his face and shake some sense into him. Did he forget the bottom line? This was her job! If Bryce wanted to, he could complain to her boss and she'd be replaced—and fired— without warning.

"Lilac, I love you," he said, looking as relaxed as her, though she knew he was on edge as well. "I hate that you dislike your name. If I could, I'd bury those nasty bitches for making you feel like you couldn't use your real name. I'm sorry if that embarrasses you, but you'll always be Lilac to me."

"God, I hate it when you make me want to cry with your caring. Stop it," she mumbled, feeling the tears well up.

She knew her brother loved her. She also knew he'd do anything for her, including ruining anyone's life who hurt her. He couldn't do that very thing with the girls who teased her in school because she refused to let him know who the culprits had been. It was done and over with. She moved on. Life moved on.

He sat up, grinning like the devil he could be. "It's just your luck you land in a situation where the dude you're working with is going through a divorce. I met his wife today. She's a piece of work."

"She's a bitch and I'm glad Bryce is divorcing her. He deserves better."

"I don't know him well, but I agree with you because I met his wife." Aster laughed as he sat back again. "You know she came on to me."

Lila rolled her eyes, not surprised in the least. She hoped

Aster didn't flirt in return. He had a horrible habit of flirting with all women. Big, small. Short, tall. He loved women. They loved him.

"Don't worry, Lilac, I told her I was taken."

"Ha! You don't do girlfriends."

He feigned shock by placing a hand on his chest. "But I treat all women with respect. There is never any doubt what's between us. It's sex and they know it."

"So why lie to her?"

"I didn't." His devilish grin grew. "I have my eyes on another woman here."

She groaned, closing her eyes for a brief moment, looking for strength. "Please do not sleep with the mayor's sister." Because she knew exactly who he was talking about.

"Too late. I'm getting together with her after I leave your place."

Lila leaned forward, grabbing his shirt and pulling him closer. "Do you want me to lose my job? Is that what you're trying to do?"

"What does me hanging out with the mayor's sister have anything to do with your job?"

"Hello! Idiot!" She shoved him away and knocked on his head. "Anyone in there? You mess around with her and it doesn't end well, which it's been known to happen. She goes to Bryce who then goes to my boss, and bye-bye job!"

Aster chuckled as he relaxed back into his seat. "Not a chance. That man has the hots for you. If he wasn't going through a nasty divorce, I guarantee you he'd be trying to get in your pants."

"No, he wouldn't."

She would've noticed if Bryce was attracted to her. He'd been nothing but respectful and professional with her. He hadn't made any rude, sexual comments. He didn't look at her funny. He always kept his eyes on her face. Some men had trouble doing that, staring at her breasts as if she'd offer an invite to touch them.

"Well, he's not going to try regardless. So you don't have to worry."

She had the sinking suspicion Bryce left out a few more things he and her brother had chatted about.

"Did you seriously tell the mayor, the man who controls the fate of my job, to not sleep with me?"

"Of course not. I told him to stop looking at you like a love-sick puppy. He understood my meaning."

And she thought she'd been embarrassed before. That didn't compare how she felt right now. She stood up and pointed toward the front door.

"Get out. Go do whatever you're going to do. Don't tell me any more because I don't want to know. And if you ever confront Bryce again, you'll be sorry."

Aster rose to his feet, the cockiness gone, replaced with sorrow. "I didn't mean to upset you, Lilac. I don't like people hurting you."

"Well, congratulations, Aster. You're one of the people now. What are you going to do about that? Kick your own ass?"

She walked out of the room. She didn't care what he thought, but for her, the conversation was over.

She heard the front door close, and she was grateful he understood that too.

7

BRYCE STOOD to the side while the crew delivering the ice sculptures did their thing. Large trucks and cranes were scattered around the park, but it was all coming together. Lila had been on the phone Friday and Saturday, yelling at the people to get their butt in gear and deliver the product they ordered. Now, Sunday, they'd followed through as they should've. The town was paying a lot more than Bryce wanted to for all the sculptures.

They had an ice castle people would be able to walk through. Scattered around the park were Christmas trees, a large Santa and his eight reindeer, different-sized presents. The magical sleigh was his favorite because they were going to allow people to sit on it and take a picture.

The carnival games were already set up and waiting to be played, though the festival didn't start until tomorrow. The stage for The Cackling Bellies was ready and they'd had sound checks the last few days. He had to admit they were a pretty good band. Their music was flawless. Them as decent human beings were a whole other matter. At least when it came to Aster.

The man hated him. When Lila wasn't looking, he received death glares. He made sure not to look at Lila in an inappropriate way, not that he thought he had before. But he tried his damnedest to keep the desire out of his eyes. That was harder than he cared to admit.

When Aster spoke to him, which was not very often, he wasn't amiable and easygoing like he was with everyone else. Like he was with Juliet.

They'd been glued at the hip since the man arrived. He hadn't asked Juliet, as it wasn't his business, but he had a strong suspicion his sister had slept with him. She was a single woman. She had the right to sleep with whoever she wanted, but it irked Bryce, nonetheless.

And he knew it bothered Duke.

They weren't seeing each other, but not for the lack of trying on Duke's part. He'd had a thing for his sister for as long as he could remember. She'd ended up getting married and there went his chance. She got divorced and he gave her space to recover from that. The last few months they had grown closer, hanging out more. Duke hadn't asked her out, but Bryce had figured it'd only be a matter of time. And then Aster arrived.

"Hey, what's the matter?"

He flinched, then smoothed out his harried expression with a smile. Lila stood close to him, and he wasn't sure why it bothered him that she had been able to get that close without him realizing it.

"Oh, I'm fine. Lost in thought, I guess. They're doing a wonderful job setting everything up," Bryce said as he motioned toward all the chaos in front of them.

"They broke Prancer. I told them we better be getting a discount for that and a new reindeer before tomorrow."

With how assertive Lila could be when it came to her

job, he had no doubt the company was already rushing to do her bidding.

"I didn't see that." He looked around the park, the trucks, the cranes, the people, and knew all the commotion was why he hadn't. Thank goodness Lila was on top of everything. Of course she was. It was her job. Something she excelled at, and he couldn't be happier with the company he picked to bring their town back to life. And maybe a little happier that it had been her the company chose for the assignment.

In less than two weeks, she managed to throw together a large winter festival, get new billboards up for the realty company, advertise the delicious places to eat around town, spread the word about the wonderful shops, and people were coming. They'd rented nearly all the places available to rent, and the ticket sales to enter the festival were higher than he'd anticipated. He could kiss her for that accomplishment alone. Which of course he couldn't. He wasn't divorced yet, and it would also be unprofessional.

"Despite that little hiccup, it is all running smoothly. Don't worry, Bryce. This will be the best winter festival this town has ever seen."

With confidence like that, he believed her.

The day went fast. Too fast. Almost like Valentine's Day had on Friday. He knew Griffin had celebrated with Eve, making her a romantic dinner. Even Aster had taken Juliet out for a nice supper. He had thought about asking Lila out for a meal so they didn't have to celebrate the holiday alone. But he figured that would send the wrong message and ended up spending the night alone in his room.

The next day arrived, and he was feeling more optimistic than he had in a very long time. He and Juliet were dressed and ready and out of her house before eight o'clock. Griffin and Eve, along with Lila and the band, were at Yuletide Park when they arrived. So were all the people working the event. At nine o'clock sharp, the doors opened. The people flooded in. Seeing so many people in their town again made his eyes water for a brief moment. Tears of joy he hadn't experienced in a long time.

His beautiful town was coming back to life.

Aster and his band played off and on throughout the day. As the opening day, that had been the plan. For the rest of the week, they'd play two times a day. Once in the afternoon and once in the evening. Friday night would end the festivities, and they planned to play their longest concert yet that night.

People mingled with others. They explored the castle and the other ice sculptures around the park. The games were played and sent wondrous sounds around the area. Food was devoured. Laughter could be heard. All in all, the festival was a huge hit.

By Friday evening, an hour into The Cackling Bellies playing, Bryce felt the first moment of relief. They'd done it. They made it through the week with much success. They'd made more money than he predicted. The amount of people had even been over the estimation they'd had. The rental properties around town were even starting to book further out in the year. Sleighville was returning to normal.

His eyes sought out Lila near the side of the stage, swaying to the music. She'd done such a great job, he hated it. Because she'd leave soon, and he wasn't ready for her to leave.

"They're pretty good," Griffin said, sidling up next to him with a coffee cup in his hand. Bryce figured there was either coffee in it or hot chocolate, and the sound of a hot chocolate sounded good.

He nodded at his brother's comment. "I have to agree."

Griffin chuckled. "Which irritates you. Juliet is a big girl. She knows what she's doing."

Bryce knew that. It didn't make it any easier to swallow the knowledge she was sleeping with Aster.

"Or does it irritate you because he doesn't seem to like you. Why is that?"

Bryce shrugged. Now wasn't the time to be getting into that.

"What's next on Lila's agenda for the town?"

Bryce tossed up his shoulders carelessly again. "I'm not sure. We haven't talked about that. The festival has been our focus." The sadness swept through him once more. "She did such a damn good job, I'm afraid we might not need her anymore."

"It's impressive how well this festival did. It's a good thing, Bryce." Griffin slapped his shoulder as if trying to slap some sense into him. That there was no reason to convince Lila to stay longer.

"Come on." Griffin squeezed his shoulder. "Let's go do our rounds. You've been standing here for too long. You'll turn into an ice sculpture if you don't get the blood flowing."

Griffin wasn't wrong. His feet had lost feeling a while ago. That hot chocolate was starting to sound better and better. Plus, that's what they did. The chief of police and the mayor of the town—they mingled, they chatted, they made everyone feel safe and welcome.

"First, I want a hot chocolate."

He tore his gaze away from Lila, knowing it wouldn't do any good to stare anyway. She'd be leaving soon. Why get attached?

SHE FELT a little awkward standing next to Juliet waiting for the band members to end their last song and pack up and leave. But she told Aster she didn't want to know what he was doing, and she wasn't going to pry into their affairs. Not like he had with hers! So that meant even prying into it via Juliet. And Juliet thankfully didn't offer any details on her own either.

She had refused to let him ruin her time here. The night she told him to get out, she woke up the next morning and treated Bryce no differently than the day before. He might've left out one detail he'd chatted with her brother about, but he'd done it for a reason. To not embarrass either of them. So she left it alone. She pretended none of it happened. That decision had been a good one. They'd flown through the week with no awkwardness. No further mishaps or arguments. Everything had gone so effortlessly. Maybe too well.

She hated to think she did such a wonderful job on the festival that she had to leave soon. One, because the cheery holiday town was starting to grow on her. Hearing Christmas songs anytime she stopped into any store didn't faze her anymore. Seeing the merriness splattered all over town made her smile instead of gag. The upbeat positivity the townsfolk portrayed seeped into her own veins. She liked it here.

And two, because once she was done here, she had to return to California to a boss that hated her. No doubt he'd send her on another assignment that would be impossible to fix. Well, she sure showed him! She fixed this little Christmas town, and in less than two weeks.

Yay her!

And three, the one she didn't even want to admit to herself. She liked Bryce. Sure, he was getting divorced, and by the looks of it, it could drag out for a while. She would never dally with a married man, even if it was ending soon. So even though her time was almost up, it was better she left. It would reduce the temptation dangling in her face every single day. Every single moment she was near Bryce.

"Lovely job on the festival. You must be proud," Juliet said, being the one to break the silence between them.

"Thank you. I am, but it was a group effort. I couldn't have done half of this without Bryce and his staff. You and Eve, Griffin. Everyone helped."

Which was true, but she appreciated the shout-out to her skills alone. It was nice to be recognized.

"Aster says he and his crew are leaving tomorrow afternoon."

Lila heard the sadness in Juliet's voice. Damn it. This was the part where she had to be brutally honest. Be the bearer of bad news. That no matter what Juliet said or did, she couldn't change who he was. Because some women thought they'd be the one to change his mind. Make him a boyfriend and a one-woman man.

"He doesn't do relationships. I'm sorry, Juliet."

Juliet giggled, waving her hand in the air as if to say don't worry about it. "I know that. He's not shy about how he feels or what he wants. I have to say, and I'm sorry if I'm being too open with you, but it's refreshing. I've never had something like this. Sex with a man knowing it's not going anywhere. He made me feel alive and special and..." Juliet's gaze swept to the ground. "I'll stop there."

Lila couldn't stop her own chuckle along with her snort. "Hey, I know my brother has skills in the bedroom, otherwise he wouldn't get as many women as he does. Not that I want to hear details." She covered her ears, singing la-la-la until Juliet laughed again. "He's a good guy, but he needs to grow up. I'm not sure he'll ever settle down. He likes living on the edge, on a whim, not knowing where the next moment will take him. I could never live like that. I don't know how he does it."

"I don't know why I brought it up. I figured you knew he leaves tomorrow. I like you, Lila. It's been nice getting to know you. I didn't know how long you're staying, and I didn't want things to be awkward between us because I..." Juliet's voice trailed off, her unspoken words just known. *Because I slept with your brother.*

"It's okay. No awkwardness here." Lie! She had felt awkward, but now having this chat, she felt better about things. It was always nice to know where she stood with a person. "And I don't know how long I'll be staying either. Bryce and I haven't talked about it. The festival...well, it went better than I think we both expected."

"I hope you stay a bit longer. It's nice having you around."

Before she could respond, not sure how she would, the guys were leaving the stage with their gear, and the festival was over. The crowd was dispersing, and it all came to an end. It made her sad.

She stayed until the park was empty. The police were left, of course, making sure everyone made it out of the park without any issues. And Bryce.

She met him by the entrance, an ice sculpture made into a trellis that one had to walk through to enter the festival.

"Congratulations on a successful festival," Bryce said with a giant, triumphant smile.

"Congrats to you as well. It was a team effort."

"Yeah, but without your vision, it wouldn't have been as great. You saved us."

Well, she wasn't sure she'd go that far, but she'd take the compliment.

"I'll walk you to your car."

His words reminded her that she had driven with Aster and the gang. Who had already left the premises. She wasn't sure whether to be annoyed or grateful for her brother forgetting he'd brought her here. What an asshat. She'd ream him out later for that mishap.

"I don't have a car here. Would you mind giving me a ride home? Aster brought me and we both forgot that." She chuckled, embarrassed by the situation.

"Of course. I don't mind at all."

She followed Bryce to his car and rubbed her hands in front of the vents, despite them blowing out cold air. It didn't take long for the car to heat up. She felt frozen to the bone and couldn't wait to curl up on her couch with a hot drink of some kind. While she had fun at the festival, monitoring the activities to make sure nothing went wrong throughout the week, she'd been so cold. Staying outside for hours on end was not her idea of fun. She hated the cold! Using that strong word fit perfectly.

When he pulled into her driveway, his dashboard screen told her it was well past ten o'clock. She was bummed to see the night end. She knew she wouldn't go to bed right away, even with the long day they had. She wondered if Bryce would be able to go to sleep right away. Or was he as wired as her?

An uncomfortable silence filled the car.

She shouldn't say anything.

"So about—"

"Would you—"

They both stopped, staring at each other. Laughter filled the vehicle.

He gestured at her. "You go first."

Her heart was going to ignore her mind. "I need a night cap. Would you like to come in?"

He looked away but nodded. "I'd like that."

Odd, how he looked away from her.

They exited the car without delay, jaunting up the side-walk to her front door. She unlocked it with quick finesse, dashing inside, undoing the alarm while Bryce shut the door. He re-locked it as well.

They both tossed off their shoes, then she headed for the kitchen, gesturing at the couch. "Have a seat. I'll make us a drink. A hot drink."

She heard his low chuckle but didn't turn around to look at him. That weird feeling in the car was still in the air.

She didn't want to be wired for the rest of the night where she couldn't sleep, so she made hot chocolate instead of coffee. But she needed more than the chocolatey taste and added some Baileys in it. She took a seat next to Bryce, handing him his mug.

At his first sip, his eyes widened before a smile formed. "Is there a touch of Baileys in this?"

She remembered the first time she had asked him that same question. He wouldn't say either way because he hadn't made it. She had no such qualms about the matter.

"Yes. Two shots of it, actually. I debated on three."

They clinked mugs to cheer that statement, sipping in silence for a while.

"So, what were you going to say in the car?" she asked, deciding she despised the silence.

He blew out a breath. "I don't even remember now."

Her brow rose as her lips pursed in a comical manner. "Is that so?"

His cheeks bloomed a bright red as he took another sip.

Perhaps to find the right words. "It's not a conversation I want to have. Yet."

She curled her feet under her, wrapping the blanket around her waist, though her feet did poke out from the blanket, wondering if she should push the issue. She imagined it wasn't a conversation she wanted to have either.

But she also didn't like to shy away from things. Get the hard parts over with was her motto.

"Now you have to tell me."

Bryce stared at his mug instead of her. "I was wondering about this weekend. Whether we were going to talk more strategies for the town tomorrow or wait until Monday. Or if we...even needed more strategies to begin with."

He wanted her to leave. Her job was complete.

He lifted his gaze, and for the first time she saw the desire her brother had mentioned. Though he didn't make any kind of move toward her. But his intense stare told her all she needed to know. The man had feelings for her, and she couldn't deny she had some in return. Bryce was easy to like. He respected others. He always had their interests at heart. He was kind and courteous. He made her laugh with ease. She felt safe and comfortable around him. It helped that he was handsome as sin. Those other traits made him even more attractive.

His words said her job was complete. His eyes said he didn't want her to leave.

"Why don't we wait until Monday to talk about it? It's the weekend, and I think we both deserve some days off."

She saw and felt the pressure leave his body. The heavy weight that had been sitting on his shoulders from such an innocent question.

"I like that plan."

Silence filled the room again. This time she understood what the tension in the air was—sexual tension.

"Do you want to watch a movie or something?" She wasn't ready for him to leave. Of course, she also wasn't ready to do anything about the attraction between them.

One, her job had to come first. She couldn't afford to lose it. Two, he was technically married. The last thing she wanted was to give his wife real ammunition in the divorce. Right now, her lies were just that—lies. If she did anything with him, even kiss him, they wouldn't be lies any longer. The more times she reminded herself of that, the easier she'd have the control to resist him.

Hopefully.

"A movie sounds great."

They put on an action flick—the first thing they found when browsing through the channels. Though she felt the tension shift between them, neither acted on it. They finished their drinks and got lost in the movie. She must've fallen asleep as had Bryce because she woke up dazed, wondering how the movie had ended. Whatever was on the TV now, she didn't recognize it.

Somehow her head had found his shoulder. She didn't want to move from her position. He was warm and comfortable...and too much temptation.

She sat up.

Her movements, as slight as they were, jostled Bryce awake.

"What time is it?" he asked, rubbing his eyes. She hoped he'd been unaware she'd used him as a pillow.

She reached for her phone on the coffee table in front of them, lighting it up to see the time.

"2:03 in the morning. We fell asleep. I didn't even see the ending, and I wanted to know how it ended."

He chuckled, standing up. "We can try finishing it another night. I should go."

She stood as well, feeling the charge in the air again. The desire pulsing between them.

"It's late. You can sleep on the couch."

His gaze glided from her to the couch, shaking his head. "No, I think it's better I go." He headed for the door, putting on his shoes and coat without waiting for her to respond. "I'll call you tomorrow. Maybe we can finish the movie."

She nodded, too afraid to speak. To ask him to stay again, but this time in her bed.

"Good night, Lila."

She smiled, a tremble shooting down her spine when he closed the door.

Maybe it was best that her job was complete. If she stayed in Bryce's presence much longer, she might lose the control she barely had right now.

8

BRYCE LOOKED up from his phone when his brother strolled into the kitchen. Griffin frowned at him, then headed for the coffee pot.

"Why are you in my house? And how did I not hear the alarm go off?"

Bryce chuckled, setting his phone down and picking up his mug, taking a sip. "You must've been in a dead sleep because I came inside around two in the morning."

Griffin turned around from the coffee pot, mug in hand, and took a sip before replying. "Why were you even around here at that time? I thought you were staying at Juliet's. Did you two argue about something?"

Because Griffin knew Bryce didn't like her having a relationship with Aster. He hadn't given his opinion about it yet. Which Bryce took to mean he didn't care. Maybe Bryce cared more because Aster didn't like him, while he had no issue with Griffin.

"No. I drove Lila home last night and I stayed to watch a movie. We both fell asleep. When I woke up at two, I left. I didn't feel like driving all the way to Juliet's, so I crashed here. I hope that was okay."

Griffin chuckled. "You're always welcome here." He paused, eyeing him as if weighing his next words. "When does Lila leave? I know her brother and his crew leave today."

"We'll be talking about that on Monday. We're taking a much-needed break."

His brother was kind enough not to add anything else. He didn't have the mental energy to have a conversation about his attraction to her. When she had offered her couch last night, he nearly caved. It would've kept him closer to her. And that was not something he could let happen. Not while he was still married. He might be getting a divorce, but he took his vows seriously. He wouldn't step out of line, even if Denise didn't hold the same belief.

"So what are you doing today?" Griffin asked.

He knew his brother and Eve had the weekend off. No doubt they'd be spending it together doing whatever they loved doing together. They were inseparable, and he hated to admit how much that made him jealous. Despite loving Denise in the beginning of their marriage, he couldn't say they were ever inseparable.

"I might supervise and check in on the clean-up today."

Griffin lowered his mug to the counter, heading to the fridge. "Or you could take the day off like you told Lila you were doing. You know they can handle the clean-up. You work too much, Bryce."

Yeah, but if it kept him busy, it also kept him away from Lila. While he'd mentioned finishing the movie, he knew it wasn't a good idea.

"Maybe. First, I need to run home and grab more clothes."

The fridge door shut hard, making Bryce flinch. The tight expression Griffin wore wasn't hard to decipher, especially when he vocalized his feelings. "She should be the one vacating the house. Not you."

Bryce stood up, went to the sink, and poured out his coffee. "I don't want to have this conversation right now."

"I know. I'm sorry. It upsets me to see you hurting like this."

He swiveled around from the sink, producing a smile he didn't feel. He knew Griffin saw through it right away.

"Have a good day with Eve. We'll chat later."

He left before his brother could say anything else about Denise. Of course, it wasn't fair he was the one being booted out of the house. But sometimes it was easier to let her have her way. He was tired. Exhausted and mentally drained dealing with her antics. He couldn't wait until the divorce was finalized. Fighting over the house—one he bought with his money—didn't even feel worth it. He wanted to wipe his hands of her.

It was eight o'clock in the morning. Too early to be up after such a long week and barely any sleep last night. He'd tossed and turned more than he liked at Griffin's. So he figured knocking on Lila's door right now wouldn't be wise. She'd still be asleep. Plus, he was supposed to be keeping his distance. He fought the urge to look at the cottage.

He drove slower than normal toward his house, praying the entire way Denise would be gone. He had no desire to deal with her.

His heart sank when he saw her car in the driveway. It was going to be one of those days. Parking next to her, he sat for a minute before even turning the car off. He had to find some calm and center himself before he walked inside.

When he unlocked the door and stepped inside, the air

felt off. He couldn't explain why. The lights were off. The alarm hadn't been set. Though Denise had been known to forget to set it now and again. The place was silent. Eerily silent.

She wasn't a late sleeper. She woke up at the crack of dawn, even on the weekends when she didn't have to work.

Unless she wasn't home, even though her car was in the driveway.

"Denise?"

Nothing but silence echoed back.

He tossed his car keys in the bowl on the bench near the door, then jaunted up the stairs. The sooner he packed some clothes, the better chance he wouldn't run into her. He passed the bathroom and spare room with quick steps, and didn't pause in his long strides until he entered the main bedroom. The bed was made, but no sign of Denise. Even the lights to the master bathroom were off. He hadn't heard any noise in the kitchen. So where was Denise?

Most likely she slept the night at her lover's place. He obviously picked her up last night. Disgusting how she was being so blatant about her affair now that the divorce proceedings were in motion.

Whatever. He'd be grateful he didn't have to deal with her.

Grabbing a suitcase from the closet, he figured he'd pack as much as he could. Less chance for him to have to come back and run into her.

That's what his life had come down to. Being afraid of seeing his soon-to-be ex-wife.

Though he wanted to be quick, he took his time folding his clothes before setting them in the suitcase. He zipped it up and grabbed it by the handle. He swiped a few more suit jackets as well and left the room. He set the clothes and suitcase by the front door, deciding to check the kitchen for her. He didn't like how quiet the house sounded.

She didn't generally let other people drive her around. She liked being in control of every little thing. If her car was here, it meant she had to be here. He found it odd if Eric had picked her up. But, of course, what did he know about Denise anymore? They'd grown apart.

The smear of blood on the entryway into the living room made him pause. Even with the lights out, he could see the evidence marring the wooden frame. He flicked the light switch, confirming his eyes weren't playing tricks on him.

Bryce let out a slow breath and made his way inside the room with quiet footsteps. He didn't see her body until he rounded the couch. Denise lay on the floor near the Christmas tree. Still undecorated, the branches bare besides the specks of blood. Her body was positioned at a disjointed angle. Blood covered the room everywhere. The ceiling, the walls, the floor, the couch. The boxes of decorations that hadn't been unpacked yet. The weapon still embedded in her chest told him how she died.

Somehow, he found himself moving closer to get a better look. He wasn't sure what was protruding out of her chest.

An icicle.

A Christmas ornament meant to hang on the tree. A tree she had meant to look merry for some odd reason.

He knew the icicle well. It was part of a set. Six total icicles. They were crystal glass, about ten inches long. Very delicate. At least he had thought so. If one was sticking out of her chest, they weren't as delicate as he thought. His grandparents had purchased them overseas on their honeymoon when they went to Prague. When his grandma passed, his grandpa had passed down the things that meant a lot to them to each one of his grandchildren. Bryce had gotten the crystal icicles.

Now they were tarnished, used as a murder weapon.

That thought jarred him out of his stupor.

Denise was dead!

He backed out with wobbly legs, his hand shaking as he grabbed his phone from his pocket. His fingers fumbled on the screen until he managed to find Griffin's number.

"Did you forget something or is she already giving you problems?"

"She's dead."

His brother inhaled a sharp breath and neither spoke a moment.

"What do you mean?"

He'd moved away, circling the couch, but he could still see her. Her vacant eyes staring at the ceiling. The droplets of blood on her cheeks. The sharp angle of the icicle as it protruded from her chest.

"I mean, she's lying on the living room floor with blood everywhere and an icicle in her chest."

"A what?"

Bryce swallowed, continuing around the couch, unable to look at her anymore. "The icicle ornaments Grandpa gave me. The ones from Prague."

Griffin sighed. "I know the ones. Do not touch anything. Do you hear me, Bryce? Nothing."

He didn't need to be told that. He knew what would happen here. The husband was always the first suspect. It didn't help they were going through a nasty divorce.

"I haven't. Just the front door to get inside. Well, the closet too. I packed a suitcase. But hell, Griffin, I live here. My prints are everywhere."

"Don't touch anything. Go outside and wait for me. I'll

be right there. I'll call the county to investigate this. It's a conflict of interest for me. You understand that, right?"

Yeah, he understood everything.

He turned around and walked as quickly out of the house as he'd walked in.

"Bryce? Did you hear me?" Griffin asked. He could hear the sound of a door slam, so he knew his brother was already in the car and leaving.

"I'm a suspect. I know, Griffin. I didn't kill her."

Griffin groaned. "I know that. Everyone will know that."

He doubted that.

Maybe people in town who really knew him would believe his innocence.

But others?

Like Lila.

What were the chances she'd believe his innocence?

And what were the odds she wouldn't run away the moment she heard the news?

SHE ROLLED OUT OF BED, blindly grabbing for her robe hanging behind the bedroom door, annoyed at whoever wanted to knock at such an unreasonable time in the morning. When she glanced at the clock on her nightstand, she figured she wouldn't ream the person too much. Nine thirty wasn't too early. She was used to getting up and at City Hall by eight the past two and a half weeks. But after a long day yesterday and sleeping fitfully after Bryce left, she wasn't ready to get out of bed.

To be safe, she looked through the peephole before opening the door. She was surprised to see Aster standing there. The band wasn't leaving until noon as they had booked an evening flight out of town.

She undid the alarm and opened the door.

His harried expression confused her, and when he crushed her into his arms, that further baffled her.

"Thank God you're all right. I was so worried."

She frowned, prying herself out of his arms. "I don't know what is wrong with you, but I'm too tired for whatever this is." She waved her hand in a circle, gesturing toward him, and shut the door with a little too much force.

She beelined it for the kitchen. She needed coffee for whatever nonsense he was talking about.

"So you didn't hear?"

Her hand paused on the cupboard door, looking at her brother. "Spit it out. Whatever drama is going on around town, I don't care."

"Bryce murdered his wife."

The coffee container slipped from her fingers. Unfortunately, she had taken off the lid. Coffee grounds scattered all over the floor.

"He did not."

Aster stared at her as if she'd lost her mind. "He found her body."

"That doesn't make him a killer. And what was with the worry about me?" She slammed a hand to her hip. "So you think he killed his wife and he would also hurt me. Why?! Why would he do either of those things?"

Aster opened his mouth, then closed it. Clearly not having a good enough answer for her.

"How do you even know this happened?"

"Griffin called Juliet."

She rolled her eyes, then swept her gaze over the coffee

mess. So much for a cup of java. Something she desperately needed.

"And you were with her when he called." She shoved past him, not even caring she'd clipped his shoulder, and grabbed the broom from the tiny closet.

With jerky movements, she swept the coffee mess into a small pile.

"Stay away from him."

Her hands tightened on the handle as she glared at her brother. "No matter how difficult things might've gotten between them, he would never have hurt her. Not even a little bit. So don't stand there and tell me what to do."

"You barely know the guy!"

"Same goes for the sister, and yet that didn't keep her out of your bed!"

The muscles in Aster's cheek pulsed, telling her he was exerting all his energy to keep his cool. They'd gotten into some volatile arguments. Words could fly without thinking things through. They'd had to apologize to each other more times than she could count on two hands. But they always moved on. They loved each other. But right now, she wanted to hit her brother over the head with the broom for thinking such disgusting thoughts about Bryce.

Aster turned toward the closet and grabbed the dustpan, stooping down to set it up next to the pile of coffee grounds. This time she had to use all her energy not to swipe them into his face. But that would be childish, and she knew why he was acting this way. Because he cared about her and he couldn't help his overprotectiveness when it emerged.

They cleaned the mess up in silence. Aster took a seat at the table while she washed her hands. When she turned around from the sink, he looked crestfallen.

"I'm sorry, Lilac. My temper got the better of me. I don't like the guy."

"He hasn't done anything to garner your dislike."

Aster shrugged. "I don't like any guy that looks at you like he does."

That produced a tiny smile on her end, which helped form one on him as well. That statement couldn't be truer. Aster had an issue with any guy that she, Poppy, or Zinnia dated. He was too mollycoddling, and she knew he couldn't help it.

"Juliet said Griffin called in the county to investigate it. I can respect him for that."

"Did you tell Juliet your suspicions that her brother did it?"

Aster looked chagrined, glancing away.

"So you have no issue sleeping with her, but you don't have the guts to tell her you think her brother is a killer."

"What makes you think he didn't do it? It's normally the spouse."

She understood why Aster would jump to that conclusion. Why others who didn't know Bryce would as well. And she couldn't say she knew Bryce, like all heart and soul. But what she did know in the short time she'd known him was he could never hurt another living soul, even if he had no other options. He wasn't that kind of person.

"I know in my gut he didn't. And if I say he didn't, my brother should trust me enough to be on my side."

Aster stood up, stepping closer to her. "I think it's time you leave this town. I'd feel better if you did."

"You know I can't now."

He shook his head, wanting to deny the truth.

"Aster, this murder just canceled out the amazing festival

we had. I can't leave." She left off adding Bryce to the end of that sentence. She couldn't leave him. Not like this.

He closed the distance, gripping her shoulders. "I'm not leaving yet either."

That was the last thing she needed.

But once he got something in his head—like her—there was no stopping him.

"You're not staying here."

He chuckled, then pulled her in for another hug. This time she didn't push him away. She soaked up his love, appreciating the fact he cared so much, but despising it at the same time.

He stepped away first this time.

"I don't foresee the other guys leaving yet either. We'll stay at the place we have, as long as it's not rented out to someone else."

"Why would they stay too?" Her brows drew low as she crossed her arms. "What aren't you telling me?"

Aster blew out a breath, chuckling with no humor behind it. "Lucky for Bryce, there is more than one suspect. There's the dude she was sleeping with. I can't remember his name." His gaze swept across the floor, telling her he was nervous to admit the next suspect.

"I know you're not that stupid since you wouldn't sleep with two women at once, but which other band member did?"

His gaze shot to her. "Stan. I told him not to even go there, but she had an effect on men. I will make sure he tells the police everything, but I know he didn't do it."

"Okay, he didn't do it. Bryce didn't do it. Perhaps the lover did."

Aster snapped his fingers as if saying, "Bingo!" "Not to

mention, if she was sleeping with the lover and Stan, who's to say she wasn't sleeping with any other guys?"

She waggled her hand in his face like she wanted to slap him. And the urge was so strong she had to back away from him. "How dare you come in here, right off the bat, accusing Bryce, when you knew there were more possible people who could've done it. Don't ever reference his name with that crime again."

He nodded. "Only for you."

"Now go find me some coffee while I shower. It's your fault I don't have any."

She left the room, Aster's laughter trailing behind her.

9

BRYCE ARCHED HIS BACK, twisting to and fro. He'd been in an interrogation room for the past three hours sitting in a chair waiting for someone to grill him. He'd be damned if he'd get up now and start pacing the room after holding out this long.

Denise was dead. While he would grieve her loss, he wasn't going down for her murder. The less he made himself look guilty, the better.

His brother had called in the county, and they responded promptly. He'd been put in the back of a patrol car and brought to the Sleighville station as soon as the first officer arrived. Griffin didn't argue. He didn't argue. Though it had been embarrassing as hell. He was already being treated as the killer. As if he'd do something as despicable as murder.

Never!

A small part of him—a tiny part inside his heart—had been starting to hate Denise at the cruelty she'd been dishing out at him. But he'd never go as far as murder. Maybe talk nasty things about her around town—if he got really riled up—but never in a million years would he have laid a hand on her.

He hoped the rest of the town knew that about him. That they would believe he was innocent.

After another thirty minutes—he guessed since he didn't have a watch or his phone—the door opened.

Sheriff Carter from Walker County entered the room and took a seat across from him. He smiled and Bryce didn't feel the friendliness behind it. While the sheriff and he interacted on several occasions, he knew they weren't friends at the moment. This was all business.

"Sorry to keep you waiting, Mr. Stuart."

He knew that was a lie as well. They wanted to make him sweat, as if that would get him to confess to a crime he didn't commit.

He returned a short smile and nodded. Not much would come out of his mouth unless necessary. He knew how all of this worked. Crime shows were his favorite. He even enjoyed the true crime shows on occasion. Though fiction was more up his alley.

"I'd like to ask you a few questions. Would you like a lawyer? Were you asked that yet?"

He had been. Though his rights weren't given to him as he wasn't officially arrested for her murder.

"At this point in time, I'm not requesting a lawyer. I'd like to know who killed Denise as much as you."

Some people would call him an idiot for not retaining a lawyer, but wouldn't that signify guilt if he did? He wasn't guilty! If the time came and he had no choice, he knew Darcy would step in and help. Hell, if she caught wind he was in here alone, he wouldn't be surprised to find her walking into the room without him asking.

Sheriff Carter nodded, then proceeded. "Where were you last night? Give me a rundown of your evening."

"It was the last night of the festival the town held. I was there until it ended around ten o'clock. Lila—she's the PR consultant the town hired—needed a ride home. I offered her one, and we decided to watch a movie together. It had been a long week, and we wanted to unwind and relax. We fell asleep and woke up around two in the morning. I left and walked across the lawn to my brother's house where I crashed the rest of the night. I left his house around eight and went home where I found Denise's body in the living room."

"How close are you with Lila?"

She was going to hate him forever for this debacle. He despised that he'd gotten her in this mess.

"She's a colleague. We've been working closely since she arrived in Sleighville about two and a half weeks ago. You know about the incident with Mark. She's been helping turn the image of our town back to something people will love."

And now this murder was setting them backward again. Not that he was going to voice *that*. Though it would be a good reason for him not to have murdered his wife. He was trying to improve Sleighville's image, not make it worse!

Sheriff Carter nodded again, increasing his smile. "And that's all? Just a working relationship?"

"I have not had any sexual relations or even touched her in an inappropriate way. The rumors going around town that you might have heard that we were sleeping together were created by Denise."

"And did that upset you?"

Oh, he saw where this line of questioning was going. They were going to pin this murder on him. He felt it to his bones.

"Yes, but more so that it was affecting Lila. She hasn't done anything wrong but do a wonderful job of putting on an amazing festival."

"Yes, I went to it myself. It was a wonderful event. I have to agree with that statement. So the divorce has been..." Sheriff Carter shook his head as if finding the right word. "Would you say volatile?"

"Mentally, sure. She's been spreading rumors about me. About a relationship with Lila when she's the one having an affair. She's trying to get the house and clean me dry of all my money. Basically, she's putting me through the ringer."

"She was, you mean?"

Bryce forced himself to remain calm and not act affected by the sheriff's condescending attitude. "Of course. That's what I meant."

"Who was she sleeping with? Do you know?"

He hated to throw Judge Riner's son under the bus. He had a deep respect for the judge. His son, though? He slept in his wife's bed, he could make it too. He didn't feel bad for Eric. Only Judge Riner, that his good name was being soiled by the affair.

"Eric Riner. He works in the same building as me. First floor. I have proof from a private investigator."

Sheriff Carter's brows lifted as if surprised by that information. "Can I have copies of that?"

"Yes."

The questioning went on for another hour. Within that timeframe, Darcy showed up. He was grateful for her intervening. It felt nice to have support on his side. She couldn't believe he murdered Denise if she'd shown up, right?

The sheriff repeated the same questions but in a different manner, as if that would trip him up in a lie. Yet, it didn't. Because he wasn't lying. Not even the hard questions where he really, really wanted to lie. The ones that painted him in a bad light and made him a damn good suspect. Darcy stepped in now and again, signaling for him to remain quiet. It riled the sheriff every time.

He had to have faith that justice would work out in the end.

Sheriff Carter stood up, gesturing toward the door. "You are free to go, but do not leave town. I might have more questions."

"Of course."

He walked out and didn't look back once. He felt eyes all over him as he walked through the station. Since he had been driven there in the back of a patrol car, he stopped heading toward the door. He needed a ride home.

"You did great in there."

If Darcy thought so, maybe he had. But it sure didn't feel like it.

"They think I killed her. I didn't."

Darcy set her hand on his shoulder. "I know that. You would never hurt anyone, even if they deserved it."

Bryce cocked a brow. He hadn't expected the statement or the venomous way it left her lips.

"We both know Denise was not well loved around town. Not lately, anyway."

Oh, he understood her meaning just fine. Denise hid her vicious ways, until recently when she decided she'd had enough of being married to him. It's as if the dam broke inside her and she didn't care what anyone thought of her.

"I shouldn't say she deserved what happened, but it doesn't surprise me. I won't let them pin this on you."

He appreciated her support. No doubt he'd need it going forward, if the way the sheriff interrogated him was any indication.

Yet, he felt lost. Like floating in a boat in the middle of the ocean, no rescue in sight.

Duke appeared next to them. "Come on. We'll go out the back. I'll give you a ride home."

Thank goodness for great friends.

He said another huge thanks to Darcy and then goodbye before slipping outside without anyone stopping them and into Duke's patrol car where he finally let out an audible breath.

"He's just doing his job. You'll be cleared before you know it."

Duke's calm, reassuring voice did nothing what he assumed he had intended it to do.

"I appreciate the support."

"You know the town has your back."

Bryce gave a merciful laugh. "I don't think the whole town will."

Duke scoffed. "Anyone who knows you will know you could never do something of that nature. I saw..." Duke paused, swallowing hard. "I saw her body too. There's no way you could ever do something like that. We got your back."

He stopped at the end of the alleyway. "Where am I taking you?"

Bryce had no idea where he should go.

"Juliet's, I guess. That's where I've been staying and where most of my stuff is." So much for the suitcase he'd packed.

An awkwardness entered the space, and Bryce wished he would've said Griffin's house instead.

"Sorry, we can go—"

"No, I'll take you to Juliet's." Duke's hands tightened on

the steering wheel briefly before relaxing. "I don't understand what she sees in that guy."

Oh, they were having the conversation. Bryce had hoped he'd keep it to himself. He didn't know why—or what—Juliet saw in him either. It was his own fault for suggesting her house.

"Not a clue. I don't get along with him myself."

Duke frowned, then chuckled. "Why? I know why I keep my distance from him, but I didn't know you two didn't like each other."

"He thinks I have feelings for Lila."

Another bout of silence entered the vehicle.

"I know you didn't sleep with her, despite what Denise was spreading around."

"Unlike her, I took my wedding vows seriously."

More silence. Duke cleared his throat. "I'm sorry, Bryce. For all of this."

He nodded, too many emotions clogging his throat. He wasn't a crier. Maybe as a child when he skinned his knee. But as an adult? He couldn't remember the last time he shed a tear. He wasn't going to start now.

They made it to Juliet's without any other chatter. Lila's rental car was in the driveway. Damn it! He should've picked Griffin's house. He wasn't ready to face her.

"Looks like we both get to be in an awkward situation," Duke muttered under his breath as he parked the car.

That garnered a chuckle out of him. "So you're coming inside too?"

Duke grinned. "And miss all the good stuff? Yeah, I'm coming in."

He exited the vehicle, wondering what would happen inside the house. The police suspected him of murder, and Lila most likely thought no different.

The husband was always suspect number one.

He didn't blame anyone for their suspicions of him.

Duke slapped him on the back and urged him on when he'd been standing frozen by the car.

"Don't forget we have your back. No matter what any outsider might think about you."

That's the motivational speech he needed to move forward. As long as he had his friends and family by his side, he'd be fine. God, he didn't even want to tell his parents what happened. They never liked Denise. Lucky for them, living in Arizona, they never had to deal with her much.

Now he would never have to either.

SHE COULDN'T FIGURE out why she had let Aster talk her into coming over to Juliet's. While she knew Bryce had nothing to do with it, this felt like a family matter. She and Aster were not family, even if he was sleeping with Juliet.

The front door opened and Bryce, along with Duke, stepped inside. She jerked upright from the couch, nearly running to Bryce and throwing her arms around him. He looked as if he'd aged at least ten years since she'd last seen him. Which was only ten hours or so ago.

"Hi." The simple greeting from him came out more cautious than she liked. He had nothing to be worried about concerning her. She believed in his innocence.

"Hey." She tried to widen her smile to ease the tension she felt building in the room. "How are you?"

Dumb question! Of course he wasn't okay. She couldn't believe those words came out of her mouth.

She waved her hand in the air before he could respond.

"Forget I asked that. Of course you're not okay. I'm so sorry about your wife."

He cringed, glancing away.

Right. She'd meant his soon-to-be ex-wife. Maybe he flinched because she should've said ex-wife instead. Or he reacted that way because he was distraught over her death. Well, duh! Bryce was ready for the divorce, but she knew he still had loved her at one time.

"Where's Juliet?" Duke broke in, surveying the room like the cop he was. He wore his uniform, which increased his intense look even more.

"Oh, her and Aster are in the bedroom." Her eyes widened, then she blinked rapidly, shaking her head. "Talking. They are in the bedroom talking."

A few minutes ago, Aster asked Juliet for a word alone. Anything else and she would've left his ass here without a backward glance.

Despite fixing her misguided words, Duke's expression didn't change at all. If anything, the scowl increased along with the fire in his eyes. Something she assumed was rage. Bryce had mentioned that Duke had feelings for Juliet. The relationship Juliet had with her brother wasn't easy on him.

"Umm...so I had a chat with the police this morning," Bryce said. The conversation switch should've eased the tension in the room. Instead, it intensified.

She could only imagine how the chat as he put it had gone.

Duke looked uncomfortable and averted his gaze away from her. Bryce's eyes stayed connected with hers though.

"I told them the truth about everything. I had to tell them I was at your house last night. I wanted to warn you that you'll have to talk with them as well."

She let out a collective breath, more noticeable than she should've made it.

"I didn't kill her," Bryce blurted.

Idiot!

Her reaction had made him think she thought he killed his wife. Not once, from the moment Aster told her, had she thought him capable of murder.

She didn't even know why she'd tensed up when he started talking about speaking with the police. Probably because she felt horrible that he even had to deal with all that mayhem.

"I know that."

The frown on Bryce's face said he didn't quite believe her. The way his eyes shattered with disgust as well that she could think something so callous of him.

"Bryce!" Juliet rushed across the room and swung her arms around him.

The moment felt personal, so Lila looked away, deciding another cup of coffee was in order. She'd already had four cups, but she didn't want to disturb them. Not to mention, Bryce didn't seem like he wanted her around.

Tears echoed behind her, either Juliet's or Bryce's, she didn't turn around to find out as she walked out of the living room toward the kitchen. Less than a minute later, Aster joined her.

"You okay?"

She nodded as she poured herself a cup of coffee.

"You're going to be on a caffeine high if you don't stop drinking that shit."

She was pretty sure she was immune to that by now. The amount she drank daily said her body had gotten used to it.

"How did your chat with Juliet go?" She turned around

with a fake, cheery smile. Aster rolled his eyes at her display of nonchalance.

Why was she pretending everything was okay when everything had turned to utter shit? Because she had to or she'd go insane.

"I wanted to warn her about Stan."

Lila's brows puckered low as she thought about that simple statement. "What does that even mean?"

"That he slept with Denise. That the police will question him and stuff. That he's a good guy that makes horrible decisions when it comes to women but he's not a killer."

"Well, of course he's not." She never once thought Stan had done it either.

That begged the question...who killed Denise?

Bryce didn't do it.

Stan didn't either.

The lover was too obvious.

But it had to be someone close to her. It usually was.

"You left the room pretty quickly. Are you sure you're okay?"

Her mannequin smile was back on. "I thought Bryce and Juliet deserved time to themselves."

"I need to head to my place. Talk with the guys. Are you okay here or do you want to come with me?"

They'd driven together and left his car at her cottage. So if he left, she'd be stranded with Juliet. Not that that was a bad thing. But if Bryce intended to stay, she didn't want to impose on family time. She also didn't want to intrude on whatever conversation Aster intended to have with the band. He could also drop her back off at home. But a small part of her wanted to stay with Bryce. To comfort him somehow.

"I'll be fine here."

Aster turned around to leave.

"Oh, Aster."

He looked at her over his shoulder.

"I'd take a wide berth around Duke. You stole the woman he likes."

Aster's lips turned up into a sly smirk that said he wasn't sorry at all. "Can't steal something that was never yours to begin with."

He walked out of the kitchen.

Lila looked at the black liquid swirling in the mug, tossing that statement around her head. He had a point. One she hated to admit. Duke had all the chances in the world to ask Juliet out and he never did. He couldn't be mad that someone else swooped in and did what he didn't have the guts to do.

Of course, what did she know? She wasn't acquainted with their entire backstory. There could be things she didn't know about their past. She and Juliet were friendly, but they weren't exactly friends where they shared all their secrets.

The air felt different the moment he entered the space.

She looked up, catching Bryce's potent gaze directed at her.

"Am I disturbing you?" he asked as if unsure of himself.

"No." She waved a frivolous hand in the air that said he was free to come inside.

He did, and to her surprise, stepped right next to her. He paused for a long moment before grabbing a mug from the cupboard and pouring himself some coffee.

"I'm sorry, Lila."

She tilted her head, hating the forlorn expression on his face. "For what?"

"For getting you into this mess."

A short laugh escaped. "It's not like you planned it out."

He set down the mug so hard, the coffee jostled over the rim, spilling to the counter. "I swear I didn't kill her. I would never—"

Her hand rose, cupping his cheek, surprising him into silence and her as well. She had no idea what came over herself. But to hear his desperate pleas that she believe in his innocence was too much.

And damn. She liked touching him—way too much. Now was not the time to be showing her true feelings. Except, her hand didn't move. Her darn heart overriding her mind again.

"There has not been one moment where I thought you hurt her. I am on your side, Bryce."

He closed his eyes, letting out a deep breath. As if her words had finally gotten through to him. A calm swept through the kitchen. She knew she should retract her hand, but feeling his bristled skin was a treat. A sweet, unforgivable treat, and she wanted to soak up a few more moments.

She regained her senses, letting her hand fall. The moment she did, his eyes snapped open. She took a sip of coffee, using both hands, as if that would help keep her distance from him.

"I suppose you're leaving with Aster."

"Are you kidding me?" She shook her head, soulless laughter releasing. "My job just got even harder. There's no way I can leave yet." Her eyes rounded, embarrassment flooding her. "Unless you want me to leave."

Like last night, she saw it again. The flash of desire erupted in his gaze.

"No. I need you more than ever."

Damn her heart. She wanted that to mean something more than it actually did. And that was wrong to want on so many levels.

"Well, this is going to require more than a festival."

A teeny smile emerged on Bryce's lips that she wanted to suddenly kiss. "I know whatever you come up with will be amazing."

Yeah, well, she wished she had the same optimism as him.

Because dealing with a creepo spying on people was a whole different ball game compared to murder.

If she didn't know any better, she'd think Denise got murdered on purpose to make Bryce's life even more hellish than it had been before.

10

"Good morning, Becca," Bryce said with more cheer than he felt. Her downturned expression said she wasn't falling for his lackluster performance.

"I'll grab you a cup of coffee." She stood up and rounded her desk so fast he had no chance to stop her. Not that he wouldn't take a cup, but she didn't need to get him one.

He unlocked his office door, set his briefcase near his desk, and took a seat. For a few brief moments, he sat there. Tried to center his mind into work mode. It sort of helped.

The past week had been a week from hell. He'd been interviewed several more times, each one more intense than the last. They were still trying to trip him up in a lie. But that was the thing. They never would because he'd been honest every single time.

Lila had been interviewed as well, and while he had wanted to ask her how it went, he held back. She might be on his side, but talking about it still worried him. He'd lose his mind if she left him now. She'd become his rock. His focus. Without her near, his entire world would come crumbling down. He knew he shouldn't put that much significance on one person, but he couldn't stop himself.

Eric Riner had been interviewed, though he had no idea how that went. He hadn't been arrested, so they didn't have enough evidence to say he did it. They had no evidence to round up a good suspect to arrest! Not even Stan, who'd been interviewed and confessed to sleeping with her, had been arrested. He'd had a solid alibi. Passed out with Toby and Carson at their rental place.

While Griffin shouldn't have told him, he had been privy to a few details of the murder.

The set of icicles from his grandparents were missing. Only the one left in her chest was present. So whoever killed her had taken the box with the rest of the ornaments with them. No prints had been found on the murder weapon. Griffin—and the police—couldn't figure out why the killer took the box. What was the point?

The time of death had been estimated to be between three and six in the morning on that Saturday. Another thing he had been thankful for was Griffin and his obsession with security cameras. Griffin's cameras had captured him entering his house a little past two o'clock in the morning and not leaving until eight, as he had told the sheriff. He had an alibi. A pretty damn solid one as Griffin also had cameras in the back of the house. No one had been detected leaving through there either. After the horrifying incident with Eve and her deranged brother, not to mention Mark and his perverted ways, Griffin didn't take any chances with their safety. It had saved his life from being thrown behind bars.

A total of twenty-eight stab wounds had been found on her body. Which, according to Griffin, indicated a crime of passion. Someone had been in such a rage, they couldn't stop themselves. He could understand that sentiment. The hell Denise had put him through. The many times she put him down, broke his soul, crushing it without a care. He had no trouble understanding why someone would keep stabbing her. Not that he'd ever capitulate to that extreme. He wasn't a violent man. He never would be, no matter the soul-crushing hurt dished his way.

Besides that, no other fingerprints, DNA, or latent evidence had been found to point them in a good direction. Unlike Griffin, he hadn't installed cameras in his driveway or near the front door. Did that make him a bad husband? Not concerned about Denise's safety like Griffin was with Eve? He didn't want to answer that question. But it would've helped to have the killer on camera entering the house. No footprints were detected by the back door or near any windows, so that meant whoever had entered had done so through the front door. Denise let them in? If so, that meant it was someone they all knew. Someone who lived in town.

He'd taken the week off to avoid the questions swirling around town. It had been a suggestion by Lila—and his family—so he listened. His mind had been mush anyway. Zoning off at times thinking about Denise. About the good times they had. About the way they turned into a couple that couldn't even stand the sight of each other. About how he could've handled things differently. It all left him very confused.

His parents had wanted to come home as well. For the funeral. To support him in general. He declined, talking them out of it. He had enough people around him trying to comfort him, he didn't need more people in his face. While he loved his parents, when his mom had lived in town, she could smother a little too much. That was the last thing he needed.

"Here you go." She set his mug down on his desk. "You do have a busy week as I pushed things from last week to this week. You have a meeting at ten with the city commissioner about St. Patrick's Day. It'll be here before we know it."

"Thank you, Becca." He picked up the mug, nodding in thanks.

She walked out, leaving his door open. It was typically how he went about his day. He felt it signified an open-door policy. Come on in and chat. Today, he wished she would've closed it. He wasn't sure he was ready to mingle with people yet.

He'd had a whole week to hide from the world and it didn't feel long enough. Juliet's spare bed was starting to give him a backache, but he couldn't go home. The thought of walking inside of it gave him the chills. And sleeping in his bed again? No way in hell. He had no idea if Denise had sex with other men in it.

He was jerked out of his thoughts when Lila stepped through the doorway. She wore a beautiful smile, and it was exactly what he needed.

"Can you close the door?"

A lone brow rose because she knew he liked it open, but she didn't question him. The door shut with a quiet click, and then she sat in the same chair she'd been using since she arrived in town.

He set the mug down again without even taking one sip yet and rubbed a hand down his face. "I didn't realize how hard it would be to come back to work."

She made a quick glance at the door, understanding why he wanted it shut. He wasn't ready for an audience. For anyone.

"You look good though."

Did he? Because as he stared at himself in the mirror this morning, he saw the bags under his eyes. He saw the shadows hiding in the depths. His hair looked duller, as if the past week had drained all the life out of it. His cheeks were roughly bristled, forgoing shaving this morning because his hands had shook too much. He hadn't wanted to cut himself. Though his goatee was still visible, so he wasn't to the full beard stage yet.

He'd seen Lila over the course of the week, but he hadn't seen her as much as he would've liked. He'd stopped by her cottage after visiting Griffin a time or two. Having coffee and chatting. Or she had dropped by Juliet's, hanging out with them for the evening. Any moment with her, he had soaked up and cherished. She made his world brighter in such dark times.

"You don't have to come back yet," she added when he remained silent.

He didn't know how to respond to the compliment about his looks. He felt terrible, so he imagined he looked the same.

"I also can't sit around doing nothing anymore. A week was too long to take off. I didn't even make a statement. I need to do that."

Lila's eyes enlarged, her lips pursing in a severe manner. "You will do no such thing. You might be the mayor, but you were also the husband. It won't look good."

"I always make a statement," he muttered, like a child getting reprimanded for being naughty.

Lila relaxed in her seat, her eyes twinkling with laughter. "Okay. What would you say?"

That was a good question. *I didn't kill her.* Though that didn't say much. People would either believe that or they wouldn't.

"Fine. I won't make a statement."

Her head tilted down in a slight nod, her lips curling even further into a delectable smile that he loved witnessing. She was trying so hard not to laugh at him. He wouldn't even mind because he loved the wondrous sound out of her mouth.

"We have a meeting at ten o'clock with the city commissioner about St. Patrick's Day." He shrugged, laughing. "Well, I have a meeting and I want you to come with me. It's the first holiday since the festival. We need to make this the best damn St. Patrick's Day Sleighville has ever seen."

"Of course. That's three weeks from today. Were we doing something special in between?"

They should. But what? What would help mask and make people forget his wife was murdered?

"Whatever ideas you come up with, you know I will love."

Her smile wavered. Which meant he said something wrong. It snapped back into place as if it never happened. Odd. But he wouldn't say anything. Keeping things good between them was all he wanted to do. Because a happy Lila kept her in town.

"Well, Juliet's cafe will be ready to open full service next week. I'd like to do something big about that."

Maybe that's why her smile wavered. Because while he was happy about Juliet making progress on the cafe, he wasn't happy about who'd been helping her fix the damage.

Aster.

The irritating man hadn't left town yet.

Though he gave the band a bunch of kudos. They all had pitched in to help her fix the fire damage. If they hadn't, Bryce figured the cafe wouldn't be opening next week.

"That's a great idea."

"Good!" She picked up her notebook she loved to carry around and jotted something down. "I will contact Harper and have her start shouting out on social media about the reopening. I'll also talk to Juliet to see if she'll be having a sale or anything. Something to entice people to come check it out. New people, anyway. I'm sure the regulars will stop by no matter what."

"Like me, if you say something should be done, Juliet will follow it."

There it was again. Her smile wavering and springing back to life as if she hadn't meant to let him see it.

THE PRESSURE WAS MOUNTING. Anytime Bryce told her how much confidence he had in her or how much he loved her ideas, more weight landed on her shoulders. As much as she wanted to pull this town out of its turmoil, she wasn't a hundred percent positive she'd be able to. Not anymore, anyway. The murder put a huge dent in the progress they had made.

The festival was a success. While the newspapers and social media had positive reviews about it, it had been over-shadowed by Denise's murder. That horrible crime had canceled out all the good they had done. She wasn't sure how to bounce back from it.

So, she was starting small. The re-opening of the cafe was a good start.

Something she tried to tell her boss this morning. He was ready to pull her from the job. Ready to call it quits and show everyone at the office how much of a failure she was. It wasn't her fault someone got murdered!

She had managed to talk him out of making her leave,

but she was on a short timeline. Three weeks was a long time until St. Patrick's Day. She didn't even know if she'd still be here. Not that she had any intention of telling Bryce that. She imagined he'd break down and lose his shit. She felt it to her bones. He was on the precipice of cracking under all the weight he'd been enduring.

"I want to get started on this. I'm going to run to Harper's office and chat with her. I'll be back before the ten o'clock meeting." She stood up, hating the panic that spread across his face. "Should I close the door behind me?"

He glanced at it, then shook his head. "No, it's fine to leave it open. Thank you for all you do, Lila. I couldn't do this without you."

She gave him a weak smile and left before her entire face crumbled. There it was again. The attitude that she was his savior. She couldn't be. Because if she failed—again—he'd blame her. Those moments she witnessed the desire in his eyes, they would disappear. Disgust would replace it.

She wanted that desire to remain.

In fact, she wanted him to act on it. Kiss her or something. Of course, it was too soon. His wife wasn't even in the ground yet. Next week she would be, but that would still be rushing it. Like slapping it into people's faces. Hey, we weren't sleeping together before but now we plan to! That was the last message she wanted to send. So as much as she wanted Bryce to make a move, it was better he didn't.

The day went by in a blur. It reminded her of how the days played out when they worked on the festival. So many meetings. So many ideas rolling around the room. She felt better by the end of the day they were making good progress.

Juliet planned to do a buy one get one free sale and have

decent-sized samples of all the delicious treats they would sell sprinkled around the cafe.

Harper had the website updated with the re-opening blasted on the front page. She also spread it around the town's social media channels. She even told Aster to make a shout-out to his fans. If nothing else, they'd fall back on the band's fans again.

Despite the murder, not all people who had been renting after the festival had fled town. Some had and left horrible reviews. But others stayed. It was those people that gave her hope they still had a chance to make people see Sleighville wasn't about mayhem and murder. It was, at the heart of it, the town to fill you with Christmas joy.

Though, maybe they should play on the mayhem and murder angle. The town's name gave off that vibe. But it was too soon to say anything in that respect to Bryce. It would be disrespectful.

The idea didn't go far away though.

She bid her goodbye to Bryce, who still looked sad and so unsure of himself. Juliet, when she had spoken with her earlier in the day, had invited her to join her, Aster, and the other band members for supper. As much as she would've enjoyed hanging with all of them, she wanted time alone.

She needed to be on her A-game for this assignment. It would devastate her—and Bryce—if her boss pulled the plug.

Her cottage looked dark and lonely when she pulled into the driveway. Griffin's house was lit up inside and out. She still couldn't get over the fact most houses around town had Christmas decorations and lights on outside. But she had to admit, it made her smile when she looked at them, even if she had seen them a million times already. There was something about Christmas lights that filled a person with exhilaration.

That had another idea popping in her head.

She pulled her notebook and pencil out of her bag as she walked up the sidewalk, scribbling as she went. If she didn't write something down right away, she'd forget it. Now wasn't the time to be forgetting things.

The motion sensor lights kicked on as soon as she loomed closer to the door, which had her movements faltering. A small-sized box wrapped like a Christmas present sat on the doorstep. A large red ribbon adorned the top.

Her notebook and pencil disappeared into her bag as her steps drew closer to the odd object. Who would leave her a Christmas gift? It wasn't even Christmas!

Well, the town celebrated the holiday year-round, so maybe this was a thing some residents did.

Still.

It creeped her out.

She sidestepped the present, unlocked her door, disarmed the alarm, and turned around. For unknown reasons, she didn't want to pick it up.

She did anyway.

Curiosity would get the best of her if she didn't see what was inside.

Her bag dropped to the chair around the kitchen table as the box made a slight thump as she set that down as well.

Something told her to open it carefully.

The ribbon untied with ease, drifting to the table. A knife would be better than ripping it open, so she grabbed the largest one she found and carefully sliced the sides open where the tape held it together.

She unfolded the wrapping paper, the paper itself giving her the heebie-jeebies. It was black with red bells and green

Christmas wreaths sprinkled all over it. But all she saw was red spots mimicking drops of blood.

Once the box was revealed, she had to slice the tape on top to open. She lifted the flaps and peered inside.

Leave now or you'll be next.

She stumbled back, gripping the counter to catch her fall.

What the hell?

Who would write something like that and send it to her like a present?

And why?

It didn't make sense.

What she did know was she couldn't keep it to herself.

With her shoes and coat still on, she left her house and walked across the lawn. Maybe she was being too jumpy about the entire matter, but it was better to err on the side of caution. A woman had been murdered. They had no suspects yet. What else could the note mean but that? She'd be the next victim.

Eve answered the door after she rang the bell. "Hey, Lila. Come on in." Her brows drew low as the concern flickered in. "Is everything okay?"

"I'm not sure. Is Griffin home?"

"Yes, of course. Griffin!" Eve hollered, looking down the hallway. He emerged a few seconds later. "Lila stopped by."

He saw her distress as easily as Eve had. "What happened?"

"Someone gave me a present. I don't like it."

"What is it?"

A chill rushed down her spine. She couldn't say it out loud. That would make it feel more real. "Can you come look at it? Tell me what you think. Maybe I'm overreacting."

Doubtful, but in case he thought it was nothing, she had

to prepare the stage for herself. She didn't want to be thought of as a dumb blonde or a woman who freaked easily over foolish nonsense.

He nodded, grabbing his jacket from the closet and slipping on his shoes. He kissed Eve and told her he'd be right back. They walked together back to her cottage, and she let him approach the box by himself. She stood in the kitchen, but far enough away she couldn't read it herself.

Griffin read the note, his mouth tightening and his eyes filling with rage. "Where was this? Not inside I hope."

"No, it was waiting on the doorstep."

Griffin pulled out his phone, fiddling with it for the longest time. She was too afraid to ask what he was doing.

He eventually looked up at her and waved her closer. She didn't want to come closer, but she also didn't want it to appear like she was afraid. So she obliged his command. He showed her his phone and hit play on a video.

"Whoever it was knew where the cameras were located. Not to mention they wore a ski mask. The clothing is too bulky to tell if it's a man or woman."

She watched the video of the person walk to her door, set the package down, and leave. Their head was down most of the time, but as Griffin had pointed out, they had worn a ski mask anyway to hide their face.

She backed away, not needing to watch it again. "I don't understand. What does this mean?"

"That's my job to figure out. But that message doesn't mean anything good."

Lila swallowed hard before answering. "It means ending up like Denise."

Griffin gave a sharp nod as if he agreed. "Which we will not let happen."

Oh, she had every faith in the police department here.

Griffin and Duke were fine men who cared about the citizens. As were the other officers she assumed, though she hadn't had as many dealings with them as she did with Griffin and Duke.

"Why does someone want me to leave? Because of my job?"

Griffin tossed up a shoulder in a careless gesture. "I have no idea. I texted Bryce. He'll be here soon."

For some reason, that statement made her even more nervous. And she wasn't even sure why.

Maybe because Bryce would demand she leave, for her own safety. She wasn't ready to go.

Not now.

But that would be the worst-case scenario. With the sexual tension between them building every day, she shouldn't worry he'd ask her to leave. His eyes told her every day he wanted her to come closer, not farther away from him.

Even before this nasty note had been delivered, she wasn't ready to leave. So no, leaving wasn't an option.

Whoever was messing with her didn't know her that well. She didn't give up.

She would see this through to the very end.

11

BRYCE SPED THE ENTIRE WAY. If a patrol car would've seen him, he didn't even know if he would've stopped. A speeding ticket could be paid. Lila's safety was more important than a dumb ticket.

Of course he was overreacting a bit. His brother was the one who texted him, so he knew Griffin wouldn't leave her alone until he got there.

He pulled into her driveway at the same time Duke pulled up to the curb.

"You were fast," Duke noted.

Bryce cocked a brow. "So were you."

Duke flashed a glance at his patrol car, indicating he had the legal right to speed. It was a police matter. Bryce didn't.

He shrugged, a low chuckle slipping out as they walked with long strides to the front door.

"I get it," Duke said in a low voice. "I honestly get it."

He still hadn't admitted out loud to Duke he liked Lila, but the man wasn't dumb. He knew. Everyone knew.

Duke opened the door before Bryce could answer, not

that he had one. There was nothing to add to that statement. He knew how much Duke cared about Juliet and would do anything for her. Even if she was with another man. He wasn't going to contradict anyone anymore when they insinuated he liked Lila.

Because he did.

A lot.

More so than he should.

As horrible as it was, he was free to act on those feelings now. Denise was dead. He was a widower. There was nothing holding him back. No marriage vows to tarnish a budding relationship.

But he wouldn't act on his feelings because Lila wasn't here for a fling. She had a job to do, and he wouldn't be the one to risk it. So while he could do something about his feelings for once with the freedom of no wife, he still couldn't make a move. Not if he wanted to remain a professional.

He closed the door behind him without looking at it, jumping himself when it slammed harder than he intended it to.

His gaze caught Lila's right away. She was curled up on the couch with a blanket covering her, her toes, as usual, peeking out from underneath it. He loved how she relaxed, her toes always visible. She didn't look frightened, but he saw the worry just on the edge.

"Duke, I want this dusted for prints on every inch," Griffin demanded as Duke met him in the kitchen to examine the box.

He wanted to see it himself, but he also wanted to comfort Lila as well. The indecision must've been written on his face because she gestured toward the kitchen with a gentle smile as if she knew one wrong move and he'd break. She wasn't mistaken.

Too much had happened in such a short time, and he hadn't processed it all yet. Now this! He wanted to punch something, anything to get the anger building from the very depths of his soul to go away.

He nodded and joined Duke and his brother. Duke had pulled out his phone to take pictures. Bryce didn't look inside until Duke stepped away, relaying he had to grab stuff from his patrol car to handle the evidence.

Leave now or you'll be next.

Computer generated note. It didn't leave many clues as to who could've sent it. Doubtful it even had any fingerprints to point them in the right direction.

"I don't like this, Bryce," Griffin whispered close to him, not wanting Lila to hear.

He didn't like it either.

The message was crystal clear. They were threatening to kill her if she didn't leave. But why?

"I know you'll hate to do it, but—"

"Don't!" Bryce quipped sharply under his breath. "Don't say it."

"We don't know who killed Denise. We can't afford to take this threat lightly. At this point in time, we need to let everything settle down before we can talk about hiring another PR company."

Another PR company? Not Lila's?

He pressed his lips together so tightly, his teeth grinded. What his brother was saying all made sense, but it didn't make it any easier to hear. Except the company part. Why would he have to hire another company if they solved this problem?

"Bryce?"

"I want to know who sent this and now."

He walked away from his brother before he did something stupid, like hit him. He was saying what needed to be said. He shouldn't be mad at him for that.

Bryce took a seat on the loveseat, making sure to stay as far away from Lila as he could. It was a small couch, so it wasn't easy.

"Did you call your brother?"

A short chuckle came out. "Are you insane? No. Aster would flip a lid."

"As he should. This is serious, Lila."

She frowned. "At what point did I make it seem like it wasn't?"

Okay. Wrong choice of words. The anger inside needed to settle down before he made a complete mess between them.

"I'm sorry. I didn't mean to make it sound like that."

Her smile was gone. This time her eyes were filled with annoyance, not worry. "Apology accepted."

But was it? Because it sounded forced.

He was making a muck of things, and he didn't know how to handle this. It was supposed to be a job. Hire someone to turn the town around. Not fall under her spell and wish for things he shouldn't even contemplate.

"In light of this new development, I think it's best we postpone our business venture until things settle down."

Her eyes burned with fire, the annoyance disappearing in a blink of an eye. "Are you firing me?" She threw the blanket on the floor and stood up. "How dare you use that smarmy politician voice on me!"

Smarmy? Since when did he sound like that when speaking?

He rose from the couch himself so they were on an even level.

"I'm not firing you. I'm saying—"

"Oh, I heard your words just fine, Mr. Mayor. *In light of this new development*," she started, mimicking his words sarcastically. "It's as if you wrote that speech before you arrived. That's how your statements you love to make sound. Fine. You want me gone. I'll leave."

She rounded the coffee table and stormed out of the room, slamming the bedroom door. It wasn't an accidental slam as the one he'd done.

He stood there, wondering what to do. Go after her? And say what? He wasn't saying anything right. Damn it!

Griffin joined him. He looked over at the kitchen, not even realizing Duke had re-entered the house at some point. He was fiddling with the box, pretending he hadn't heard any of that.

"That went...well. The best thing for her is to go back home."

Bryce laughed, no humor behind it. "You thought that went well? Which part? Because I'm pretty sure I screwed up the moment I sat down."

Griffin lifted his hands in a careless gesture, wincing. Yeah. That's what he thought. No part of that interaction went well.

"She's scared. I'm sure once she calms down she'll understand."

"Do I really sound like a smarmy politician when I give speeches and such?"

Griffin hesitated, and Bryce knew that whatever he said would be false. To shield his feelings.

"I do. Oh my gosh. I don't mean to sound fake or anything. I care about the citizens of this town. I want—"

Griffin clasped his shoulder, stopping his rambling tirade. "No one thinks you don't care. Do you change your tone of voice when going into mayor mode? Yeah, a little. Your speech becomes more articulate and"—he winced again— "matter of fact. Could you have worded what you said to her better? Sure. It did sound a little too polished." He squeezed his shoulder, leaning closer. "I know you care about her. I know you haven't admitted it out loud, but I can see the way you look at her. Sometimes when we're scared for the one we care about, we do or say things we shouldn't. It's going to be okay, Bryce. She'll go back to California and she'll be safe. That's what matters the most."

Another true point from his brother. It didn't make it any easier to deal with. He didn't want her to leave.

But he also didn't want her in harm's way.

He still saw Denise's mangled body in his mind when he closed his eyes at night. If he saw Lila the same way...it would destroy him.

"I'm done," Duke interrupted, holding the present in a large evidence bag.

Griffin let go of his shoulder, stepping back. "Let me know as soon as you find anything."

Duke nodded and left.

"You can go too, Griff. I need to talk to Lila. I can't let her leave like this."

"She should call her brother. She shouldn't be alone until she leaves town."

Calling Aster didn't sound like it would happen, not based on her opinion on the matter. But he nodded anyway to appease his brother. He left, and only Bryce and Lila remained. He locked the door, double checked the sliding door, then made his way to her bedroom.

He stood for the longest time in front of the door,

working up the nerve to knock. Words—the right words—
still hadn't sprung to mind. He had no idea how to erase the
last few minutes.

A LIGHT KNOCK SOUNDED on her door. She ignored it.

If it was Griffin, she was embarrassed that she'd had
such an outburst and didn't know what to say to him for
getting upset with his brother. Not that she was sorry
about it.

If it was Bryce...well, more harmful words might come
out still. How dare he fire her! After all the hard work she
put in. After everything she did for this town—for him.
She'd been by his side from the first moment she heard
about the murder. One nasty little note and he was tossing
her aside. Making her leave.

Another knock sounded. Still light. A bit tentative, as if
the person was unsure of themselves.

It made her think it was Bryce. He knew he'd messed up.
He would be one who'd want to fix his mistake. A trait she
liked about him, just not right now.

When a third knock sounded on the door, she decided
she had enough. He didn't get her message the first time.
She'd make sure he understood her this time.

She whipped open the door, gripping it hard. "I'm sorry
I forgot to add you need to leave as well. Get out of my
cottage."

He flinched, not expecting that. "Lila—"

"As we no longer have a working relationship, Mr.
Mayor, you have no reason to be here."

"Well, Duke is gone, and so is my brother, and I can't
leave you alone."

"You most certainly can."

"With that threat. No, I can't."

"I said—"

"Because I still can't get Denise's body out of my head, so there's no way in hell I'm going to let the same thing happen to you." His voice cracked at the end, his eyes filling with water. "Do you think I want you to leave?"

She froze, watching as his features crumbled. As the wall he'd built to hide his worries fell.

"Apparently, I have two tones of voices. My regular one and a smarmy politician one. I've never noticed I do that. I am so sorry from the bottom of my heart how I handled everything out there. I said it all wrong."

She knew he wasn't lying because it was his regular voice he was currently using. Not that he lied when he went into politician mode.

"What were you trying to say?" She'd give him one chance to correct his mistake. Only one. If she didn't like what she heard, she'd slam the door in his face.

He exhaled with a large, audible breath, visibly relaxing. He wasn't out of the waters yet, but she could see her small reprieve was a blessing to him.

"I don't know...I don't know how to say everything." He clenched his jaw, then it slackened, biting his bottom lip. "The last thing I want is for you to leave. I don't want that at all. But I also don't want your safety in jeopardy, and that threat does exactly that. So it's best that you leave. That's what I was trying to say. Evidently, in a polished and articulate way that came out wrong."

A tiny smile emerged, one she couldn't hold in. They had been precisely that. It made her wonder if Griffin told him how he sounded. It didn't mean she liked these new words any better. He still wanted her to leave.

"For how long?"

His brows furrowed low. "What?"

"How long do you want me to stay away? I mean, you still need a PR company to help this town. Or were you going to hire a new company?"

"I'm not sure."

"About what?" She let go of the door, crossing her arms.

"I can tell you I have no intention of hiring a new company. I want you."

Her heart pitter-pattered for a second that those words meant so much more than he intended. She wanted them to mean more. She wanted him to want her. To drop all pretenses and kiss her. Hell, throw her on the bed and make sweet love to her. Declare some sort of feelings and tell her to stay.

Not that she had to leave. Anything but that.

"I don't want you to leave hating me. I'm not asking you to leave because I don't want you here."

And he was choosing the wrong route. He wasn't going to ravish her or even attempt to kiss her. Damn the man!

"Actually, Mr. Mayor, you're telling me to leave. There was no asking."

His frown turned into a scowl. "Can you please stop calling me Mr. Mayor?"

"Why?" She should stop needling him, but she was still too pissed off by his insistence she leave. "That's what you are. We have a working relationship. You're firing me, and I'm being respectful by using your title."

"No, you're saying it in an impertinent way and like you hate me. I'm not firing you. At a later point in time, I'd like you to come back."

"You're still using fancy words. It's annoying me." Her nails dug into her arm to stop herself from saying anything further on the matter. He knew it bothered her, so why did he keep speaking that way?

He gritted his teeth, the water gathering again. "I don't mean to. It's reflexive. You don't hate me, right?"

No, she didn't. Hate was too strong of a word, and she tried to not feel that emotion often. Hurt would be a better description. Or devastated.

"I want you to come back," he added when she didn't answer his question.

"When you find the killer? Which is who you are assuming sent the note."

"Yes."

"And if you never find out who killed her, what then?"

The panicked look in his eyes sprung forth. "We will. My brother will or the sheriff. I have faith they will."

That didn't answer her question.

"I don't hate you. But this was not the outcome I expected. I stood by you all week, on your side. This, right here, feels like you're abandoning me. I'll get over it though. It's just a job. I'll call my brother so you can leave."

She shut the door before he could say anything else. There wasn't anything left to say. He fired her. She had to leave.

The killer won.

She dialed Aster before she changed her mind. Bryce, in his own way, was acting protective. Making her leave to keep her safe. Her brother would be far worse.

"What's up, Lilac? Change your mind about supper? We still have food left."

"No, I need you to come over. I'm booking a flight for tomorrow morning and going home. You'll want to spend the night, so bring a bag. Please come now so Bryce can leave."

Bryce had to leave.

He'd hurt her, and she didn't want to be around him any longer. While she knew he hadn't meant to cause her pain, he'd done it anyway. Distance was needed. A very long distance. She couldn't wait to get on the plane now.

"What happened?" Gone was the cheeriness, replaced with the attitude she was so familiar with. Over-protective mode activated.

"Someone left a present for me on my doorstep. A note inside said to leave or I'd be next. Griffin and Bryce think it's from the same person who murdered Denise." She inhaled and exhaled, then continued. "So Bryce fired me and I'm leaving."

"I'll be right there."

She tossed her phone on the bed and stared at her bedroom door. She was surprised Bryce didn't knock again and try to continue the conversation. But she was also grateful for his restraint. Aster would be here soon and make him leave. She'd be gone tomorrow and life could go back to normal.

Where she didn't pine after a man that didn't belong to her. That didn't care like she had thought he did.

HE KNEW the moment Lila called Aster because Juliet called his phone. He'd relayed what had occurred, pausing at times when he found himself using those damn articulate words Lila hated hearing.

Juliet tried to reassure him that everything would be okay, but also reamed him for firing Lila. Whatever she had told Aster hadn't been good. Nowhere in their conversation had he said the words 'you're fired' so he despised it she kept insisting that's what happened.

But what really killed him inside was that she thought he was abandoning her. Was asking—telling—her to go home the same as abandoning her? Even Griffin had said her getting out of town was the best idea. He was looking out for her safety! If that's how she wanted to perceive it, so be it. It kept her alive, and that's all that mattered to him.

He'd been pacing the living room when several deep knocks sounded on the door. On the safe side, he looked through the peephole first.

Aster.

The man looked pissed.

Bryce unlocked the door and let him in.

"Where is she?"

"In her bedroom."

"You can go." Aster swung a hand at the door, nearly hitting him in the face. Bryce didn't know if it had been intentional or not.

Why was he the bad guy here?

"I didn't fire her."

Aster narrowed his eyes. "Are you calling my sister a liar?"

"No, but I didn't say she was fired. I told her it was best she left for the time being and come back another time when this is all solved. That's what I said." Bryce stepped into Aster's space. "I found my wife's body. I saw the brutality of it. Her mangled body. The blood everywhere. The walls, the ceiling, the couch." He almost shouted but managed to control himself so Lila didn't hear. "I refuse to witness Lila in the same manner. That is why I told her to leave."

The last sentence came out broken. He could feel the

tears that had threatened to flow earlier resurface. He hadn't even shed any tears for Denise yet. No emotion had erupted since her death. Perhaps he was still living in shock. He wasn't sure. But he couldn't seem to control his emotions now.

Aster's anger he'd walked in with deflated. His body relaxed. Even the hatred in his eyes dissipated. "You did the right thing. You made my job easier. So thank you."

Bryce nodded and took a step back.

"You can still go. I'm here now."

He didn't want to go. Yet, her words filtered through his mind. *I'll get over it though. It's just a job. I'll call my brother so you can leave.*

She wanted him gone.

"Tell her I'm sorry, if you don't mind. I'm sorry I hurt her in any way. It wasn't just a job for me."

"You and I both know that to be true, but I ain't saying that to my sister."

"Because you hate me."

"Because she's leaving and it doesn't matter anymore."

But she'll be back. Though he didn't voice it because it didn't sound true. She wouldn't be back. They both knew it.

Bryce put on his shoes and coat, then grabbed the door handle, staring at the door. "Thank you for what you did for this town. I am grateful for that."

"It's a quaint town. I like it."

"But not enough to stay for Juliet."

Aster laughed. "What's between her and I is just that. Between us."

"How do you do it?"

"Do what?"

"Live life without a care. Sleeping with a woman like it doesn't matter."

"You know, Mr. Mayor, I almost thought we had come to some sort of truce. Then you have to go be a dick." Aster's brows narrowed, his lips tight. "Get out."

There would never be a truce between them. And he was right. His relationship with Juliet wasn't his business because she was a grown woman capable of making her own decisions. It didn't mean he didn't worry as her brother. That he wouldn't stick up for her.

He decided to let Aster have the last word and left.

12

THE BAG of chips crinkled as she shoved another hand inside it. Her front door opened and closed. She twisted on the couch to see who had walked in without knocking. Poppy, followed by Zinnia. They took a seat on both sides of her, Poppy shoving her hand in the bag to grab a handful.

They both munched as silence filled the room.

She appreciated her sisters' support, but she wanted to be alone. It had been a long day of travel. She, Aster, and the other band members all left this morning. While she hadn't expected all of them to leave, they had decided it was time. Stan, while on the suspect list, was permitted to leave town. Their flight had been at eight o'clock, so they had to leave before the sun even rose to the airport. Then a nearly four-hour flight to get home. Another hour stuck in traffic before Aster dropped her off at her apartment. Not to mention the time change. She'd gained two hours, but it didn't feel like it. She was exhausted. Aster had stayed for a while before she kicked him out, reassuring him she was fine. She would be fine!

He had to go and call the calvary.

"So, you wanna talk about it?" Zinnia asked, grabbing her own handful of chips, munching softly on them.

"No."

Poppy chewed loudly on her end. On purpose to show she wasn't walking on eggshells around her. Something Zinnia would do to keep the peace and not send her further down the rabbit hole of despair.

"You're going to anyway." Poppy smirked, throwing a chip in her mouth, chomping.

Well, yeah, she would because she knew her sisters wouldn't leave until she did. She didn't want to start at the beginning though.

"Aster told you everything."

They both nodded with Zinnia adding, "Yeah, but his version could be off from yours. He's seeing it through the eyes of an overprotective brother who loves you. Now dish on your version so we have the full picture."

Poppy pointed a long finger at Zinnia. "What she said. Spill, woman!"

So Lila did. The wonderful time she had working with Bryce and the other members in the town. How welcome they all made her feel. Until Denise butted in and some looked at her like a home-wrecker. All about the murder and the rumors and suspicion that toiled around town. Who could have killed her? The random glances of desire she swore she saw from Bryce, though how he always remained an utmost professional. Coming home last night to a disgusting present and horrifying threat. The way it made her feel. Scared yet determined not to let it affect her. She hated how it felt like she ran away instead of facing the problem head-on. How Bryce demanded she leave and fired her. To where they were right now sitting on the couch devouring a bag of chips that would add five pounds to her weight by tomorrow.

"That's shitty. Like, all of it." Poppy shook her head, rolling her eyes. "Small-town nonsense. You don't need that in your life."

Zinnia put a hand on her knee, though it was covered by a blanket. "I think she was starting to like that kind of life."

Her eyes stayed trained on the bag of chips in her lap as she gave a subtle nod. "For the most part, people liked me. I felt part of a community. I mean, here, it's too busy. People worried about themselves and that's it. It was nice."

"You liked him, uh?" Zinnia murmured, as if she said it too loud Bryce himself would hear it.

She rolled the top of the bag down to close it. "He was a nice man. Kind and thoughtful. Very good at his job. It didn't hurt that he was handsome." She stood up and stalked to the kitchen, snapped the chip clip onto the bag, and then tossed it into the pantry. "He was married and I hated that I liked him. I hated Denise for putting awkwardness between us when it wasn't even true. I hated that he told me to leave like he didn't give a shit."

One arm hit her right shoulder, then another one hit on her left, her sisters cocooning her in a double-sided hug.

"You don't hate things," Poppy reminded her. "So if you're using that strong of a word, you like him more than you want to admit."

"It doesn't matter. I left and I won't be going back."

"It matters," Zinnia said, resting her head on her shoulder.

Poppy did the same.

The tears released without notice. She cried in her sisters' arms, letting out all the anger and anguish she'd felt since Bryce blindsided her with his decision. She figured someone would've watched her more carefully. Followed her home and around town. Safety in numbers and all that jazz. But she hadn't seen it coming when he told her to leave. To listen to the killer's threat. That's what hurt the most.

When no more tears emptied out of her, she dried her eyes and took the offered spoon from Poppy, who had grabbed the mint chocolate chip from the freezer. The three of them took a seat back on the couch, each scooping ice cream right out of the bin.

"So what's next?" Poppy asked.

"Whatever assignment my boss gives me. Because like I told Bryce, it was a job and I'll move on."

The next morning, when she went into work to relay the latest news, she left a few minutes later.

Fired. Again!

This time it couldn't be misinterpreted. Her boss literally used the words 'you're fired.' He blamed her for the fiasco as if she killed the woman. As if she sent herself a threatening note. Whatever. She hadn't enjoyed the job as she had some of the other ones she had. While she had enjoyed her time in Sleighville, it would've come to an end at some point. She would've been thrown on another assignment and done it because she had to make a living somehow.

Aster showed up later that evening, Chinese food in hand. She didn't confess about her job until they were halfway through their meal.

"Can I say I'm happy about that?"

She rolled her eyes. "I wish you wouldn't."

"I didn't want you going back to that town anyway."

"Well, I have no reason to now. How about you? Will you ever go back?"

Aster tossed around some noodles in the container, shrugging, not meeting her eyes. "Probably not."

"What about Juliet?"

"We had a nice time. She knew when I left it was over. I mean, she knew when it started it wasn't anything serious. She didn't seem heartbroken or anything."

Lila threw broccoli at him. "She's not going to show you that emotion. You don't know how she feels."

Aster chuckled as he picked up the piece of broccoli that hit him in the chest and popped it into his mouth. "Look, neither of us are going back there. Agreed? That town is worth more trouble than we need."

She couldn't disagree with that. Trouble was the last thing she wanted. Having a target on her back wasn't fun. Although Aster slept in the living room, she had a fitful night the last night. Tossing and turning, worrying about who might try to break in.

Even back home now she had trouble sleeping last night. Logically, she knew the killer wouldn't follow her all the way to California. They issued a warning and she followed through on the demand. There was no need to follow her. It didn't mean scenarios and her wild imagination didn't run away from her.

"What's the next job you're hitting up?"

She giggle-snorted, tossing her shoulders up in a careless gesture. "I haven't decided yet. I'll have to go down the list of what I've done so far and pick something new. Why be boring and repeat something?"

"That's the spirit." He pointed at her plate. "You gonna eat that egg roll?"

She picked it up, taking a huge bite. "Yes. Paws off."

From there, laughter rang around the table and the conversation moved on to more lighthearted matters.

Just as her life would move on. Because she wasn't one to dwell on the past. Bryce made his choice. She would live with it and forget the tiny blip that Sleighville was in her past.

IT HAD BEEN a full week since he'd last seen Lila. Seven miserable days. Bryce had gotten used to seeing her every day. Her laughter. The tiny quirks she had while working. Even when she wasn't working. She'd gotten under his skin and then some. He wanted her back so damn badly.

Of course, the sheriff was no closer to finding Denise's killer, so that made it very dangerous for Lila to return. Her safety meant more than his desire to see her.

She was safe and he had to live with that.

He fiddled with his phone, taking a sip of beer. He'd gotten into a bad habit of stopping at Frost's Pub and Grill after work the last few days. One beer, sometimes two, and then he left. But still. It was something he should break. What kind of message did it send the townsfolk the mayor was having so many drinks after work?

But at this point—his wife being murdered—did it matter what the town thought of him anymore?

He'd always been so worried about his image. How people perceived him. Did they like him or hate him? It was one of the reasons he stayed with Denise for so long. Portraying a happy marriage was better than dealing with the fallout of a divorce. Now he was left with much worse.

"Hey, stranger." Melody slid onto a stool next to him at the bar.

Funny how he'd been coming the last few days and people didn't bother him much. It's as if they knew he needed some time to himself. Have a beer, muse in his own thoughts, and leave.

Melody didn't hold that same belief. He wouldn't be rude, even though he didn't want to chat with anyone. Since their last interaction, they hadn't seen each other. He wasn't too sad about that.

"Hi."

"I'd ask how you're doing, but I know that's a ridiculous question." She turned away from him when Anson approached. "I'll have a glass of Chardonnay, Anson. Thank you." He walked away to retrieve her drink, and her attention went right back to him. "I haven't seen you since... Denise passed away. I'm sorry for your loss."

Passed away?

That was an interesting way to put it. He supposed murder sounded too harsh. It was what had transpired though. Why dodge the truth?

"I'm sorry for yours as well. I know you two were like sisters." Now he felt like a huge asshole. "I should've reached out sooner, Melody. I'm so sorry I didn't."

He hadn't even gone to the funeral. Her parents hadn't been kind in their words when he saw them at the precinct one time. He figured they wouldn't want him there, so he didn't go. Griffin and Juliet didn't make him or even try to convince him. Some people probably thought it odd, but it was to the point he didn't give a shit what anyone thought anymore. Life had derailed so much he wasn't even sure how to get it back on track.

She and Denise had known each other since they were five years old. Best friends on the first day of school. Losing her—and so violently—couldn't have been easy.

She put a hand on his thigh, smiling. "Thank you, Bryce.

I understand though. You've been through so much. Don't worry about it."

He didn't like the feel of her hand on his thigh. It lingered until he shifted and she got the message to remove it.

For the longest time Denise had tried to get Griffin and Melody together, even knowing Griffin had no feelings whatsoever for her. Melody never took it personally, not that he'd been aware of anyway. She'd always been in his life because Denise had wanted her there.

And now...

It wouldn't bother him if he never saw her again.

He downed the rest of his beer and stood up, grabbing his wallet to throw some bills on the counter for Anson. The man himself reappeared, setting down Melody's drink in front of her. He grabbed the cash, nodding in appreciation toward Bryce.

"I have to go. It was nice seeing you, Melody."

Her smile brightened, then she took a sip of wine. "It's always a joy to see you too, Bryce. We should have dinner sometime."

"Yeah. I'll be swamped the next few weeks preparing for St. Patrick's Day." That was his polite way of declining. Having dinner with her was the last thing he ever wanted to do.

And he would be very busy. That wasn't a lie.

Too much to do to erase the memory of a brutal murder out of everyone's minds. Though he didn't voice that. Not to mention, he had to do it on his own now that Lila was gone.

"I haven't seen Lila around. Where did she wander off to? Isn't she helping?"

He forced a weak smile to hide his real feelings on the

matter. "She had to get back to California on another matter. I'll see you around, Melody."

Her goodbye trailed behind him as he walked away before she could get it all out. But if he didn't leave, he'd fall apart in front of her.

Thinking about Lila crushed his heart. Pulverized it into tiny little bits where he feared it would never be back to normal again. Such a short time, but she had weaved her way into his heart and soul with ease.

He missed her like crazy.

When he got home, he crashed on the couch, pulling out his phone, fiddling with it again. The urge to call her was strong. Every time he had his phone in his hand, he wanted to do just that. Call her. Text her. Anything to know how she was doing. Yet, he never did.

He needed his own space, so the same day Lila had left, he moved into the cottage where she'd been staying. Juliet had not minded that he left her house. Griffin didn't care he stayed in the cottage, even though it could've been used for renters. They knew he couldn't go back to his own house, despite it being available for him. The crime scene crew had done its thing. The mess in the living room had been cleaned up, thanks to Griffin. But to go back there...even for clothes...he still couldn't do it. He imagined his suitcase still sat by the front door.

Now that he was in the same domain Lila had been, he saw her everywhere. Curled up on the couch with her little toes sticking out from under the blanket. A cup of coffee in her hand as she sat at the table in the kitchen. Looking full of rage as she stood by the door in her bedroom, wanting to murder him for making her leave. That was the image he saw the most.

The hurt in her eyes.

The hatred...

She said she didn't hate him, but the eyes never lied.

He tossed his phone on the coffee table, listening to it as it clattered and nearly flew off the edge.

He had so much work to do concerning the next big event in town and he didn't even care if it went well. All he cared about was how Lila was doing, and he couldn't even call to ask her.

She wouldn't pick up anyway.

13

LILA WAVED to Roger after she swung open the door and kept running to the elevator. She appreciated he saw her coming and buzzed her in so she didn't have to find her key. She even kept running in place as she waited for the elevator to arrive.

"I have a letter for you. It got mixed up with Mrs. Danburry's mail." Roger held out a long white envelope with typewriter style writing on the front.

She smiled at her doorman and took the envelope, when every fiber in her being didn't want to. "Thanks, Rog!"

Hopefully, her peppiness didn't display the sudden fear slithering up her spine. The elevator swished open, and she jogged inside, pushing the third-floor button. By the time she got to her door, the envelope was burning a hole in her hand.

She tossed it on the kitchen counter and headed straight for the shower. After running two miles, she needed to rinse off the sweat. It might also help her mentally prepare to see what was in the envelope.

After getting ready and having a bite to eat, she focused

on the white rectangular object. The return address bothered her. A lot.

Sleighville, MN.

Who could be writing to her and why?

Bryce?

It had been a month since she last saw him. Last week, St. Patrick's Day had arrived, and it pained her inside not to call him and ask how everything went. Well, with whatever they had come up with for the event. The first meeting with the city commissioner they had mentioned putting up some leprechauns in the center of the town wearing a Santa hat, holding a present filled with gold. She had even suggested a treasure hunt of some sort for the kids. Something fun and engaging. Did they do it? Did it go well, if so?

She hadn't been paid by City Hall in Sleighville for working there. All her checks had come from her boss. So it couldn't be a paycheck. And she already got her last check from that asshole.

Why would Bryce write to her anyway? He hadn't even called or texted to check in with her. And damn the man, but she had wanted to hear his voice more times than she cared to admit.

She missed him.

Way too much.

He'd wormed his way into her heart, and she couldn't seem to get him out of her mind. She wanted to hate him for doing that to her.

"Open the damn thing!" she hollered at herself, as she grabbed the drawer where the silverware was and damn near pulled it all the way out she yanked so hard.

Carefully with a knife, she sliced the top open and pulled out the lone sheet of paper. It fluttered to the counter after she unfolded the page to read it.

Bitch! You should still die.

What. The. Hell.

The last note hadn't yielded any results. Although Bryce never contacted her, Griffin had once. To relay the news that no evidence had been detected on the present or note to offer any clues who could've sent it. She imagined nothing would come from this either. It had to have passed through multiple people to get to her. Numerous prints would be all over it.

She called her sisters and brother anyway. They would want to know, and she needed help making a decision on what to do.

None of them delayed coming over.

Zinnia bit her bottom lip, staring at the note. "I don't get it. You left. You haven't contacted anyone there." Her gaze zoomed to her. "Have you?"

Her head shook fast, making her dizzy at the motion. She grabbed the counter behind her to keep her balance. "I talked to Griffin when I first left, but that's it."

Poppy stood by Zinnia, looking like she was ready to jump into the ring and pound the owner of the letter to a pulp. "Whoever they are, they don't know who they're messing with."

Aster chuckled. He was leaning against the counter with his arms crossed. "You wouldn't hurt a fly, Poppy."

"Nobody threatens our family," Poppy snapped back. "You should bring it to the police."

"They won't find anything. They didn't on the last one." Lila didn't feel like wasting her time with that.

"It can't hurt," Aster said, standing up. "I'll do it for you."

She slapped her hand over the top of it before Aster could touch it. Her prints were already on it, so it didn't matter if she handled it.

"I will handle my own problems, thank you."

"Okay, who had a problem with you in that town?" Poppy asked, ready to get to finding the culprit.

Lila shrugged. "Denise. And we know she didn't do it. I got some weird looks from the rumor she started, but not to the point I'd think someone would want me dead."

"I don't like this," Zinnia muttered. She was always the more timid and worrywart out of all three of them. She didn't like confrontation and avoided it at all costs.

Poppy would face anything head-on.

And for herself....well, she was more like Poppy. She tried to delay confrontation, avoiding it somewhat, but she wouldn't shy away from it.

So why start now?

"I'm going back to Sleighville."

"Like hell!"

"I don't like that idea."

"That's what I'd do."

Aster, Zinnia, and Poppy all spoke at once. Aster would fight her tooth and nail. Zinnia would worry but support her. And Poppy would help her buy the plane tickets.

"Leaving didn't solve anything. Whoever this person is has a personal vendetta against me. How am I any safer here?" She picked up the envelope, waving it. "Why am I such a threat to them? Because I have to be for some reason, if they sent this. I need to know why."

Aster stood to his full height, though relaxing his rigid stance. "If you're going, I'm going too. No discussion about it."

Hey, she knew when to back off and when to press.

"Fine. What about the band?"

"We don't have any gigs until May. I have the next month free to do whatever. It's fine."

She still had yet to find a new job, so she had nothing to worry about there. Zinnia was a fifth-grade schoolteacher and couldn't leave during the school year, not that Lila thought she'd offer. Poppy worked at the zoo. While she could take time off, Aster would be enough. Poppy knew that too.

"Okay. I want the next flight out. I'm done messing around and waiting. This person wants a fight, they're going to get one."

Aster rolled his eyes toward the ceiling, letting out a strangled breath. "Don't do anything stupid, Lilac." His gaze hit hers again. "Promise me you stick by my side the entire time."

"Ha!" She giggled, rounding the island counter to venture to her room to pack. "You're hilarious. You know I'm not going to follow that rule. I won't be dumb and put myself in a dangerous situation, but you're not going to be overbearing."

"Watch me!" Aster shouted at her back.

She slammed her door for added effect to that asinine request. A few minutes later, it opened and closed with a quiet click. She looked up from her suitcase to Zinnia's worried expression.

"Aster has a point. You need to be careful."

"I'll make sure I'm not alone at all times. I have other people there I can trust."

A tender smile emerged on her face. "Like Bryce?"

Lila turned her gaze to her rumbled clothes in the suitcase. "He hasn't called once."

"And neither have you. It doesn't mean you don't care about him."

"He'll tell me to leave again. I might slap him in the face if he does."

"Or kiss him. That would get your point across too."

Her head shot up to Zinnia's where her eyes were filled with laughter. Lila couldn't hold in her own. They both bursted out with the joyous sound, her snorts mingling in there.

"How do you think he'd react if I did?"

"Well, if Aster's assessment is correct,"—Zinnia rolled her eyes— "and he's usually right. So annoying. That man has been wanting to kiss you from the beginning."

Well, she'd play it by ear. If Bryce told her to leave again, she wasn't sure what would come out. A slap or a kiss.

Either way, he'd have to deal with her whether he wanted to or not.

A WHOLE MONTH and he still couldn't control the urge to stop at Frost's. He had stayed at work until six, catching up on paperwork he'd let slide. Something not normal for him as well. Now he sat nursing beer number two with the strong, uncontrollable yearning for a third. He rarely had three, but tonight he might succumb to it.

Anson strolled over to him, nodding at the bottle. "What are you thinking?"

"That I should stop coming." The answer was more reflexive than it should've been.

Anson leaned against the opposite counter, getting comfy to chat. They did that every night. Chatting about this and that and inconsequential things. Bryce rarely brought up how he was feeling.

"The question is why you keep coming."

Bryce picked up his beer, finishing it off. There were too many reasons for it. A dead wife. Her murder still unsolved.

Lila...never coming back. Because at the rate the sheriff was going with the investigation, that's what was going to happen. Her staying away forever.

He pulled out his wallet and threw money on the bar. "I should go." This conversation could derail further into a territory he wasn't ready to face.

Anson nodded, grabbing the cash. "I'm never not going to welcome you in here, but I won't be sad if you stop coming in."

That was Anson's nice way of telling him to knock it off. Stop making his way to being the town drunk. Though was two beers a night something that would label him that? But if he didn't stop it soon, he might get to a point where he didn't stop at two.

"I hear ya, Anson."

"Oh, I forgot to tell you, Melody stopped by before you came. She said to tell you hi if you stopped in."

He smiled and said nothing else. There wasn't anything to say. Anson knew he had no feelings for the woman. Anson also knew it aggravated him when people bothered him here. He wanted to come to drown his sorrows in a pint or two and leave. Not chat. With Anson, he didn't mind. Anyone else, it annoyed him. Not that he ever let it be known it bothered him. He'd seen Melody in here more times than he cared to. She wasn't the only person who tried to corner him in some sort of conversation.

"Thanks. I'll see you around, Anson."

He made his way out and to his vehicle. Another night almost over. By the time he got home, it was a little after seven. The lights were blazing through the windows at Griffin's. He knew if he knocked he'd be welcomed without an issue. But he didn't. Like every other night.

Griffin and Juliet had already made a few comments to

him over the course of the last few weeks on his behavior. Going to Frost's. Not always shaving. Refusing to come over for dinner more often than not. Juliet even chided him for becoming a recluse. Not quite yet, but he was making his way there.

He didn't have the energy for company. Not anymore. Not since his life had turned upside down and inside out. He didn't recognize himself in the mirror anymore. After a quick shower, that's what he did. He stared in the bathroom mirror wondering who the hell stared back. Bloodshot eyes from the lack of sleep. No matter how hard he tried to turn his mind off at night, it was impossible. His hair getting too long because he couldn't be bothered to get it trimmed. Emmy, the sweetest hairstylist at HO HO Hair did an amazing job on his hair. She wouldn't hurt a fly, but she would talk his ear off. She'd want to gossip as if he'd dish every sordid detail about his life.

He scrubbed at his chin and cheeks, figuring he should shave since it'd been awhile. He couldn't remember the last time he gave himself a good shave. The motivation still wouldn't come.

Instead, he flicked off the lights, threw his dirty laundry and towel in the bin in his room, and ventured to the kitchen. He didn't cook. That took too much effort. So he popped in the TV dinners he'd been buying and ate one, not tasting a bite of it.

For a few seconds he even debated on grabbing another beer, before stopping himself and plopping down on the couch. Where he sat in silence. Even the thought of turning on the TV felt like too much to handle.

His phone sat on the coffee table where he had set it when he came home. If he looked at it, he knew what he'd see. A few missed calls or texts from Griffin and Juliet. Maybe one from Duke as well.

But nothing from Lila. And why would she?

He should look at his phone. Make sure no emergencies or anything had happened. But he knew it would read at least two texts from Griffin wondering if he wanted to join him and Eve for supper. Typical of him. One or two from Juliet asking the same. Duke liked to change it up every other day, chatting about this and that. But not to eat. Out of the three of them, Duke knew he wasn't going to cave until he was ready.

When would that be?

Nope. He wasn't looking at it.

Over an hour had passed since he arrived home. Nearing nine o'clock, something joyous to him, it meant he could venture to bed and lay in silence there instead of sitting in silence in the living room.

Pathetic.

And he didn't know how to stop the horrible routine he'd set for himself.

He should go to bed.

Start the whole depressing routine for tomorrow.

Standing up, he swiped his phone from the coffee table but didn't look at it. The walk down the short hallway felt longer than it should've because his feet dragged as he went. He didn't want to go to bed. He didn't want to act the way he'd been. Except he didn't know how to pull himself out of it. Even with his brother and sister's undying support to help him.

He set his phone upside down so he wasn't tempted to look at it, then crawled into bed. His gaze ventured to the ceiling instead of his eyelids closing. Because that was what he did. He stared for a long time before attempting to sleep.

Once he closed his eyes, it turned into tossing and turning until his alarm went off.

Time passed. He wasn't sure how much before he decided he needed something to drink. Something, anything to help his mind settle down.

It didn't take long to down a glass of water. He even popped two pain pills in because he felt a headache forming in the front of his head.

One bathroom stop, then back under the covers he went. His eyes trained back onto the ceiling.

It was going to be a long night.

Beep. Beep. Beep. Beep. Beep.

He shot up in bed as the cottage alarm went off.

Someone was breaking in.

Finally, something to disrupt his routine. And a chance to unleash some of the anguish and rage that simmered in his belly for too long.

14

UGH. Lila was ready to crash. Crawl into bed and not wake up for twelve hours. Poppy had booked her and Aster the first flight out of California to Minnesota. It had given them three short hours to pack, get to the airport, and onto the plane. They barely made it because Aster was way slower than her. No doubt it had been his plan to thwart her efforts to return. Nothing would stop her. She was here now, and there was no going back until the threats were solved.

While in flight, Poppy also rebooked the cottage for her. Her sister was on top of it all. It was too bad she couldn't join her. Poppy was the only one in her corner about the entire matter.

They rented a car when they landed in Minneapolis. Aster driving, of course. When they hit Sleighville, he stopped at Joy's to get the key for the cottage. Since he called Juliet in advance, he dropped her off and headed to her house. Thank! Goodness!

While she appreciated his concern, she did not want to be smothered by him. She had put her foot down on sharing a place. Since Poppy had already booked the cottage, there wasn't anything he could do about it. She knew he wouldn't want to sleep on the couch. She'd have to thank Poppy later for helping her get some distance from their brother.

It had taken quite a bit of convincing for him to call Juliet and crash with her. She hadn't objected once. Not that Lila thought she would. Aster had a way with women. She reminded him the cottage had a top-of-the-line security and the chief of police himself next door. She would be fine. Not that he appreciated the reminder, as if he was an idiot and forgot that little detail.

She made sure to wave goodbye that she was good before closing the door and undoing the alarm. She reset it and locked the door again. She already felt better.

With her hand still wrapped around her suitcase handle, she flicked on the light and turned around. Then screamed.

Bryce stood by the hallway, a baseball bat dangling from his hand, and his other one covering his heart as if she had scared him. No way. She was the one who had been startled way more.

"Lila," he said breathlessly, his brows puckered low. He even blinked a few times. It made her think he was waking himself up, trying to make sure he wasn't dreaming.

"What are you doing here?"

His brows lifted. "Ummm...I could ask you the same thing. I moved in here."

She lifted the key Joy had given her. "I rented it."

His eyes flashed from the key back to her face. "Griffin must've forgot to tell Joy not to rent it out right now."

Well, this put a damper on her plans. It also gave her a mental note to tell Joy she should change the locks after each rent. Someone could make a key. Burst into the place like she had done to an unsuspecting tenant.

"How long have you been here?" Not that it was her

business, but she needed to keep the conversation going. Awkwardness was filling up the space.

"The same day you left."

That upped the awkwardness to dangerous levels.

She wasn't sure what to say to that, so she remained silent. And stared.

He looked different. Tired and worn-out. His hair was longer and in disarray as if he hadn't taken care to comb it. She was surprised to see what looked like the start of a beard. He'd always taken care of his goatee, not having a full-on beard. Sometimes, he had the start of scruff on his jawline. The look always enticed her to want to kiss him along that path.

What happened to make him change his appearance so much?

He set the bat against the wall and moved closer to her. "What are you doing here?"

Well, he'd answered her question why he was here. Sort of. She could infer why he'd moved in. Going back to his house where his wife had been murdered wouldn't be on the top of her list either. Fair was fair. She could answer his.

But she wasn't ready. He wouldn't like it, and he'd demand she leave. She'd get pissed at him all over again. She was ready to stop being mad. Why give him more ammunition to increase the anger?

He took another step closer. "Lila?"

"I should go." Before he made her leave anyway. Except Aster dropped her off and she'd have to call him to come back. She didn't want to do that either.

"Where would you go? It's late."

Juliet's, obviously. Since that's where Aster went.

He closed the distance so he was an arm's length away. "Why won't you tell me why you're here?"

"Because you won't like it and you'll tell me to leave again."

He winced, as if agreeing with that statement. "I never meant to hurt you. I wanted to keep you safe."

A ragged laugh escaped as she let go of her suitcase she'd been holding onto with a death grip. She dug through her purse and held out the envelope and letter she'd put in a plastic bag. She hadn't turned it into the police in California, but it didn't mean the department here wouldn't want it. They might want to do some checking for fingerprints and such.

He took the bag, glancing at it, his features morphing into rage. She knew he was on the precipice of taking that anger out on her.

"When did you get this?"

"This morning."

His gaze shot to her. "And you thought coming back was the best decision!"

Wagging her finger in his face, she took a step closer. "Don't you dare. It's my life, my choice. Leaving didn't do a damn thing."

He deflated right before her eyes. "It crushed me is what it did."

Well, that was news to her. He had acted as if he didn't care.

The bag drifted to the table as he tossed it in that direction. "I'm sorry we ended on bad terms. I wanted you to leave to be safe."

"So you keep saying. What do you call that?" she snapped, jerking her hand toward the evidence bag.

"I don't understand why anyone has their eyes set on you. I don't get it, and it makes me so mad," he muttered through gritted teeth, following the direction of her hand.

He stood staring at the bag, and she couldn't help but keep her eyes locked on him. When he didn't look away, she realized she would have to make him.

Reaching out, she grazed his cheek, letting her hand fall to her side when he jolted his gaze back to her.

"I'm okay, Bryce. I wasn't happy leaving because I don't like running away from things. If I'm honest,"—why hold it in any longer?— "I didn't like leaving you either. I was very angry at what you did. I wanted to hate you for it."

"But you don't, right?" he whispered, the plea in his tone so desperate that she couldn't even think about hating him. That he'd succumb to whatever hell he'd fallen into.

"If you tell me to leave again, I might and not take it back."

"I've been a mess since you left." He rubbed his chin as if pointing out how much. "I don't think the town knows whether I'm losing it because Denise was murdered or because you left."

"Losing it, how?"

He glanced away, laughing. "I don't think I should tell you."

She touched his cheek again, this time not letting go right away, cupping it until his eyes turned back her way. "You look tired."

He nodded, leaning into her soft touch. "I can't sleep anymore. I find shaving a chore. I shut myself off in this cottage." He closed his eyes. "I stop at Frost's way more than I should after work. Like every day." He opened them. "I missed you. I wanted to hear your voice so many times over the course of the day that I had to shut my phone off to stop myself."

That was more than she had hoped for.

He was confessing his feelings at long last. Honest words to go with his heated looks.

"I would've answered."

Apparently, that's all he needed to hear.

His hands wove around her waist and pulled her closer. Right before his lips would've touched hers, he whispered, "I can kiss you, can't I?"

"As much as you'd like."

Then his lips were devouring hers. Scorching her from head to toe. Her other hand met his free cheek, then she smoothed her hands up and through his hair. Her mouth fell open and his tongue dove in.

The kiss morphed from want to craving. She had envisioned this between them on too many occasions as they worked together. Now it was happening.

"Stay," he whispered between hard presses of his lips against hers.

Finally. The one word she wanted to hear from him. If she ever heard the word leave slip from his lips again, she wouldn't forgive him. She swore she wouldn't.

She giggled, then a tiny snort followed it. "I have nowhere else to go unless I want to crash Juliet and Aster's time."

That had him pulling away, though not completely. His hands were locked around her waist.

"Aster came with you?"

She cocked a brow as if asking if he was insane. "He would've never let me get on the plane by myself."

His features tensed. "Yet, he dropped you off here without coming inside. He was going to leave you alone!"

She smoothed her hands from his cheeks up through his hair again. She loved the breathy sigh he released as she did. Something to note for the future. Something that calmed him down. The tight lines in his face decreased as did the anger fueling in his gaze.

"Aster and I already had that chat. A very heated chat. I will not be dumb while I'm here. I won't go anywhere alone." The pressure in her hands increased on the back of his head, her nails digging in when it appeared he wanted to interrupt. "Except in this cottage. I feel safe here. Your brother lives next door. He's the chief of police. I can't be smothered or I will lose it."

His lips found hers again, starting the kiss slowly before increasing the tempo. She let out a small cry when he ended it.

"Well, you won't be alone here because I'll be here. I can't promise not to smother because..." He sucked in a sharp breath. "I can't bear to see you the way I did with Denise. I can't."

She didn't want that to happen either. But she also wouldn't be frightened into a corner by whoever was playing sick jokes on her with those threats.

"So we're, like, moving in together?" she asked with a short chuckle. "Seems kind of fast."

Her words had the effect she had planned. His eyes relit with happiness and gone was the horror he had witnessed. Of what he didn't want to ever lay eyes on again.

"All I've wanted since you left was for you to return. I swear to you I never wanted you to leave in the first place. Now that you're here..." His grip tightened. "I'm afraid I won't be able to let you go."

Except, her plan wasn't to stay forever.

He knew it too.

By the fierce look in his eyes, she had better prepare for a battle on the matter.

She came back to Sleighville looking to stop the threats

and find the culprit. Not lose her entire heart and soul in the process. Sure, she wanted to make things right between her and Bryce. But she never expected he'd bear his feelings.

"What's happening here, Bryce?"

His fingers gentled on her waist as another soft, feathery kiss hit her lips. "I'm not sure yet. But I'd like to find out. What do you say?"

Her answer was to keep the kiss going. No more talking, especially the heavy will-you-eventually-leave-me part.

HE WAS STILL IN SHOCK, wondering if he had fallen into a deep sleep and was having the most wonderful dream of his life. Yet, the tiny sounds of delight coming from Lila couldn't be fake. She was here in his arms. This was as real as it could get.

While they would talk more about the second threat she had received, right now, he had more important matters at hand. Convincing her to stay—permanently.

He was done telling her to leave. Since the day she had left, he wanted her back. Now she was, and he wasn't ruining anything between them this time. He was going all in.

He slowed the kiss, peppering light pebbles across her chin and down her neck. "Let's take this to the bedroom."

She inhaled sharply, then let out the breath, her face cocooned in his neck as he continued to place tiny kisses on her soft, delicate skin.

Too fast?

She didn't respond, and he was nervous to say it again. He was going too fast. He'd gone from trying not to look at her with desire in his eyes to wanting to love her body from head to toe. What had he been thinking?

He needed to ease into this budding relationship, not dive in headfirst without looking at what was before him.

Of course, she had asked if they were moving in together. Part in jest, but also being serious. Where would she sleep if not with him? Unless she wanted him to sleep on the couch, which he would. Making her uncomfortable was the last thing he wanted to do.

"I can—"

She lifted her head, cupping his cheeks, causing him to stop speaking. She ran her hands up and through his hair. He couldn't stop the throaty sigh that escaped. He loved when she did that. It sent the pleasure tingling down his spine and straight to his cock.

"I'm not one that jumps into bed on the first date. I like to get to know a guy first."

Well, that didn't sound promising for him. This didn't even constitute as a date.

"I—"

Her hands slid down his back, making him pause again. A silent plea to let her continue.

"I do feel like I know you pretty well, Bryce. The kind of man you truly are. So giving and kind. Always thinking of others before yourself."

Okay. Maybe all hope wasn't lost. He remained quiet.

"What will the town say tomorrow about us? I didn't come back here to make matters worse for you."

Screw the town!

His hands tightened around her waist, then he relaxed, not wanting her to get the wrong impression. The anger had welled up so fast, he hadn't been able to control his reaction.

If anyone said something derogatory or rude to her, he'd let them have it.

"I don't care what anyone thinks about me anymore. I cared for far too long, which made my life a living hell. I should've left Denise a long time ago. I put up for too long with her breaking me down and making me feel like I wasn't worthy of anything. And for what? So the people in town wouldn't make comments about me. To me. I'm done caring about my image. I—"

"No, you will care about your image. It's important to you."

He leaned in closer, brushing her lips with his. "You're more important. I got too many things wrong with Denise. I'm not repeating the same mistakes. Plus, I've already shot my image to hell since you left. It can't get any worse. Screw them. All of them. You matter to me more than anything has in a very long time. It scares me how much I care about you. So much that I'm afraid of losing you."

Her hands wove around to the front of his body, smoothing up his chest, pausing over his heart. It beat so erratically he wouldn't be surprised if she could also hear it.

"Well, if you don't care what anyone says, I don't either. But I'm afraid they'll think this"—she pressed her hands hard to his chest to emphasize their closeness— "started when Denise was alive. I'll be the bad guy in the scenario."

"The people who matter know the truth. At this point in time, that's all I care about."

She chuckled. "You're starting to use your fancy words. At this point in time..." Her words trailed off as more laughter left her lips.

He couldn't help himself. It would take serious effort to choose his words carefully with her. Because he didn't even realize he was doing it until she pointed it out. He never wanted to make her feel as he had done a month ago though. So he'd try his damndest to stop it.

Of course, part of him also couldn't hold back a bit of teasing.

"I think at this juncture we move to the bedroom."

She giggle-snorted some more, pressing her face into his chest. His hands traveled to her ass where he lifted her, eliciting more delightful giggles from her as she wrapped her legs around his waist.

"Is the current item on the agenda sufficient for you?"

She pretended to look stern and annoyed. "I'm going to spank you if you don't stop with that shit."

"Promise?" He winked, then turned around toward the bedroom.

Once inside, he closed the door with a quick kick of his foot and deposited her on the bed. He hovered above her, swiping a lock of hair that had fallen near her lips.

"It's been a long time for me. With...Denise,"—he winced, hating to even say her name while they were locked together in a sexual embrace— "we didn't use condoms. I don't have any."

She brushed her hands over his cheeks and through his hair. He closed his eyes to relish in the soft touch. When her hands slid down his back and to his front and started lifting his shirt, they snapped open. He didn't say anything while she pulled off his shirt and threw it to the floor.

"There's so much more we can do without a condom. Tomorrow is a new day." Her wicked smile told him they weren't about to let a little obstacle get in their way of pleasure.

He stood up, shucking off his pants and boxers while she removed her clothes as well. She settled into the middle of the bed, and he joined her, resting on top. His cock twitched, aching to dive in. He mentally told his throbbing body part that it would happen, just not tonight.

He couldn't resist rubbing against her though. Hell, the temptation was right there. How could he stop the motion?

"Bryce," she whispered, closing her eyes as her hips met his movements.

Lowering closer, his lips started at the end of her shoulder, pressing tiny kisses as he pumped slowly against her, torturing them both.

Her hands found his back, dragging her nails up and down. The movement urged him on, building the ecstasy coursing through his veins. If he didn't slow down, he would come sooner than he wanted to. After so many months of celibacy, he knew it wouldn't take much to lose it.

His kisses continued their path across her chin, down her neck until he hit a soft, plump breast. His lips attacked one nipple while his hand played and massaged the other one. Her delectable moans filled the room. He switched, sucking and nipping on the other breast while his hand kneaded and built the pleasure within her.

From there, he kept trailing downward, his lips touching every inch of skin. Around her stomach, kissing her belly button, circling her thighs. He wanted his touch everywhere. To brand her, to make her see—and feel—how much he adored her. That he always would.

His mouth hit the ultimate prize. She sucked in a sharp breath, her hips lifting off the bed when he kissed her. His tongue dove in and her low moans turned into loud cries of pleasure. His tongue swept around, pulling the delight out. A finger slid inside, jolting a 'hell, yes' from her lips.

He pumped his finger a few times before adding another, thrilled at the way she moved and moaned at his touch. His deep kisses and thrusting of his fingers continued until the moment she fell apart, crying his name so loud he couldn't stop the smile. He kept up the ministrations until he felt a sharp tug on his hair.

He lifted his head, grinning with satisfaction. "I love the sound of my name on your lips."

"And I love your lips."

A heavy chuckle erupted, the feeling so damn gratifying. He didn't need anything else to happen because her happiness filled him with so much joy he hadn't felt in the longest time.

But she had other plans.

She sat up, pointing to the bed. "Lay down. It's my turn."

He obeyed because he wasn't going to argue about something like this. He would've been fine without it, but his body tingled with the pleasure he knew was coming.

She cupped his thick, throbbing cock and licked her lips. "I felt like you teased me for a long time before I came. It seems only fair you suffer the same fate."

Yeah, fair was fair.

When she deep-throated his cock, his eyes slid shut as a low growl filled the room. Damn! He didn't think he could withstand the suffering. But he laid back and let her do as she wished with his body, loving every second of it.

15

WHEN THE LOUD alarm went off, she groaned and turned away from it. The sound miraculously turned off, and a warm arm slid around her waist, pulling her closer. They'd fallen asleep naked after a very thorough bout of lovemaking. Bryce's cock was hard and pulsating against her ass, telling her he was ready for another round.

"I don't want to leave this bed for a week," he mumbled against the back of her head, swiping her hair out of the way before kissing her neck.

She twisted around in his arms, receiving a kiss on the lips. "Me either."

"So I'll call in today."

Her eyes widened at the truth in the words. No joking tone whatsoever. "Absolutely not. I can handle some talk about us, but not a full-blown attack."

His left hand cupped her back, pulling her even closer. A tender kiss hit her lips. "I don't want to leave you. Not alone."

She wiggled her hand out of being cocooned between their bodies and held his cheek. "I can come with you, if you don't mind. You didn't tell me how the St. Patrick's Day event went. I know Easter is around the corner. There's a lot of work to do."

His eyes brightened at the idea. She enjoyed that look much more compared to the terror from moments before. "We didn't exactly talk a lot last night." He smothered her neck with kisses, making her giggle, yet relishing his touch and the playful manner.

He retreated, the happiness not as bright, and she knew a serious talk was coming.

"St. Patrick's Day didn't go as well as I hoped. We didn't utilize your idea, and it irritated me, but I also didn't speak up. I've been..." He twisted his lips, averting eye contact. "I haven't been myself lately. And I hate that I acted the way I did. I have a lot of groveling and making up to do with the town."

"We all have rough patches in life. Give yourself some grace, Bryce. It's okay to fall apart sometimes." She didn't want to ask the next question, but she had to. They couldn't have anything standing between them. Something that could tear them apart before they even began. "Have you even grieved for Denise?"

When he still wouldn't make eye contact with her, she knew the answer.

"You need to do that."

He shrugged. "I don't know how. She died with too much tension hanging between us. A lot of hatred on both sides. I would've never gotten an apology from her for the way she treated me throughout our marriage—and the divorce. But now I don't even get that chance to demand one. I don't know what to feel. Sad? Angry? Heartbroken? I cried..." His gaze found hers. "I cried when you left. I tried to stop it, but the tears came anyway. I haven't even found that kind of emotion for Denise. What does that say about me? Cold-hearted and cruel. That's what."

She applied pressure to his cheek. "Never. You are the most kindhearted man I have ever met. You haven't grieved yet because you're bottling up too many emotions. You have to let it go. You don't have to forgive Denise for anything she did to you because she died in a horrific way. But you should forgive yourself."

He lifted her hand holding his cheek and kissed the inside of her wrist. Then he wrapped it with his hand, pressing them to his chest. "I don't deserve you. I don't feel like I deserve this happiness. I feel like..." He frowned. "I feel like I'm looking at someone's life, jealous of what he has. I know you're in my arms right now, but I'm afraid of it slipping away. That it won't last. That it's all in my head."

"She really did a number on you. And that is unforgivable. She doesn't deserve your forgiveness. I'll never forgive her for what she put you through. But I need you to absolve yourself of any guilt. You did not do anything wrong." She pressed her lips hard against him, hoping it would instill some of her strength into him. "You are not doing anything wrong. I'm real, and what's happening between us is real."

"You seem too good to be true. Sometimes, I think it was fate that you were the one who came to save our town."

She winced. He was at it again, making her his savior. He noticed her reaction and went into panic mode. She knew because his heart rate sped up and his hand tightened around hers.

"What did I say wrong?"

"What happens when I can't save this town? What does that do to you and me?"

His features relaxed and a soft chuckle slipped from his

lips. "Nothing. We remain the same. I'm so sorry I said it that way."

"It's a lot of pressure on one person, Bryce. I felt it before I left. I don't want to feel it again."

He shook his head. "We're in this together. I won't say it again. I'll make sure your boss knows that too."

She cringed again, dipping her head to hide from him.

He kissed the top of her head, sighing. "I said something wrong again."

"I don't work for that company anymore." Her voice was muffled because she still couldn't look him in the eye.

"Why not?" He let go of her hand, forcing her to look at him. "What happened?"

His fingers still held her chin, not giving her the chance to avert her attention elsewhere. Well, they'd been honest with each other thus far, why stop now.

"He fired me. The first day I came home. Well, the second day when I reported to work for the first time. He blamed me for everything that happened."

The fire lit up Bryce's eyes. "He blamed you for receiving a death threat?"

She nodded once. The movement alerted Bryce he was still holding onto her chin in a firm grip. He relaxed it, bringing it to the back of her head and pulled her closer, placing a hard kiss to her forehead.

"I'm so sorry. I never meant for that to happen."

She gave a helpless shrug. "I didn't like the job much anyway. He gave me all the shit assignments."

They stared at each other as she realized how that sounded.

"I mean, most of the assignments were shit. Not here though."

A sweet grin lit up his face. "Of course not here. Why would you ever think that? It was the easiest job you had."

Ha! She knew he was joking about that, so it didn't require a response.

"Where do you work now?"

"I've been looking around but haven't found anything yet. I'm jobless, Bryce. You're starting a relationship with someone who has no part of her life together."

His grin intensified to the point the happiness burst through his eyes. What was so happy about that statement? It pictured how pathetic she was.

"And you're starting a relationship with a murder suspect. My life isn't much better."

That had her heart flipping in turmoil. "They don't still think you killed her, do they?"

"Griffin's cameras saved my ass. But I imagine I'm not off the suspect list. Nobody is."

She hated to think anyone, especially the authorities, thought Bryce had anything to do with her murder. He would never. He wasn't the violent type.

"But can we backtrack?"

She wasn't sure she wanted to. Nothing they had been talking about was great. But she nodded anyway.

"You said we're starting a relationship."

"I did." How else would he describe this? She wasn't like Aster. Sleeping with someone for the hell of it and walking away like it didn't matter. She was putting her heart on the line. Didn't he understand that?

"Last night when I said we should take it to the bedroom, I thought maybe I moved too fast. I might be putting my foot in my mouth again, but..." He licked his lips. "But does starting a relationship mean you're thinking about staying?"

When she decided to come back, no, that hadn't been her intention.

"Because I want you to. I want you to stay in Sleighville."

She didn't know how to answer that. But she had to try. Only honesty would be between them from now on. No more holding in what they wanted to say.

"It means I don't take what's happening between us lightly. I don't know what the future entails, but I'm willing to find out. I don't want to upset you with false hope. Things are new and we should both make sure what's happening is what we really want."

"Right. Yes. Of course."

His words said he agreed.

His eyes spoke the truth though. She didn't say what he wanted to hear. He looked devastated and like she had crushed his heart.

"You haven't even come to terms with Denise's death. I don't think we can move forward to something serious like you suggested until that happens. It's not fair to me. Or to you."

While she spoke with honesty, his eyes still betrayed him. He didn't want to hear anything she said.

BRYCE TRIED to push Lila's words—honest and true—out of his mind as he got ready for work. He wanted her to shout it as loudly as she could that she would stay. That she would build a life with him.

Instead, she shot the idea down.

He understood why. It didn't mean he liked it. He wasn't ready to come to terms with anything concerning Denise.

She was gone, and yet she was like a virus, still infecting his life at every turn.

He showered first, then she hopped in. He didn't know if it was the serious conversation they had that put an awkwardness back between them, but he would've enjoyed it a lot more if they had showered together. But baby steps. They were heading in the right direction and the less he did to derail that, the better.

Coffee brewed and the food he wrangled up was ready by the time she emerged. She looked beautiful in a casual shirt and black pants. Her hair was down in soft waves with light makeup on. He could stare at her all day and soak up her beauty. Too bad he couldn't.

"I would like you to come to work with me. I feel like we got sidetracked from that conversion."

"It'll look odd."

He lifted his mug to his lips, taking a sip. "The city will hire you to help with the Easter event. Nothing odd about that."

"I don't work for a PR company though."

"We'll hire you as an independent consultant. The city will pay you directly."

"If you're sure..."

He hated the hesitation. Setting down his mug, some coffee spilled over the rim when he slammed it without intending to. He stalked to her, cupping her cheeks. "I've never been more sure about anything in my life."

Technically, he was talking about them as a couple. But he'd let her think it was about the job.

She might not be ready to jump all in, but he was. He would show her every second of the day how much he wanted her in his life. Forever.

"Okay. Fine. We can do it that way, but remember, I don't have all the answers to save this town."

His mouth brushed across hers, letting the kiss linger. Hoping to erase all the tension he still felt in her body. As his tongue dove in and his arms circled around her, the kiss taking on a life of its own, he felt the agitation release from her body. She succumbed to the pleasure, and if they didn't have to be at the office in twenty minutes, he would've swooped her into his arms and back to the bedroom.

"Just so you know, I don't expect you to save the town. But your ideas are a hundred times better than the ones we come up with, so trust me when I say, we need you. I need you." *In every way possible.* Of course, he kept that part to himself.

She nodded but didn't add anything. He finished his coffee while she grabbed her own cup and some of the food he had prepared. They left ten minutes later.

Becca stood up as soon as she saw Lila walking next to him. "So wonderful to see you again, Lila. I didn't realize you'd be here this morning."

Bryce smiled wide, not an ounce of it fake. He felt on top of the world again. Lila was back, and nothing would ruin the newfound happiness he had been given. He had even shaved this morning, evening out his goatee so he looked like his normal self.

"She thought she'd surprise us." He turned to her, grabbing a hold of her hand as he stared into her eyes. Hiding the desire was impossible. Why even try to mask it anymore? "I couldn't be happier by her decision."

Becca coughed, rousing him out of the trance he'd been in.

"Why don't you get set up in my office, Lila, and I'll grab us more coffee."

She got a long, warm hug from Becca before entering his domain. He ventured to the break room, making them both a large cup. He knew it wouldn't be the last one they had.

A throat behind him cleared.

He turned to find Becca waiting with an expectant look on her face. He figured she'd follow him, which was why he'd offered to get the coffee in the first place. Speaking to her without Lila around had to happen. She couldn't know how difficult it might be to get the city to pay her. They were running out of funds as it was.

"Lila no longer works for the PR company. We will be paying her directly as an independent consultant."

Becca's brow rose as her lips pursed in a thin line.

Yes, he knew it wouldn't be easy.

"Please find a way. Somehow. I don't care how." There was no use hiding the plea in his tone. He needed this to happen. He had to show Lila in every possible way she belonged here. With him. With the town.

"That's asking a lot, Bryce. I don't know if it's possible." She propped her hands on her hips. "What title do I give her? Independent consultant doesn't explain much. What is she consulting?"

He tossed his shoulders up. "How about social media expert? Or something along those lines. She's going to be doing what she did before, but not with the PR company behind her back."

"Harper handles all the social media. You know that. Try again."

Why was Becca giving him a hard time about this? She liked Lila. At least, he had thought so.

"Is there a problem here, Becca?" His tone went from cordial to dangerous in a blink of an eye. He wouldn't have anyone treating Lila like shit, not even his closest confidant at work.

She stepped closer, erasing the irritation and replacing it with sympathy. "Did you know today is the first day you arrived with a smile on your face? In over a month."

He hadn't been keeping track of how often he lifted his mouth upward like that. But if she said so, then it meant it was true.

"The day she left, you did too. You've been a person I didn't even recognize." She reached out and brushed his cheek as if she had the right to touch him like that. "You shaved. Your eyes look brighter. Even your clothes aren't wrinkled."

Wow. Really? Had he been so bad that he didn't even bother to wear decent clothes? He'd been so far gone in the depths of hell he hadn't noticed all the ways he'd faltered in his appearance.

"I have no problem whatsoever with Lila. In fact,"—a brilliant smile lit up her face—"I want to hug her for eternity for bringing life back into you. So damn easily too. And if the way you grabbed her hand means what I think it means, it's about damn time."

There was that stern expression again, as if she wanted to ream him for waiting so long to declare his feelings to her.

"The problem I have is the city is broke. I don't have the funds to pay her, even though I can see the desperation on your face that it needs to happen. No amount of me finagling and wording something in a specific way will change that."

He had done one right thing in his marriage. Keep separate accounts. While Denise wormed her way into his good graces now and again and he spoiled her, she never had full control of his money.

"I'll provide the money and you pay her with that."

She narrowed her eyes. "And if she finds out...how will that make her feel?"

He leaned closer, whispering, "I'll worry about that later. Right now, I need her by my side, and not because it makes me happy, which she does. But she was threatened again. I will die before I let anyone hurt her."

"No one else is dying around here." She shooed him away from the coffee machine. "Go away. I'll finish this. If she needs some serious convincing to stay in town, we have our work cut out for us. You handling the coffee isn't doing us any favors."

He laughed as he stepped away from the area. He never knew he could make coffee wrong, but who was he to argue with the woman who ran his work life like a captain on a ship.

"I'm glad you're on my side."

Becca looked him square in the eye. "Always. With everything. It might not seem like it, but this entire town is on your side. We always have been."

16

BRYCE CAUGHT her up to speed on how the St. Patrick's Day event went. Not good. The turnout had been low, which wasn't unexpected. An unsolved, brutal murder would do that to a small town like Sleighville. People wanted to feel safe and welcome when entering a new domain. Not fearful and looking over their shoulder constantly.

He even told her the re-opening of Noel's Cafe hadn't gone as well as they had hoped. Juliet kept her spirits up despite it. She wasn't going to quit grinding at it every day. Lila hoped she never did. The food and atmosphere in the cafe were wonderful. It would be a very tragic day if she ever closed the doors.

"I have a few meetings today that I can't reschedule, but—"

She held up her hand to stop him. What he had to say was no doubt important, but she wasn't here to rearrange anything, especially his schedule. She wanted things to go as normal, not disrupting a moment of the town's operation.

She also couldn't let him hover and smother her. That

warning had already been given to him. Why was he pretending to forget that?

"I do not need you rescheduling anything on my behalf. Nor do I need to attend all of the meetings you have. I'm here to help, not be a burden. As long as I'm around people —we both trust—there is no need for you to be by my side twenty-four-seven."

Bryce frowned, leaning toward her, outstretching his hand. She took it as he wanted her to. He squeezed it before lifting it tenderly to his lips and placing a short kiss on it. "I never want you to think you're a burden. So let's not utter that word again. It's not true." He forced out a weak smile, and she appreciated his effort to lighten whatever blow he would deliver next. "It's going to be very hard for me to let you out of my sight. Like, really hard."

She matched his shaky smile with one of her own, hoping to ease the words she'd deliver next. "It's going to happen, Bryce. You have to deal with it somehow. I refuse to let this person scare me."

He pressed his lips together, the rage simmering in his eyes. "You should be scared. I'm scared!"

She needed to remember what he had seen. Denise's body torn apart by violence. When he thought about the threats, that's what his mind conjured. It would be very difficult to fight that mental image he saw repeatedly. She didn't want to fight with him about anything, but she had to put her foot down in some instances.

"I thought we had come to some sort of compromise. I wouldn't be alone around town. You have meetings, so I'll hang around Becca or I'll ask Aster to escort me around town. We have to find a middle ground. It's not feasible to be by my side all day, every second."

He looked crushed by her words, then he wiped the

emotion off his face as best as he could, lifting her hand once again to place a kiss upon it.

"Okay. Middle ground. Compromise. I forgot Aster was here. I worry about you."

"I know, Bryce. It's going to be okay."

Though she knew by the concern still etched in his features, he didn't believe that.

Before they started their day, Bryce called Griffin to come to the office. When Griffin walked in, he looked unsure of himself on how to greet her. They started with a hi. Her sweet smile must've told him it was okay to step closer and grab a hug.

She dug into her purse and pulled out the plastic bag with the latest threat.

"I received this yesterday morning. Mailed to me in California."

Griffin took the bag, reading the contents. He flashed a glance at Bryce, then back to her. "Well, this is unexpected. Why are you here?"

His demanding question was also unexpected. Gone was the friendliness he'd displayed moments before.

"Watch your tone, please," Bryce said, his body taut and rigid as he sat in his chair.

Griffin's head swiveled toward Bryce. "I'm confused. She left for her own safety and now returns when she receives another threat. Walking right back into danger."

Lila stood up, grabbing the bag. "I don't have to explain my decisions to anyone. Not even you. I doubt anything will be found on this, but I thought I'd give it a try. But if you're going to act this way, then never mind."

Griffin snatched it back, surprising her at his reaction. She even flinched as it slipped from her fingers. "I will have this tested because it's my job." He inhaled and exhaled, releasing some of the tension from his body. She joined him, because she didn't want to fight with Bryce's brother. A tentative smile emerged as he watched her follow his actions. "I'm sorry, Lila. I didn't mean to have an outburst like that. You became part of this town and that increases my concern. This isn't an idle threat. This person murdered once, they'll do it again."

"Yes, I know. And I'm not going to hide the rest of my life. I left. I did what you two wanted me to do. They re-issued the challenge. I would've stayed away if not for that letter. But no one is going to throw that kind of shit into my face and think I'm going to take it. So do your job and analyze it. You won't find anything, I'm sure. But maybe me coming back will put a little fear into them. Show them I'm not playing around either."

Bryce pushed his chair back, standing up. "As long as we're clear that you're not making yourself bait at any point. Right?"

She turned her head his way. "No. I said I would stay with someone at all times. I'm not going to give this person a chance to hurt me on purpose. I'm not dumb."

Bryce moved closer to her. "I know that, but that speech made it seem like..." His brows puckered inward, and she couldn't help but reach out and smooth the worry lines away. "Eve made a hard decision last summer. She left to confront her demon. Almost didn't make it out alive, but she wasn't going to back down. I know it was one of the hardest things Griffin had to deal with. I think I'm starting to understand how he felt in that moment. Because I'm feeling it right now. I get what you're saying. I don't like it, but I get it."

She reached out again, this time brushing his cheek, letting it linger for a moment before smoothing it up and through his hair the way he liked it. He savored the delicate touch by closing his eyes.

"Is there something I should be aware of? Like, more than this evidence?" Griffin popped in, breaking up the moment.

She let her hand drop to her side, chuckling under her breath.

Bryce looked at his brother. "Lila is staying at the cottage with me. Aster's also back in town, staying with Juliet."

Griffin nodded, glancing back and forth between them. "Well, okay. I'll get this to the lab and let you know what I find out. It could take a few days though."

He left, and Lila didn't know what to make of his last comment. Was he not okay with her staying with Bryce? Did he not want Bryce to start a relationship with her?

"Sorry for—"

"Don't." She shook her head, not looking for any apologies. "Let's get to work."

He frowned for the longest time, staring at her as if debating whether to argue over her declining to have the conversation about his brother. He rounded his desk and took a seat.

"So, Easter. What ideas do you have?"

She had none.

At least, not yet.

———

THE MORNING HAD BEEN HECTIC, which was not the norm. Well, for the past few weeks anyway. Those weeks he had been in his shell, hiding away from the world and his work. With Lila back, his spirit, his confidence had returned. Which had made the day seem more chaotic than normal.

When in reality, it was back to the way things were prior to Denise's death.

He went to his meetings. The focus was back. Engaging with colleagues and giving rebuttals when necessary. No one commented on his attitude change, but he knew some of them wanted to.

While he took care of things needing his attention, Lila brainstormed with Becca on Easter event ideas. He'd been nervous the whole time she'd been out of his sight, but he'd also been proud of himself for not texting her or leaving his meetings to check on her. She would be okay with Becca. Repeating that in his head to the point of going crazy with it, he was starting to believe it.

When lunchtime rolled around, Lila suggested they venture to Noel's Cafe. He wasn't opposed to the idea. But he also knew going out into the open like that might go one of two ways.

Everyone would welcome her back with open arms.

Or everyone would stare belligerently at her and even make snide comments.

But if that's what she wanted to do, he wasn't going to keep pushing back on her decisions.

They rode the elevator in silence. As soon as it swung open to the first floor, he grabbed her hand before stepping out of it.

"I didn't know you liked to hold hands so much," she commented, glancing at their hands as they walked to the door, passing through security.

The guard on duty, Ronan, noted the affection but didn't say anything other than widen his lips into a silly grin.

"I didn't either." He chuckled, pushing open the door to bring them outside. "But I find I like holding your hand."

They ventured down the sidewalk, making their way to the cafe.

"It's a very big sign we're giving the town."

His steps slowed but he didn't stop. Her words caught him off guard. The last thing he wanted to do was cause a scene. According to her, they already were by holding hands.

"Should I let go?"

Her grip tightened. "I didn't say that."

They made it to the cafe. He wasn't sure what else to say, so he remained silent as he opened the door. Once they entered, their hands did part. He missed the small contact and wanted to snatch her hand back.

"Lila!"

Juliet shuffled around the counter with a huge smile on her face, wrapping Lila up in a hug. He chuckled at his sister's enthusiasm, taking one step away to give them space. Aster strolled up next to him.

"I was informed you're staying at the cottage."

He turned his full attention to Aster. The man wanted to have that chat right here, and right now. Well, he'd oblige him.

"I am."

Though he wasn't going to make it easy on the guy. Who the hell did he think he was anyway? He was staying at Juliet's house! It was the same damn thing.

"And where did my sister sleep last night?"

Bryce grinned. "Should I ask you where my sister slept last night too?"

Aster's eyes narrowed as his stance shifted from easygoing to taut in an instant.

"Okay, lower the testosterone." Lila stepped between the two, putting her hands out. She turned her gaze at Aster.

"Knock it off. My business is just that. My business. Something you love to say to people. So back off."

Aster inhaled deeply, took a step back, and laughed. The sound echoed off the walls and grated on his nerves all in the same breath. "You got it, sis."

Bryce didn't believe for a moment that Aster would let it slide. He'd be in his face again, but not when Lila was around.

She grabbed Aster's arm, guiding him away from the area and to the display case to the right, pointing at all the delicious treats that had been made for the day.

"How are you? Aster told me about the nasty note."

"I'm great." He produced a smile to go with his positive attitude. Neither one was fake. "And you? How are you?"

"Now I'm going to tell you to knock it off. Play nice with Aster."

"He started it. Not me."

Juliet rolled her eyes. "You're not a child, Bryce, so don't act like one."

"Why am I the bad guy here?"

Her eyes softened. "You're not. Neither is Aster. He's worried about Lila."

He leaned in closer. "So am I. Whether he likes it or not, she's staying with me. And if I can convince her, she won't leave at all. Ever again." He straightened his stance. "We both know Aster will leave regardless."

"I never said I wanted him to stay. For the first time in my life, I'm enjoying myself. I'm having a bit of fun. Let me have it."

He pulled Juliet into a hug, squeezing hard. "As long he doesn't hurt you, I want you to have as much fun as you can. I know that asshole did a number on you. You deserve all the happiness in the world."

Her arms tightened around him, and he even heard her sniffle. "Ditto. So if Lila is the one who makes you happy, I'm all for it." She lifted her head. "Just so you know, I have been trying to make Aster see how awesome you are."

He imagined that hadn't been easy. The man still hadn't given an inch in his dislike for him.

Juliet let go first, returning behind the counter. "The usual?" He nodded and she turned her attention to Lila. "What do you want, Lila?"

"Same as Bryce." Lila pointed to the raspberry Danish in the display case. "And two of these."

"On it!" Aster said with an over-the-top enthusiasm that made Bryce want to roll his eyes. But he resisted. Barely.

Lila took her two pastries, and they took a seat by the window. People strolled past on the sidewalk, making eye contact, and to his pleasant surprise, most of them smiled at them instead of glaring with disdain.

"After we finish eating, I'd like to walk around town. Visit each store."

He had a few meetings he couldn't get out of.

"Why?"

He wasn't asking to change her mind. Simple curiosity.

"Because people are going to talk. I'd rather get ahead of it. Make the story go my way, not the wrong way."

That made sense. Small towns had a way of spreading rumors without delay. It went from the truth to a distorted reality with too much ease.

Her hand slid across the table, her fingers wiggling for him to take a hold of it. He obeyed her command.

"I also want to talk to everyone and see their reaction. Someone here committed murder. That same someone is threatening to do the same to me. I want to know who I make uncomfortable, and I won't know that until I speak to them."

Now *that* he didn't like the sound of. Which was why she wanted to hold his hand like she was comforting a scared child.

"That's risky, and I don't like it."

She smiled with caring and understanding. "You don't have to like it. But you have to accept it."

She knew he had meetings he couldn't get out of.

He could hear Aster's loud voice coming from the kitchen. Laughter floated out as well. The man had returned as if he hadn't left on a whim. He inserted himself into Juliet's life with such deftness it shocked him.

While he should trust Aster to follow his sister around town, the man wasn't used to being on alert. He made friends, made people laugh and feel at ease. That was his forte. His magic power. What he didn't do was watch his surroundings, pay attention to things most people didn't even notice.

"You're right, of course. Do you mind if Duke tags along with you?"

Because he was far more qualified to keep Lila safe than Aster was.

Her expression was neutral as she contemplated his request.

"Why not Aster?"

Bryce tossed a lazy hand in the direction of the kitchen. "He appears to be busy. Duke won't mind."

Not that he'd asked him yet, but he knew Duke wouldn't refuse anything he asked of him. Not when it came to Lila's safety.

"You don't trust Aster."

"Your brother would never let you get hurt when he's

around. It's not that at all. But if you're going on a mission to weed out potential suspects, then you need someone with you that can help you identify those people. Someone like Duke. An officer in this town. Someone who knows these people. Things you might not know."

A sly grin built on her face. She lifted his hand, mimicking the gesture he loved to perform on her. A tender kiss hit his skin. "I like your train of thought. Okay. Let's call Duke."

He'd be more than happy to.

"So tonight, after your sleuthing, will you have dinner with me?"

An adorable giggle-snort sounded as a brilliant smile lit up her face. "Well, of course, silly. We are living together now."

He leaned closer. "No, I mean, I'd like to take you out to dinner. On a real first date. I'd love to take you to Rosetta's. They have the best Italian in the area."

Because he had some courting to do. It was best to start at the beginning. To get her to stay forever, he had to make her see how wonderful of a guy he truly was.

"I'd like that."

He stood up to lean even farther across the table and sealed their first date with a kiss.

17

LILA JUGGLED the two bags in her hand so she could open the door to the next store. She and Duke had started by Noel's Cafe and made their way down the sidewalk, stopping into each business.

Shannon, from Tidings and Joy Apparel, wrapped her in a big hug when she ventured to her store first. The greeting had been unexpected but welcome. They chatted a bit, catching up with life, though keeping it casual. They didn't touch on any heavy subjects.

Before she left, Shannon insisted she take a shirt. Since she had already gotten her free shirt, she was surprised. People who moved to Sleighville always received one free T-shirt from her clothing store. It was a gimmick to get them to come back for more. Which they did, so her way of doing things worked.

So she was baffled why Shannon gave her another free shirt. But she accepted it with a smile and big thanks. It was a tank top with the word festive written on it. Not written with a simple font, but each letter formed from something Christmassy: colorful lights, candy canes, Christmas trees,

194 AMANDA SIEGRIST

and snowmen. It wasn't warm enough to wear it yet—at least in Minnesota—but she couldn't wait to wear it.

At Mocha's Merriment, Taylor greeted her jovially and also gave her a Christmas mug with 'season greetings' written on it with a voucher for one free coffee.

Farther down at the Jolly Scrooge where they had a wide variety of candy, they gave her a whole box of candy canes and a bag of caramel.

And down the line she went, receiving something free from each establishment and a warm welcome. No one seemed contrite or even full of wrath toward her. Not in their words or their facial expressions. She made sure to keep a close watch on their eyes. The eyes always betrayed a person. She knew Duke was as vigilant of the people and his surroundings as she was. Maybe even more than her.

By the time they made it to the other side of the street, they had one more place to stop, which was Frost's. She doubted Anson wanted her dead. He'd been nothing but kind to her every time they interacted. But she couldn't discount anyone. They were all suspects in her eyes.

Duke pulled open the door and let her enter first, something he'd done at every store. Such a gentleman. Not to discount her brother because he had manners too, but Duke was a keeper. Juliet should date him. He'd be more secure than her brother, who never had any intention of maintaining a long relationship. And one out of state? No way!

She was up to four bags now, setting them on the floor near the bar, and took a seat on a stool. Duke joined her.

Anson strolled over, smiling affectionately. "So good to see you returned, Lila." His expression fell into sadness. "I'm sorry to hear the reason why."

She wasn't surprised he'd heard about the latest threat.

Most people had, though not all were as forthright about it as him.

"Me too. Although I am enjoying being back. It made me realize how much I missed it here."

"Can I get you something to drink?" Anson asked, his smile returning with no difficulty.

"You know what? Why not. I'll have a chocolate martini. The last one you made me was delicious." She hadn't ventured into Frost's often the last time she was here, but the few times she had, she'd ordered different flavored martinis, loving the chocolate one the most. He made it to perfection, and she would know as it was one of her favorite drinks.

He dropped his head slightly to acquiesce, then turned to Duke. "How about you?"

Duke chuckled, pointing at his uniform. "I'm on duty."

The answered laughter said Anson knew what he'd say. He made her drink with quick precision, and she moaned in delight with the first sip.

"You have magic in your hands."

He lifted them, grinning. "These old things? Yeah, I'd have to agree."

She'd loved his confidence and wily remarks from the beginning. She still wasn't getting any murderous vibes from him. Besides the tasty drink, this had been a wasted stop.

"So on duty, but strolling around town?" Anson questioned Duke, his easygoing smile still displayed. But she felt the slight undercurrent for the first time.

"The department is taking the threat against her seriously."

Anson nodded. "As you should."

They were all silent. She assumed their thoughts went

the same way as hers had. Imagining Denise's brutalized corpse.

"I don't want to throw anyone under the bus. I'm not that kind of person."

Duke leaned closer, his eyes alert and his entire body tense. She couldn't help but react the same way. What was Anson about to reference? Or better yet, who?

Anson also leaned closer, though only two other patrons were in the bar, and both sat too far away to hear the conversation.

"While Lila was away, Bryce came here a lot."

She found it comical how he mentioned her absence as if she had always intended to return. She also knew Bryce had stopped at the bar after work. He'd been honest about himself last night. The behavior he'd fallen into. The actions he wished he could've done better.

"If you're about to suggest Bryce had something to do with Denise's murder, Anson..." Duke let his voice trail off, the venom in each word. Things would not end pretty if he agreed that was where he was going.

"Absolutely not!" he uttered in a whisper. "That man would give his life before he'd take another one away."

Duke gave a sharp nod, but his scowl remained.

"I only bring it up because someone else came in here a lot as well. Someone who normally didn't until Bryce started to."

That had them both leaning even closer. Could they be on the cusp of revealing the killer?

"Melody. I think she tried to hide that she was coming to see him, but I knew what she was doing."

Duke straightened, blowing out a breath. "She had a thing for Griffin..." He shook his head. "Denise was her best friend."

Anson tossed his hands up, shrugging. "I'm telling you something I observed. Something I thought was odd. If she had a thing for Bryce, which I think she does, jealousy and shit like that can take a dangerous turn in the blink of an eye, best friend or not."

Lila had to agree he made a good point. She'd interacted with Melody a time or two, but nothing to give her a clear picture of her as a person. And definitely not about her feelings toward Bryce.

"I'll look into it." Duke stood up, looking at her. "You ready?"

She glanced down at her drink, realizing she'd been sipping the whole time and it was all gone. It sure had been a tasty one. Part of her wanted another, but she knew right now wasn't the time to keep drinking.

They had a lead.

A small one. Kind of an iffy one too.

"Yep." She stood up, dug through her purse, and put a twenty on the bar.

"On the house."

"It's not," she insisted, pushing the twenty to his side. "You've been very helpful. And you make a mean martini."

Anson chuckled, accepting the money and giving her change. He grabbed a piece of paper from the opposite counter and a pen, scribbling on it. "For another day then. I won't be the only place not giving something away."

She burst out laughing, her signature snort trailing it, and took his makeshift coupon offering one free drink to her. "I still haven't figured out why everyone did that today, but thank you."

It also showed how word spread around town with deftness. She and Duke had been venturing around town for about three hours, and Anson had already heard about the freebies given to her.

"One more tidbit," Anson started, his expression turning serious. "I don't know how true this is, but I heard Melody has been seeing Gregory. Maybe he'll have some insight about things."

Interesting.

Gregory ran the homeless shelter in town. She didn't know what to make of him. He'd been pleasant to her whenever she ran into him. But he was also the brother of Gerald, Juliet's ex-husband. The man who beat her to the point she nearly died. According to Juliet, Gregory blamed her for his brother in prison. He was never friendly when Juliet went to the shelter. And she went often since she donated the food that didn't sell from Noel's Cafe so it didn't go to waste.

"I appreciate that information as well," Duke noted. "That isn't a rumor I had heard before."

Anson shrugged. "That's why I'm not sure how true it is."

They thanked him for his help—and the drink—and left.

The day hadn't been a complete waste. She got a ton of free, fun goodies, and a new direction in the case.

But in all likelihood, nothing would come of it. The police had investigated the people closest to Denise in the beginning, as one did in a murder investigation. If Melody had anything to do with it, they would've found that out before now.

But it couldn't hurt to check again.

Maybe Bryce had some insight into Melody as well. He should know her pretty well being best friends with his wife.

Ex-wife.

Dead spouse.

Ugh. Lila didn't know how to picture Denise anymore and how she related to Bryce. So she wiped the confusion of the matter out of her mind and thought about all the good things that happened today.

Because bad, negative thoughts would bring her down, and she didn't want to feel that way. Not with a tiny morsel of a lead in their hands.

"Oh, I have one more stop to make. The drug store."

Duke nodded, but didn't ask why. And she didn't want to say it out loud. Buying condoms was already an awkward thing to do, which was asinine. It was human nature to have sex. To join as one and find release.

Except this town had a horrible fascination with talking about each other. Anson proved that by informing them he knew all about their day before they even arrived.

Duke walked into the store with her, the bell jingling merrily. It went perfectly with "Jingle Bells" playing over the loudspeaker.

She hummed along with the song as she headed for the aisle that she needed. When Duke saw where she was going, he stopped following her. His cheeks even turned a bit red. She giggled but didn't point out his embarrassment. Hell, she was mortified herself. But if she wanted sex tonight—the real kind of sex—condoms were necessary.

She stopped in front of the many varieties of condoms and snorted out loud. All she needed was a normal package full of foils she and Bryce could put to good use. But the options before her... How could one person not lose their shit with laughter at the craziness?

Merry Dickmas. The stockings were HUNG. Well HUNG. HO HO HUNG. Naughty? Nice? Those were some of the festive messages on the boxes of Christmas-filled condoms.

Her head bobbed back and forth between the normal, generic boxes and the fun, ridiculous Christmas-themed ones.

When in Rome...

Merry Dickmas was her favorite, so she grabbed that box, filled with twenty-five condoms, and made her way to the checkout counter.

Duke stood near it but didn't come any closer. She heard a snicker from him, so she knew he could see quite fine what she'd placed on the counter from where he stood.

Bonnie, the young girl running the register, scanned the box, as if not fazed whatsoever "That's thirty-two dollars and five cents."

Talk about a rip-off! Maybe she should go with the plain box.

Hoping it would put a smile on Bryce's face, she paid the outrageous price.

Bonnie made eye contact with her when she handed her the change. "Oh, Lila. Hi."

"Hello."

Everyone she'd chatted with today had never broached the subject about her and Bryce. Would Bonnie be the first? It was quite obvious why she was buying them and for whom.

She took the change and tossed it into her purse instead of messing with her wallet, then snatched the box of condoms and hid those in her purse as well.

Bonnie smiled. "Merry Dickmas!"

Lila burst out laughing. The snort came out extra loud. "You too, Bonnie."

What did that even mean? You too? She was now going to die of mortification.

She turned around and walked out of the store, hoping Duke would not say a word about what happened in there.

Another snicker echoed in her ear.

She stopped, facing him head on, unable to hold her smile in. "Okay. Say whatever you have to."

Duke shook his head, holding his lips together with a smirk a mile wide.

"Can't have sex without condoms!" she blurted, then started speed walking away.

"And definitely not the merry kind of sex without the right kind of condom."

His unexpected response had her pausing in her long stride. "Admit it. You've bought the Christmas kind before too." She giggled, feeling another loud snort rising up her throat.

He shrugged. "I would love to be a fly on the wall when you show Bryce what you purchased." He couldn't hold it in any longer, his laughter ringing around the sidewalk, loud and clear.

She joined him, letting the embarrassment wash away. So she bought condoms. Big deal!

The expedition into the drug store made her forget all about her other worries.

THE TEMPERATURE in the room was rising and it wasn't because a fire blazed in the fireplace right by him. Lila had returned to City Hall before he had finished his meetings. One went longer than he anticipated, and Duke had brought her to Griffin's house. He was the last one to arrive. Eve and Juliet were working on supper while he, Griffin, Duke, Aster, and Lila sat in the living room. Well, they all sat while he stood by the fireplace. He was too wired to sit, especially after the news Lila and Duke delivered.

"What do you think, Bryce?" Duke asked, leveling a very intense gaze his way.

Not like he was a suspect, but one that said he was still in cop mode. The uniform still on also helped the severe look he sent his way.

He had no idea what to think. Melody? A killer? He couldn't picture it. Now Gregory on the other hand. His brother was an abuser. Damn near left Juliet for dead. Violence could run in the family. But why would he kill Denise? That's what made no sense.

"I don't know. I don't know what to say to that."

"Let's start with the basics," Griffin offered. "You frequented Frost's the last few weeks. Is Anson correct in his assessment? Did Melody approach you more than normal?"

Well, him going to Frost's as much as he had wasn't normal to begin with. "She did happen to be there a lot when I was there. Anson even mentioned she would say to tell me hi if she missed me."

"She was best friends with Denise. You hung out with her a lot. Her saying hi isn't abnormal," Griffin said.

"Yeah, but Anson said she didn't normally come in before Bryce started coming in. That's abnormal for her," Duke pointed out.

Bryce, somehow, found a smile when he looked at Lila, who had a notebook out and was jotting things down in it. "What are you doing?"

She met his gaze. "I need a clear picture of things. I'm writing this stuff down."

"You're not a detective, Lilac," Aster drawled, the only one not sitting on the edge of his seat like the other three were. He was the most relaxed in the room, and Bryce wished he would join Juliet and Eve. His mere presence irritated him.

"It doesn't mean I can't take notes, Aster." She enunciated his name with derision, so much so that he sat up a bit. As if realizing he needed to take this conversation more seriously.

Oh, Bryce knew that Aster understood how serious this matter was. But his nonchalance said otherwise.

"Did you ever get the impression she has feelings for you?" Griffin asked, returning to the matter at hand.

Bryce shook his head. "Not like she did with you."

"Yeah, she was always trying to get you to go out," Duke said.

"True," Griffin started, giving Bryce a potent look, "but she never looked at me the way she looked at you. I never understood her infatuation with me."

"Unless it was to get closer to Bryce, who she knew was taken." Lila didn't look up from her notebook as she said that. She winced, jerking her gaze to Griffin. "Not insinuating you were second best or anything. Or that you are."

Griffin offered her a gentle smile, indicating he knew she meant no harm. "I get your point you're trying to make. What better way to be around a man you like than to be around his family. She couldn't go on dates with Bryce and Denise as a third wheel, but as a double date, well, that's another story." He swiveled his direction to Bryce. "How many double dates do you think I was forced to go on?"

Bryce scowled at his brother. "Forced? I never forced you."

Griffin's brow rose. "Your wife did. On several occasions. Each time it was hard to get through it. Melody knew how I felt. I was clear on my feelings, yet it kept happening."

He shrugged. "I don't know what to say. I never noticed anything weird from Melody."

"You wouldn't. You were devoted to Denise." Duke didn't look at him when he said that. But his tone told him enough. That he hadn't approved.

"Was it wrong of me to be devoted to my wife?"

Lila's head shot up from her notebook, and he hated the way she cringed. He had been married before. He had loved Denise once. He couldn't erase his past. But the way she looked at him right now said she was disgusted at him. That she couldn't believe he ever loved his wife.

"That's not what Duke is saying," Griffin said. "You didn't notice Melody's behavior because you loved Denise. You would've never cheated on her. So looking at another woman like that, it wouldn't happen. Maybe you subconsciously ignored the signals coming from her."

Bryce did not like where this conversion was going. Lila looked upset. The more it went on, it was making him angry as well.

"Okay. So we're going with Melody has a thing for me. How does that translate into murdering Denise? We were getting a divorce. I would've been free for her to make a move."

"Except a best friend—a true best friend—doesn't date the ex-husband." Lila wouldn't look at him as she spoke. "Based on what I know about Denise, she would've made Melody's life a living hell if she would've made a move like that with you."

"I have to agree with Lila on that," Griffin said. "Maybe she confessed her feelings to her. Wanted to see if she'd approve. It didn't go well and..." His words ended because they all knew what ending Denise met with.

"What does Gregory have to do with all of this?" Aster

asked, a little more alert than before. As if Aster had noticed Lila getting uncomfortable and refusing to look at him.

Why was he the bad guy again? What had he done or said wrong?

Duke stood up. "That's what we need to find out. I need to confirm if the rumors are true. I need to question them both."

Griffin also got up from his position. "Sheriff Carter needs to do those things. You know we can't be involved in the investigation."

"Fine. I'll go share our findings with him." Duke headed for the front door.

"At least stay and eat with us." Griffin's tone sounded demanding, as if he knew why Duke was leaving already.

He didn't want to be around Juliet and Aster. They could get touchy-feely, not caring who saw their affection. Bryce didn't blame him for leaving. If he could leave, he would too. He didn't like the feeling of the atmosphere. He hadn't since the moment they told him about their day interviewing people.

"I'm good. Thanks for the offer though." Duke made eye contact with him, a weird laughing twinkle in his eye. "Don't let this conversation ruin your evening. Have a fun one."

He left.

What an odd thing to say.

"I'm going to check on Eve." Griffin left the room.

Now was Aster's chance to leave too. He wanted to talk to Lila alone. Of course, he wasn't going to point blank tell the guy to exit the room. Aster would get in his face or even throw a punch because his anger was always just on the surface whenever they spoke.

Lila had no such trouble though. "Why don't you go check on Juliet."

Aster rolled his eyes and stared him down as he stood up from the couch. Then he was gone too.

As soon as they were alone, he took the empty spot next to her. "I feel like you're mad at me. Tell me what I did wrong."

She reached over and smoothed a hand across his cheek. The tender touch gave him hope that she wasn't too angry over whatever had upset her.

"I'm sorry. I don't mean to seem angry. It's...sometimes when we talk about Denise, it gets weird for me. She doesn't feel gone all the time. Like she could walk into the room at any moment. When you call her your wife...those weird feelings I have intensify. It's a me problem, not a you problem."

She had been his wife only a few weeks ago. He didn't know how to think of her now either. She'd been a part of his life for a very long time. High school sweethearts, if one wanted to put labels on it. Though the sweetness in the relationship died after college when she realized he didn't have ambitions for a higher office.

"No, it's an us problem. You were right last night. Telling me that I have to come to terms with her death, I don't know how to do that quite yet. Calling her my wife feels weird even to me. Which is also weird because she was just that over a month ago."

He placed a hand on her waist. She didn't flinch or move away, so his grip strengthened. "I know we're jumping head-first into whatever is happening between us, but I'm not afraid of the fall. Being with you makes me happy. You make me so damn happy I can't even describe it. So when I mess up like I did, please forgive me. I will come to terms with everything, but it might not be a fast thing. I only ask for some patience."

Lila cupped both his cheeks, smiling, her eyes shimmering a bit as if tears were on the verge of releasing. "Patience never has to be asked for. I know none of this has been easy on you. That's why I said it was my problem. I'm not mad at you. I promise. I'm mad...at Denise."

That made him chuckle and he wasn't sure why. Perhaps because he was also angry with her. For so many things. Things he still had yet to let go of. That's what he needed to do. To move on, he had to let go of the anger and pain.

But how?

"I know the feeling well." He kissed her, feeling better for the first time that evening. "I wish we could leave like Duke did. I want you to myself. I'm sorry we didn't get our first date tonight. I wanted to take you out."

"Tomorrow is a new day. Oh, and I have presents." She giggled, then snorted.

The sound made his chest burst with happiness. He'd never get tired of hearing her adorable laugh.

"Now I'm intrigued. What for?"

The sly smile said he wasn't going to know yet.

"Are they wrapped? Like, actual Christmas presents?"

"You'll have to wait and see." Another captivating laugh-snort erupted. "You're going to love it."

It? So one present. If he had known she was going to get him something, he would've returned the favor.

The night couldn't go fast enough.

18

THE EVENING WENT SLOWER than she had liked. After their conversation on the couch, she wanted to go home and have her wicked way with him. But the meal was delicious. No surprise there because Eve and Juliet could bake and cook so well.

She sat next to Bryce, of course. And maybe it was her teasing him about a special present, but he was unable to keep his hands to himself. Touching her thigh underneath the table. Running a hand down her arm. Holding her hand for a while as well. Each touch, nothing too sexual, sent the desire straight to her core.

She wanted to leave, and she wanted to leave right this instant.

But dessert had to be eaten.

That was delicious too.

A tiramisu that she couldn't believe was homemade, though she shouldn't have been surprised.

After the sweet treat, Griffin offered drinks, and they accepted. At least the conversation was light as they sat around the living room.

Finally, after what seemed like ages, they bid their good night. So did Aster and Juliet. She was grateful she and Bryce had a short walk across the lawn instead of a car ride home.

As soon as they walked in, Bryce undid the alarm, and she re-locked the door. She took her coat off, listening to the beeps as the alarm was set again. She looked at Bryce, and the heated look in his eyes was all she needed.

Her coat fell to the floor. His disappeared as well, joining hers. Then she was in his arms and pushed up against the door.

The soft touches from before were the prelude to the real thing.

His deep kiss sent lightning strikes down her spine. She gripped his shoulders, returning the fervor with as much energy as he was giving.

Her hands found a path to his cheeks and ran up and through his hair. The feral growl that left his lips had her heart jumping with joy. She loved that she made him feel so delirious with passion.

"Lila…" he whispered as his lips moved down her neck, scorching her skin along the way. His hands untucked her shirt, lifting it up and over her head, letting it drift to the floor. "I've wanted you to myself all day."

She smirked, pushing the suit jacket off his shoulders and dropping it. She started at the bottom button of his shirt, going as nimbly as she could. "You have me now. What are you going to do about it?"

His shirt was off and on the floor.

His eyes dilated with pleasure as he worked the button on her pants. She shimmied them down and off. He did the same with his own.

"You're overdressed." His wicked grin came right before

he unsnapped her bra and took a nipple into his mouth. Lightly biting, then soothing it with a kiss.

They were both naked and they hadn't even moved two feet from the front door.

"I want you so badly," he groaned, his eyes flashing with pain. "So, so badly I'm willing to risk the consequences."

Woah! Now that was speaking volumes.

So if she got pregnant, he'd step up and what? Raise the baby with her? Ask her to marry him?

Love hadn't been exchanged between them, and it was too soon for those illustrious words anyhow.

But she didn't want him to think he had to be with her because of consequences that could've been prevented.

She placed a hand over his heart, grinning. "Well, I should give you your present. So no consequences have to be had."

He looked disappointed for a second before the emotion vanished. She'd ignore what she probably didn't even see anyway. She stepped over to the side where she'd tossed the bags and her purse before heading to Griffin's. After rummaging around, she retrieved the box and held it out to him.

"Merry Dickmas!"

Bryce couldn't hold in the loud guffaw. "Oh my God. You went into the drug store to buy condoms." He held up the holiday box, his eyes large and round. "And you bought the Christmas ones."

"Don't forget Duke was with too." Her lopsided grin made him laugh harder.

"He's going to give me so much crap for this." His head shook though his laughter remained.

"It was worth it to hear you laugh."

The smile he wore filled her heart with jubilation. He

hadn't smiled like that in a long time. The last month had been hell on him. On both of them.

His eyes grew with worry. "You know it's all over town by now. That you bought condoms."

"The town already knows there's something between us. Are you suddenly not liking that idea?"

Because the fact he brought it up made her think he didn't like the notion any longer.

He cupped the back of her neck with one hand and pulled her closer, pressing his lips hard to hers. "I don't give a shit what anyone thinks about us. But I don't want you to deal with blowback, if it's not nice."

"I'm not worried." She tapped the box in his hand. "So please proceed to wish me a merry dickmas."

He snorted but obeyed, then opened the box and removed a foil, ripping it open. She took the condom from him, rolling it on him herself. His eyes closed as she did it slowly, enjoying the way his entire body leaned her way.

His eyes popped open and his hands were gripping her waist to lift her up. She wrapped her legs around his waist as he guided himself leisurely inside her, taking his sweet, sweet time. The moment he was fully inside, he stood still.

She pressed her hands to his cheeks, holding his gaze steady. Not that she thought he wanted to look away.

"I've never had sex against a door before," he whispered, chuckling. "Are you okay? I'm not hurting you, am I?"

"I'm perfect. It's a new one for me too. I'm a fan."

He pumped his hips, eliciting a soft moan from her. "I'm a fan too. I don't know how long I'll last because you feel too damn good."

"We have twenty-five merrily condoms."

He chuckled, pressing his lips to hers. She smoothed her

hands up through his hair, then clung to his back as he started pumping harder.

She held on for the ride of her life. He didn't hold anything back. His thrusts were intense and deep. They moved fluidly, grinding against each other. Dare she say, loving each other thoroughly.

But it was too soon for love, so she dismissed the word from her mind.

Her nails scraped his back, her cries of pleasure increasing in volume to urge him on. He followed her commands, thrusting with complete abandon.

She knew it was coming to an end when she felt the pleasure rising, undulating like a tsunami. Her head fell back against the door, moaning his name as it hit her.

"Yes, Lila!" Bryce growled, pumping even harder and deeper before he tensed himself. Her name came out in a whisper along with other words she couldn't quite make out, he said them so quietly.

He stood there, holding her against the door for the longest time before either one of them spoke.

"I wanted to shower with you this morning." A feather-light kiss hit her lips. "How about one right now?"

She wasn't sure why they hadn't showered together, but there had been a slight awkwardness between them. She wouldn't have denied the request this morning, so she wasn't about to deny it right now.

"I could go for more holiday cheer under the water."

He laughed, letting her feet drift to the floor. "I buy the condoms from now on."

She swatted his ass as they made their way to the bathroom. "You're no fun. Admit it. It puts the Christmas spirit in you."

"I will never admit such a thing." He tossed the used

condom in the trash can, then popped another one out of the box, setting it on the shower ledge near the shampoo. "But I'll wear as many dickmas condoms as you want." He pulled her into the shower, wrapping his arms around her. "Because as long as you're in my arms, that's all I care about."

She had to agree with that.

No matter what people might say tomorrow, either to her face or behind her back, it didn't matter. She had Bryce the way she wanted in her life and that's all that mattered.

HE WAS in much better spirits this morning than yesterday. Not that it was a terrible morning, but he decided he enjoyed showering with Lila rather than on his own. Today, they lathered each other up, building the desire between them before he took her shamelessly against the shower wall. He was ready for the day.

Lila continued to beautify herself in the bathroom while he ventured to the kitchen to make breakfast. A small batch of eggs with toast. She seemed to enjoy it yesterday, so he'd go with what he knew she liked.

When she walked into the room, his heart palpitated. She hadn't done much to her appearance. Her hair was dry and pulled back into a loose ponytail. She wore a slight amount of makeup, a touch of eye shadow, mascara, and lipstick. Enough to notice she wore it but not enough that she caked it on or anything. Not that he thought she needed anything to begin with.

But her beauty, any way she dolled herself up, it blew his mind. It made him wonder how lucky he'd gotten that she liked him in return. That he was worthy of her affections.

That's all he wanted to do. Be worthy of her.

She strolled to him with an adoring grin on her face, then placed a finger under his chin and pushed up. He didn't think he'd let his jaw drop, but apparently he had. What could he say other than she made him speechless.

"You sure know how to let a girl know she's beautiful with no words."

"Good." He wrapped his arms around her, pulling her closer. "Because you're so damn beautiful I don't even know how to put it in words."

They shared a powerful kiss that made him want to call in sick. Not leave the cottage until he was positive she wouldn't leave him.

When the kiss ended, her eyes portrayed the same desire inside of him. To hide away from the world. But she slipped from his grasp and headed for the coffee pot.

"I had an epiphany while blow drying my hair."

His heart rate kicked up another notch, not sure whatever inspiration hit her would be good news for him. Because no matter how hard he tried, he could never shake the feeling she wasn't staying around permanently.

Of course not! She lived in California. She had returned to find the culprit threatening her. And when he told her he wanted her to stay, she wouldn't confirm the request.

Which was why he had to make it his goal to change her mind. To remain with him.

"I can't wait to hear what it is." He hoped he injected enough upbeat attitude in that sentence. Because in reality, he was deathly afraid to hear what she had to say. He couldn't pinpoint why his thoughts always turned negative.

Or maybe he did know.

He always had to walk on eggshells around Denise. It

was hard to stop that kind of reaction, even if it wasn't her he was dealing with anymore.

She turned around from the counter, the pure happiness and excitement shining through the depths of her emerald-green eyes.

The bright expression she wore looked promising. He had nothing to worry about.

"You saw all the goodies I got around town. So much fun stuff. A T-shirt, a mug, candy, discounts and free coupons. That sugar cookie candle made me want to have a whole box of cookies," she said with a chuckle. "I don't understand why everyone gave me something yesterday, but it sparked an idea."

He had no clue either why the townsfolk had done that. It wasn't unusual for Shannon to give free T-shirts, but everyone else, definitely abnormal.

"What do you think about a care package? When someone books a stay at one of the B&B's or one of the rental properties associated with Joy, they get a free care package. A good way to get each business's name out there, and an excellent way to reel them inside the store. A fun T-shirt? Love it! It'll make them wonder what other fun T-shirts there are. That candle smells amazing. Now they need one that smells like gingerbread and hot chocolate. Or like a candy cane. What do you think?"

He thought it was a wonderful idea. Honestly surprised no one else had ever started it before. But...

The elation slowly dimmed. "You don't like the idea?"

He mentally berated himself for letting part of his doubt show. "I love it. I think it's an amazing idea and something we should've already been doing."

"But?" she urged, gesturing with her hand for him to continue.

"Some of those stores can be stingy. I'm not sure how many would donate to it. Right now, a lot of them are hurting and might not be able to financially."

Lila waved her hand as if that wouldn't be an issue. "You like the idea though? Besides that concern?"

He moved closer to her, brushing his hand behind her neck. "Your ideas always amaze me. I've never not liked one of them. And if you're not concerned about getting full approval from everyone, I'm not either."

She met him halfway for the kiss he wanted to bestow upon her. It went from slow and sweet to hot and passionate in the blink of an eye. So much so that her coffee spilled, making him jump back when it hit his shirt. The hot liquid even scorched through the material and hit his skin.

She winced, then giggled. "Sorry."

He grabbed another quick peck, smiling. "It's just a shirt."

As he walked to the bedroom to change, it crossed his mind that he never had those kinds of moments with Denise. Where they chatted before work. Kissed here and there. Light touches throughout the day. It made him sad to realize how far his marriage had sunk before Denise made the decision they should part ways.

He should've done it years ago.

Maybe she'd be alive.

Wiping those negative thoughts from his mind, he changed his shirt, ate breakfast with Lila, and they were out the door.

Lila went right to work on her new idea. He had another busy day of meetings, so he couldn't trail around town with her. And he wanted to. She shouldn't have to be without him after buying condoms. People would have something to say. Not everyone could keep their opinions to themselves. Duke wasn't on duty yet, but he offered to join her again. Bryce would make sure he paid him back in some way. He appreciated Duke stepping in when he couldn't be there for her.

The moment she left with Duke, he felt her loss. Like a part of him had disappeared as well.

"She'll be okay."

He jerked his attention to Becca, who stood right by his desk. He'd been so lost in thought he didn't even hear her walk in.

"Not if they don't approve of us together."

Becca shook her head as a sly smirk emerged. "This town loves her. This town loves you." She pointed at him, her gaze intensifying as if laser beaming the point home to him.

He knew he wasn't hated around here. At least, not at the last election because they voted him back in as mayor. Now, after the debacle with Denise, then her death, he couldn't be sure how anyone thought of him.

"I wish I had your same enthusiasm about it."

She picked up his coffee mug. "You look like you need a refill. I'll do it for you." She headed for the doorway.

"Becca!" His tone had been light but quick. He didn't want to make it seem like he was hollering at her. He waited until she turned around. "You do not have to keep getting me coffee. I insist I do it myself."

"No. I will do it. Because I want to. Because it's okay to let people in and help."

She continued on her way without waiting for his rebuttal.

Was she insinuating he didn't let people help him? That he pushed people away? He hadn't thought he acted that way. But her words meant something. That maybe he had.

When she returned with his mug, he was still contemplating the entire conversation. Playing it on a loop as if that would help him understand better. The mug hit the desk with a soft thump, she smiled at him, then made her way back out of the office. The moment her feet hit the threshold, he said her name again.

She turned around, same as before. Same smile on her face. Same kindness in her eyes.

"Did you have something to do with the town giving Lila free stuff?" The idea hit him square in the chest, and he knew it would eat at him if he didn't ask.

"Now why would I do that?"

Yes, that was a very good question. Why would she?

Unless she didn't want Lila leaving either.

But why?

"It's odd they did that yesterday. A very nice gesture, but odd."

Her smile increased. "You have a meeting in fifteen minutes. Finish your coffee."

He picked up the mug, taking a sip before she swiveled around and left. She hadn't answered his question. Which made him think she had something to do with it. And if it helped in some weird way keep Lila in Sleighville, he wasn't going to argue with the method. Any sort of method Becca would continue to come up with.

Like she informed him, he finished his coffee and made his way to the meeting. Trying his damndest to keep Lila out of his thoughts and how she was faring around town.

Duke would keep her safe. He needed to remember that.

19

Lila grabbed onto Duke's arm, beaming up at him. "I can't believe it. Can you believe it?"

"That everyone said yes to your brilliant idea? Yes, I totally believe it."

They walked with her holding onto the crook of his arm for a short while before she realized how the gesture might look and let go. It hadn't been in a sexual way whatsoever, just her excitement bursting out. She had every store on Main Street agree to her plan. The last thing she needed was to turn those yeses into noes because they thought she was making a move on Duke.

"Why do you seem so shocked?"

Good question Duke posed. Maybe because Bryce had a very decent point this morning. This town was bleeding dry of money. Not many could afford to give stuff away. It would be hard in the beginning. She made sure to be very honest about that aspect of the idea. But it would work out in the long run. She honed in on that point as well.

"I guess the pessimistic part of me didn't think everyone would be on board."

They made it to the cafe where they decided to meet Bryce for lunch. Duke stopped in front of the door, holding the handle but not opening it.

"I know you went through hell with those rumors Denise spread. But nobody believed her. Because it wasn't true."

But now it was. How could any of them be sure she and Bryce hadn't hooked up before her murder?

"It is now."

Duke's grin widened. "And thank goodness for that. You fit right in. You belong here. With Bryce." He swung open the door, gesturing for her to enter first.

She didn't know how to respond to his kind words, so she chose not to.

They were early. Bryce hadn't arrived yet and she didn't want to order without him. Duke remained in front, but she ducked into the kitchen to say hi to Juliet and Aster. Eve was in the front with Tabitha. She'd make sure to chat with her as well before she left.

Juliet was at the counter rolling out dough while Aster stood to the side staring at her with stars in his eyes. It made her pause in the doorframe, in awe of the look. He never looked at women like that.

Could her brother be falling for a woman for once?

"Hey!" Juliet beamed at her, not stopping once in her rolling technique. "How did it go? Who said no so I know who to bother?" The fierceness in her eyes said she wasn't kidding. She'd get into someone's face if they declined to be part of the welcome gift idea.

"They all said yes."

"I knew it!" Juliet smirked at Aster. "Did I not tell you they'd all say yes?"

"You sure did."

Lila feigned a hurt look. "Hey, did you not have complete faith in me, brother?"

"I always have faith in you." He winked, though little devils danced in his eyes.

She rolled her eyes and directed her attention back to the dough. "What are you making?"

"Sugar cookies for Shannon. She's attending a craft fair tomorrow two towns over and wants some refreshments at her table along with the T-shirts and such she'll be selling."

"I love that!" Lila walked closer, eyeing the cookie cutters waiting to be used: a Santa, a snowman, a reindeer, a circular ornament, and a candy cane. "Will she be advertising they're from your cafe?"

Juliet shrugged. "No big deal if she doesn't. She'll reel in customers for her store. I hope, anyway. She hasn't done one of these craft fairs in years, but..." Juliet's voice trailed off. There was no reason to explain why she was doing it this year. Anything to make money and get people to come back to town.

"Well, she should."

Juliet set the roller down. "It's okay, Lila. I'm not worried about it. She's paying me for the cookies, so it's not my business what she does with them once I get paid. It'd be different if she wanted them for free."

Lila didn't like it, but she hadn't been involved in the initial talk about the craft fair. "Why didn't you sign up for the fair as well? That would be a great way to get your name out there."

"I don't have the manpower for that. We're bare bones at the cafe as it is. Me, Eve, Tabitha, and Chip. And Marcy only works weekends. I can't blame Dawn, who I hired a few months ago, that she didn't last long. I just can't swing that kind of thing right now."

"I'll do the booth."

Juliet shook her head. "It's too late to sign up, Lila. Maybe the next one."

She would add looking up the local craft fairs to her to-do list. In fact, Sleighville should host their own craft fair.

Aster had pulled his phone out, holding it up and directed at Juliet.

"What are you doing?" Lila asked with a giggle.

Aster's face dusted a light red. "Grabbing a quick picture of Juliet. She's cute making cookies."

"Stop it," Juliet jested, her cheeks blooming a light red as well.

That simple action sparked another idea in her head. The ideas kept rolling in.

"That's a great idea."

Juliet and Aster trained their attention on her, both frowning at her enthusiastic outburst.

"Does Noel's Cafe have social media?" Every store in this town needed a social media presence. Though she wouldn't spring it on all of them at once. Baby steps. She'd start with Juliet.

"We have a website so people know our menu, location, and when we're open. It's a simple one."

She nodded, already aware of that. She was talking about everything else. "Aster will help you get set up on everything. He'll start filming you baking and such. He has a good eye, so he's perfect for the job."

Juliet stepped away from the counter as if that would stop Lila's idea in its tracks. "Ummm...I'm not a big social media fan. I don't even have personal accounts anywhere."

Lila walked to Juliet and thought about grabbing her hands, but they were covered in flour and small specks of dough. "Do you want Sleighville back on the map? Do you want people to flock to town and come try your delicious food?"

"Of course."

"You have to put yourself out there. The whole town does. I can only do so much. Do you know how we got so many new people to the winter festival? Because Aster and his band posted everywhere about it like crazy. It trended on several apps. So now let's get Noel's Cafe trending."

Juliet looked at Aster, who wore a confident, encouraging smile. Her brother knew she was right.

"I hate to do it," Juliet pouted. "But I will because I trust you. If you say I should, I'll do it."

"Awesome!" Lila glanced at Chip working quietly at his worktable. "Make sure you get a few pics and videos of Chip. The ladies will love his handsome face."

Chip winked, but also blushed at the compliment.

Aster already had his phone at the ready, focused on the device as his fingers rushed across the screen. "I'm on it, Lilac. This place will be crazy busy in a week. Tops!"

And she had no doubt he was correct. They were a lot alike in that respect. When an idea popped in their head, they put their full focus on it.

She left them to it, baking and starting the new journey of social media, and went back to the front. What a productive day. And the ideas kept popping out of nowhere. How long would it keep up?

She stopped in her tracks at the scene before her.

Duke was near the front door, toe to toe with Gregory.

"I told you to leave," Duke said through gritted teeth.

"Not until I speak to Juliet," Gregory spat back. "I don't appreciate having the cops on my doorstep accusing me of murder!"

Oh, dear.

Their theory last night about Gregory sleeping with Melody and having something to do with Denise's murder was causing the wrong reaction. Juliet hadn't even been a part of the conversation. Why would he think she had something to do with the accusation? Because his brother—who beat Juliet to near death—was in prison? Ridiculous.

This wasn't a headache Juliet needed.

"She had nothing to do with that." Lila jolted forward, standing next to Duke before he could tell her to stay out of it. "I learned an interesting tidbit yesterday while visiting around town. I was the one who wondered about your relationship with Melody."

She felt Duke tense next to her and she knew she'd be getting an earful from him later for putting herself as a larger target.

"So you went to the police because you think I'm sleeping with Melody?" he snarled, and so venomously she almost stepped back from the hatred in his eyes. But she held her ground. She would not let any person intimidate her.

"No, I spoke to Sheriff Carter about it," Duke stated. "I would've spoken to you myself, but since he's in charge of the investigation, I went through the appropriate channels."

Gregory straightened his stance, considering he'd been leaning closer to Duke. Something Duke had also been doing. She let out a quiet breath that they were both releasing some of the tension between them.

"I imagine you didn't like it when rumors spread that you were sleeping with Bryce while Denise was still alive."

She shrugged. "It wasn't true so I didn't let it bother me." Not a full truth from her lips, but she wasn't going to tell this asshole how she felt. "Are you denying sleeping with Melody?"

"She's not married. I'm not married. We're both single. I didn't think it was wrong of me to do so."

"It's not." Lila didn't care who he slept with. But if it had caused him or Melody to kill Denise, then that was another story.

"Well, as I informed Sheriff Carter, Melody was with me that evening. She stayed overnight and didn't leave my house until eight o'clock. Neither one of us killed Denise. Nor did we have a reason to."

Pretty convenient they were each other's alibi. Not that Lila would voice that out loud.

"How about the rumor Melody has feelings for Bryce? What do you think about that?" Gregory was being forth-coming, why not keep interrogating him.

"Again, she was with me all night and into the morning. Why would she kill her best friend?"

"Maybe she told Denise about her feelings and it didn't go well."

"That would be between her and Denise. I wouldn't have anything to do with that."

"Do you even care she has feelings for another man?"

Gregory burst out laughing. "She's not my soulmate or some shit. It's sex. Something you're engaging in right now with Bryce. You'll use him and abuse him and then leave." Gregory leaned closer to her. "Good riddance to you."

"And to you as well."

Gregory flinched and turned around at Bryce's harsh tone.

"You're not welcome in my sister's cafe. Leave."

Perhaps Gregory got the answers he'd been looking for, believing Lila when she said she'd been at the heart of further police scrutiny. Or maybe he didn't want to get into it with Bryce, afraid of him for some reason. Either way, Gregory threw her a nasty look before leaving.

Bryce looked pissed. "What the hell was that about?"

She shared a look with Duke, who appeared to not want to answer that as much as her. Because when she relayed the entire encounter, she knew Bryce would holler at her for the part she played in it.

"How dare he come into my shop!" Juliet paced back and forth in front of the cookies she was still preparing.

Bryce let her get her ire out. One of them had to.

They'd ventured to the kitchen after Gregory left, where Bryce demanded from Duke and Lila what happened. The story didn't bother him when Duke told him part of it, but as soon as Lila jumped in with her side, his anger rose to the surface.

What had she been thinking?

Was she asking for another target on her back? A much larger and deadlier one?

"He's gone now. I wouldn't have let him near you," Aster crooned, though he didn't get closer to Juliet. Not even his soft voice stopped her vigorous pacing.

"He wouldn't have gotten past me," Duke added.

Bryce had to stifle a chuckle. Both men were fighting for her attention and neither one was getting it.

Eve was the only one who managed to get close enough to Juliet, and even her presence wasn't enough to stop her jaunting back and forth.

"He's gone now and there's nothing to worry about."

Bryce couldn't hold back the glare he sent Lila's way.

"Seriously? Nothing to worry about? You practically shoved a neon sign at yourself. Hey, pick me as a target."

Lila crossed her arms, pressing her lips together as if she didn't want to say something she'd regret.

Oh, she didn't appreciate his anger? Bummer! Because he wasn't going to lessen any of it until she got it through her thick skull how dangerous her actions had been.

Juliet slowed her pacing down though. Eve took advantage of the opportunity, wrapping her arm around her. As if she didn't want her to start pacing again. "Yes, Lila, I have to agree with my brother. You shouldn't have done that."

"Just so you all know, I didn't come back to town to hide. I came to weed out the asshole terrorizing me with threats."

That statement ramped up his fury.

"I don't think Gregory had anything to do with the notes," Aster said. "If I'm going to threaten someone, I'm going to do it to their face. Gregory strikes me as the same kind of guy. He's not going to write a note and send it as a Christmas present."

Bryce hated to admit how that made sense.

"Now a woman, on the other hand..." Aster let his voice trail off when Juliet, Eve, and Lila stared daggers at him.

"So Melody," Juliet snapped, took a deep breath, and continued. "If she did have feelings for Bryce, she wouldn't want someone else in the way."

"But Lila left town with the first threat," Eve pointed out.

"Yes, she did," Duke agreed. "Melody tried her hardest to get Bryce to see her as more than a friend. She constantly showed up at Frost's and you kept ignoring her." Duke looked at Bryce as he said it. "It angered her so she sent another threat because she blames Lila for it all. She's right because now you are with Bryce. Her plan backfired. She wanted to get her anger out and all it did was send you back here."

As much as he wanted to disagree with all of that, he couldn't. It made sense.

"We have nothing to prove it was her." That irked him more than he cared to admit. "The only way to know is to ask her."

Duke grinned, as if he loved the idea. Bryce knew the cop in him would devour the opportunity to confront her. Juliet and Eve frowned, indicating they hated it. Aster looked indifferent. And Lila...well, she wore close to the same expression as her brother. He couldn't determine what she thought.

"And I don't think we'd get far doing that either." Bryce knew a losing battle when he saw one. "She'll never admit to doing it."

"So we catch her in the act," Duke said.

"How?"

Duke turned his attention to Juliet. "Only something big will do. If it's her, she won't be able to resist."

Something big?

How big?

"Are we saying Melody sent the threat and killed Denise?" Aster asked. "I want to know where we stand on all of it."

Bryce shrugged. "I can see her sending the threats. But murdering her best friend? I do have a hard time picturing that."

"That would make it two different people," Duke pointed out. "And maybe one big thing will draw them both out."

"You already said that. What's this big thing?" Juliet

sounded like she was on the verge of screaming her ire right out of her body.

Bryce felt bad for Duke because she kept letting it out on him. Duke hadn't done anything wrong but put her best interests at heart. All the time.

Duke tossed up a loose shoulder. "I don't know." He glanced at him and Lila. "Maybe an engagement. That would really piss Melody off."

Bryce swallowed hard, peering at Lila out of the corner of his eyes. She wasn't looking at him.

"A fake one?" Aster asked, his annoyance finally popping to the surface. "Because a real one is a little too fast."

"It's not your business what I do with my life."

That statement from Lila had him directing his full attention her way. Was she saying she wasn't opposed to marrying him? And if so, was he ready for that kind of commitment again? His last marriage had failed spectacularly.

"Do you love him?" Aster demanded, throwing a hand in his direction. "Are you ready to move to this small town? Absorb yourself in this kind of life? Is that what you're saying?"

"What I'm saying, *Aster*," she enunciated his name with derision, "is that the decisions I make are none of your business. You can say something is too fast and I can disagree. The same thing could be said about you."

"I have no intention of marrying Juliet!"

Silence coated the room at his outburst. Aster had the grace to look repentant, his cheeks blooming red again.

"I'm sorry, Juliet. That came out wrong."

Juliet offered Aster a short grin. "It was honest though. I can't fault you for that. I never asked for marriage. So there's nothing to be sorry about." Juliet turned her gaze at him.

"Bryce, you don't have to do anything you don't want to do. Real or fake."

He knew that dig had gone to Duke once again. He'd have to talk with his sister later and ask why she kept hurting Duke that way. It had to stop.

"Forget I said anything," Duke muttered.

Oh, he wasn't planning on forgetting anything that was said today.

"Lila, if your main goal is to flush out the person threatening you, let's do that. Marry me?" His heart pounded as he waited for her answer. It didn't look promising by the slight terror he saw deep in the depths of her eyes. "As a ruse, of course. Then you're free from this town."

And from me.

Because he saw it so clearly now.

She wasn't going to stay. She never was. Her goal had always been to find the person threatening her. That's why she returned. Not because of him. He would never forget that again.

20

LILA BLEW out a breath before picking up the mascara and applying it.

Yesterday, after the volatile discussion in the kitchen, the rest of the day had been strained. Between everyone. Even her and Aster. Of course, all of them put on a show, not letting anyone see the tension building everywhere.

The evening had been one of the worst she'd ever experienced. Sure, she and Bryce ate a meal together, but not much was said. When they went to bed, they didn't touch each other. Not even a kiss good night. She hated the strain one discussion put between them.

How did she fix it?

Short of asking the marriage to be real, she didn't think anything would fix it. Bryce had pulled away from her, and she had to accept that. She didn't expect him to want a real marriage. Not so soon after his last one just ended— brutally.

She didn't even know if she was ready for that sort of commitment either. Marriage was a huge step. A very big deal. Her parents, while she knew they had their ups and downs, had a solid marriage. She wanted what they had. Right now they were spending their retirement traveling the world. Seeing new places. Enjoying their lives together. She wouldn't accept anything less than what they had.

She and Bryce were compatible. In bed, for sure. But tying the knot compatible? She couldn't positively say yes.

They had relayed their plan to Griffin, who didn't voice his opinion about it. At least, not in front of her.

Today, she'd leave the house wearing an engagement ring. A ring Bryce had retrieved from Griffin last night.

She set the mascara brush down on the sink, turning her hand to and fro, watching as the light hit the diamond.

It was a gorgeous ring. Simple, but elegant. At least a karat, and the band pure gold.

It had been their grandmother's. Bryce didn't explain why Eve didn't receive it—or why Denise never had.

She felt like a fraud wearing it. The ring itself was light on her finger. But she felt the weight of their actions. It was massive and she wasn't sure she'd survive this farce.

They didn't intend to purposely announce anything. They'd pretend to want to keep it quiet. But it wouldn't be hard for anyone to notice the ring on her finger.

She had been right.

She and Bryce ate a silent breakfast and left right after for City Hall. Becca honed in on their farce right away.

"What is that?" Becca's eyes lit up with pleasure, rounding her desk and grabbing her left hand before she could respond. "This wasn't here yesterday."

Bryce chuckled, the sweet tune sounding real, and placed a hand around her waist. "We were trying to keep it quiet."

Becca didn't raise her head, but her eyes tilted up at him.

"Good luck with that. This ring will say everything your lips will not."

Becca wrapped her arms around her, dislodging Bryce's hand. She missed his touch. She'd missed it all night long. Everything that happened yesterday angered her. From Gregory's visit to their discussion to the wide gap that emerged between them. She couldn't even pinpoint why they were barely even speaking to each other.

She assumed he was angry for her part with Gregory, but she wasn't going to apologize for it. So if he was waiting for one, he'd be waiting forever.

"I'm so happy. You are perfect for Bryce. You two complement each other so much. Denise never deserved him," Becca whispered in her ear before pulling away, the happiness beaming from ear to ear. It wasn't hard to smile herself. Plus, she had to, to keep up pretenses.

"We know it'll get out, but let's not shout it to the rooftops. It'll be a long engagement anyway."

The longest one in the history of the world because the marriage would never happen. But she didn't add that.

Becca made a gesture as if twisting a key in front of her lips. "They won't hear it from me."

Several hours later when her phone pinged with a billion congratulations, she decided it wasn't worth it to figure out where the leak came from. Their plan was in motion.

For the objective to go without a hitch, Duke had eyes on Melody. Discreetly, of course. When she decided to send another threatening message, he'd catch her in the act.

Hopefully, anyway.

That was their brilliant plan.

For lunch, she and Bryce ate at the cafe. To keep up appearances. They both wore smiles that she knew were fake. But to everyone else, they believed it. That they were in love. Desperately, madly, and deeply.

When they returned to his office, Becca was waiting for them.

"I know you wanted to keep it quiet." Her eyes laughed at that notion as if it would've never happened. "And I understand why. Denise hasn't..." She cleared her throat. "She hasn't been gone long."

Lila didn't know what to say to that, so she remained silent. It was true.

Bryce wasn't devoid of words. "I let her put my life on hold for a very long time. I refuse to let her continue to control it."

If only the engagement were real...

"Of course, Bryce." Becca placed a hand on his shoulder, nodding. "I agree. But you know how some of the townsfolk can be. This might be a good time for one of your calming speeches."

Ummm....what?

"Why?" The one-word question came out more forceful than she intended.

Becca smiled. "He's the mayor. It might not seem fair, but his life is under a microscope. He can't do whatever he wants without the public having an opinion. To avoid the negative parts, he should address the issue. I promise you, Bryce will say the right thing and have everyone swooning and wanting an invite to the wedding of the year."

Oh geez.

Wedding of the year?

Even if it were real, she didn't want that kind of pressure on her. A low-key ceremony would be more her style.

"We haven't set a date."

Because it was fake!

Becca waved her comment away as if it didn't matter. "We'll have a town meeting at four o'clock. That should give you enough time to write something up."

Bryce nodded, smiling as if he couldn't wait to make a grand speech about their upcoming nuptials.

How had this plan gotten so out of hand so fast? And how would everyone react when they learned it was all made up?

"Well, if we're having a town meeting, I want to set up a table for social media awareness. The stores need to start having a heavier presence online. We can kill two birds with one stone at this meeting."

Becca clapped her hands with merriment. "I love how you think. I'll help you."

Lila turned to Bryce. "I'll leave you to your speech."

She walked away with his bright smile engrained in her mind. His phony smile that would be imprinted forever.

HE SCRIBBLED out the words he'd written—again—then crumbled the paper and threw it toward the waste basket. Missing it—again. There was a small pile of paper building that he kept throwing away.

Becca wanted him to write a speech that wasn't coming from the heart. He hated to deceive the town this way. Although he didn't doubt it would reveal Melody for the black heart she had. It didn't mean he enjoyed any part of this.

A light knock on his doorframe had him looking up. Aster stood in the threshold with a tentative grin.

"Can we have a word?"

He gestured for him to take a seat.

Aster closed the door and sat down. His gaze glided to the notepad. "A town meeting?" He cocked a brow. "About your engagement?"

"It was my secretary's idea. One I can't discredit. She's right when she says that as the mayor, my life isn't my own. I live under a microscope, even if I'm only a small-town mayor."

"And what does your speech entail so far?"

Bryce lifted his notepad, showing Aster the blank page.

That had Aster laughing.

"Are you here to yell at me?"

Aster shook his head. "I can admit when my sister is right. What she does is none of my business. It doesn't mean I don't like to make things my business. I worry about all my sisters."

He understood that sentiment well. He worried about Juliet.

"Juliet and I had a long talk last night when we got to her place."

That made Bryce jealous. He wished he'd had a long talk with Lila. Not much had been said between them. It killed him not to pull her into his arms last night. But he'd felt the paws-off vibe from her and didn't want to risk her wrath. Since he'd come to the conclusion nothing would keep her in Sleighville, he'd given up the fight. He let the silence remain. He held himself back by not touching her. He kept how he really felt about her to himself.

Because the moment he realized she'd never stay, was the moment it hit him how much he loved her.

"And?" Bryce prompted when Aster didn't continue. He wasn't about to confess he and Lila had done the same thing. Because it would be a lie.

Aster chuckled, propping a leg over his opposite knee. "I

apologized again for my outburst. I've always been honest to her about my feelings toward relationships. I didn't mean for it to come out so vehemently as it did."

Bryce had no idea why Aster was sharing any of this. "You don't need to be telling me all of this."

"I know. But I wanted you to know I've never had any intention whatsoever to hurt Juliet. Her feelings are always the utmost importance to me." Aster set his foot down and leaned forward. "I know you care about my sister."

More than cared. But that would remain his secret alone.

"I wouldn't be opposed to a relationship between you two. I know you make her happy."

Holy shit. Was he getting Aster's blessing?

"Since we're being honest here, Lila and I did not have a long talk last night. In fact, we barely spoke."

Aster nodded as if he already knew. Had he spoken to Lila? What had she said?

"What do you want to happen, Bryce?"

"Relating to what?"

"Lilac, you idiot. That is what we're talking about here."

He'd ignore the insult. "Why do you suddenly care?"

"Because the entire town thinks you're getting married and the fallout will be insane when they realize it's not real."

Bryce slumped in his chair. "And Lila will be back in California, so she won't have to deal with it. She'll be okay."

"She'll still feel the effects of it all. She'll worry about you even if you think she won't. This will gut her."

"Why do I have your sudden approval? Did you talk with Lila? What did she say?"

"I haven't spoken to her since yesterday at the cafe." Aster grinned. "Your marriage proposal, while for a specific reason, sounded real. In those few seconds before you added it would be fake, you meant it. You asked Lilac to marry you for real. Are you going to deny that?"

He should.

Nothing good would come from Aster knowing the truth. At best, he'd tell Lila and maybe she'd change her attitude toward him. At worst, Aster would beat him to a pulp and Lila would continue to want to leave.

"It would be insane to marry so soon again."

"That didn't answer my question."

"What do you want from me, Aster? A confession that I love your sister. That I never wanted her to leave in the beginning. That a part of me will die when she does leave me. Is that what you're looking for? A reason to gloat that I will be viscously gutted. That I can't have the one thing that has made me happy in the longest time. So long I can't even remember the last time I felt this much joy in my life."

Aster sat back. "Why isn't that shit on your piece of paper?"

"What?"

The man was confusing him left and right. Did Aster hate him or not?

"No man will ever be good enough for my sister. Unless he proves he is." Aster gestured at his notepad. "You want Lilac to believe it's real, then tell her how real it is. Tell the whole damn town. Nothing's stopping you but yourself."

He stood up and opened the door.

"What about you and Juliet?"

Aster turned slightly. "There never was a me and Juliet. She and I understood that. If your friend Duke wants her so badly, maybe he needs to man up and tell her. Don't be blaming me for his own faults."

Yeah, he was not going to share that with Duke. Though

Aster had a point. Duke had all the chances in the world with Juliet after her divorce and he never took one.

Bryce looked at the clock on the wall, noting he had another hour until the speech needed to be ready. He stared at the blank page.

To be honest or not to be honest?

According to the man who he thought hated him, he should be so honest that Lila would know his true feelings.

Wouldn't keeping those feelings to himself be the same as Duke had done? Land him in a position he didn't like. On the sidelines.

He picked up the pencil and started writing. This time the words kept flowing.

21

———

LILA STEPPED BACK and surveyed the table. She'd thrown a white tablecloth over it, nothing too fancy. With Becca's help, she had created a quick sign that was simple to understand. Sign up for help with social media. Spreading the word about Sleighville was the main goal and every store owner needed to be on board with it.

She put some candy in a bowl because people always liked to get free stuff while signing up for something. It wasn't much, but she didn't have a lot of time to prepare for this.

Right next to the sign she had a clipboard and a pen.

It could use a little more sprucing up, but it would do for now.

"It's missing something."

She agreed with Becca, but again, not much time. The meeting would start in thirty minutes. In another ten minutes, they'd open the doors for people.

"Come on. The supply closet has to have something. It needs something cheery."

She followed Becca to the basement where they stored a whole range of things. Signs for different events. Decorations for each season. The storage unit was huge.

And also dark and dusty and sort of creepy. The lights didn't illuminate the whole room, and one even flickered in and out but thankfully stayed on. It didn't help the moody vibes she felt.

"One of these boxes should have like tiny Christmas trees or something. It doesn't matter what we find, but the table needs a few festive items. It's too blah right now."

Lila chuckled. "Agreed."

Becca pointed to the right side of the room. "You look over there and I'll take this side."

They went their separate ways.

The boxes and items on her side weren't helpful. Most of the stuff was for the outdoors. Thanksgiving items that she assumed went in the center of town. The turkey wearing a Santa hat made her giggle.

She continued on down the line, going past some shelving units before reaching the back wall.

The first few boxes she opened were old election signs for Bryce. Seeing his name had her heart skipping with joy.

Why were they so distant with each other last night?

She should've never let her anger get the better of her. He had a right to get mad at her. It wasn't because it truly made him angry. It was fear. She knew that.

When this whole dumb speech debacle was completed, she'd tell him she understood. That it was okay he was angry and that it didn't change how she felt. That she didn't like the tension between them and it needed to disappear.

She opened the next box, feeling triumphant. Small Christmas ornaments for indoors. The tiny Christmas tree would go great next to the sign she made. Though it needed new batteries for the lights on it. She also grabbed a plate shaped like Rudolph, intending to use that for the candy instead of the Styrofoam bowl she had.

She pulled out a small wooden box. The top was carved with one word: Stuart.

Footsteps approached her from behind.

She lifted the lid.

The breath she released was loud enough for Becca to hear.

"You weren't supposed to come digging all the way back here."

Lila turned around with the box open and the glass icicles on display. Six slots for six crystal Christmas icicles meant for hanging on a tree. Only five slots held one. The last one was missing.

Because it was a murder weapon. Currently in an evidence bag. She didn't know a lot about the crime scene, but she knew that part. Everyone in town did. Not much stayed a secret.

"You killed Denise?" Lila couldn't fathom why Becca would do such a thing. She would've never thought her capable of such violence. Why put the evidence in a place where someone could find it? Like she just did. Maybe she thought no one would look down here. Of course, she had to give time for the murder to die down and for time to pass before she could get rid of the evidence. But still. An odd place to hide it.

"Not on purpose."

"She was killed in the early hours of the morning. Why on earth would you even be at her house at that time, Becca?"

"I'm an early riser. I always have been. That bitch was making Bryce's life a living hell! He didn't deserve any of that. She didn't deserve him. I was checking my voicemails from the office line around four when I woke up. Denise had left one earlier that evening. Around six or so. She wanted me to give her a key to his office. So she could poke around there when he wasn't around. She called me like I'd do what she asked."

Becca laughed, the delirious sound sending terrifying shockwaves down her spine. "I mean she didn't say why she wanted the key, but I knew there would be no reason for her to have one other than to snoop. If she didn't already have one, then that meant Bryce didn't want her to have it. It's his office. His domain."

"She must've been looking for something." Because it baffled Lila why Denise would snoop. Bryce had nothing to hide.

"Or plant something. She was a bitch. You, of all people, know how cruel she could be. She didn't even know you and accused you of sleeping with Bryce right away. She would've done anything to paint him the bad guy in the divorce. I wasn't going to let that happen. So before heading to the office, I stopped at their house. Denise was already awake, getting ready for the day. She let me in, probably thinking I was going to give her the key."

And Lila knew how the interaction ended. But how had it started?

"I can't picture you hurting her."

Becca's expression softened, appreciating the compliment. "I didn't mean to, Lila. I swear. I let her have it, telling her in no uncertain terms she would never get in his office. We exchanged a lot of heated words. She slapped me. I don't know, something came over me. I grabbed the nearest thing, and it was those icicles. By the time I regained my senses, I realized what I had done."

Lila glanced at the box, the lid still open. "Why hide it here? Why even take it? You left one in her chest."

"I panicked, Lila. Okay. I didn't go over to her house that morning to kill her. I wanted to let her know she wasn't going to boss me around or keep getting away with hurting Bryce. I didn't mean to kill her. You have to believe me."

Lila nodded. "I do." She closed the lid with a quiet snap. "And when we tell the police, they'll understand too. She hit you first. You can claim self-defense."

Becca laughed. "You don't honestly believe that, do you?"

Well, no, but Lila had to talk her way out of the room somehow. They were in the basement. Alone. And no one knew where they were. It wasn't as if they stopped to tell anyone.

"What do you suggest, Becca?"

"It'll be our little secret. She was not a nice woman, Lila. You know she wasn't. No one is sad she is gone."

Except her parents. Lila assumed anyway. She never met them.

And Bryce.

He might not act sad, but her death had destroyed a part of him. He hadn't grieved yet. He hadn't come to terms with her death. So, Lila would have to disagree. Some people were sad she was gone.

"Lila?"

They weren't going to agree on the matter. Which meant she had to get out of the room.

She threw the box at Becca, startling her. Then she ran around the black shelving unit to the other side, running as fast as she could toward the exit. Noises could be heard where Becca was and pounding feet going in the same direction as her.

Freedom was in her sight. If she could get the door closed, she could lock Becca in.

She made it a few feet from the door when a sharp, excruciating pain hit her shoulder and she went down hard. Twisting, though it killed her to do so, she looked up, screaming as Becca took another swing of the axe.

An axe! Which was why her shoulder wailed with pain.

She managed to roll away before the axe would've hit her square in the gut. Becca kept swinging and she kept dodging until she was able to get to her feet. Though the wound in her shoulder was bleeding profusely, causing her vision to go wonky. She was losing blood way too fast.

"Becca, don't do this." She stumbled to her right, feeling behind her for her own weapon. Becca stared at her with wide, manic eyes. "You won't be able to talk yourself out of this one."

"Sure I will. You confessed to killing Denise. Jealous of her. Wanting Bryce for yourself. I had to defend myself. I'll make sure to hurt myself and make it that much more real."

She swung the axe again, grazing her chest. More pain erupted at the slice now visible, saturating her light-yellow shirt with red.

"Bryce will never believe your story."

Becca clucked her tongue. "I've known that man for far longer than you. Don't you worry about what he'll believe or won't believe."

She swung again. Lila jumped back to avoid the sharp device, falling to the floor, taking several Christmas props with her. Becca made another charge at her. Her hands swept around the floor, grabbing the first thing they touched. She raised it at the same time Becca leaned toward her, piercing her right through the chest.

Lila stared in horror as the realization swept through Becca's eyes. That she had lost. That a wooden staff from the outdoor nativity scene had pierced her heart.

The light from her eyes disappeared. The heavy weight of her body became too much. She screamed as she shoved until Becca toppled to the side of her.

Her gaze roamed to the exit.

The very, very far exit away from her.

Dizziness attacked her when she tried to stand up, plopping back down to the floor, shrieking in agony.

She'd never make it out of here before the blood loss would make her lose consciousness. Digging her phone out of her pocket made tears gather and fall. It had been busted in the fight.

Okay.

She needed another way out.

Her hand brushed another prop. It made her gag to see another staff. The curved handle. The smoothness of the wood. The craftsmanship from top to bottom. The sharp, pointy end of it. No doubt so it would stay upright by pushing it into the ground next to a shepherd.

But it would help her walk. So she erased the memory of how it sounded crushing through Becca's skin, at the way it slid through her so easily, and used it to stand up.

She wobbled, her vision blurring even more.

All she had to do was make it to the elevator. The hallway would be full of people for the town meeting.

That's all she had to do.

Make it fifty feet or so to the elevator.

So she put one foot in front of her, crying out in pain. Then another. And another.

BRYCE STOOD outside the assembly hall, smiling and greeting people as they walked inside. The meeting would start in five minutes and his heart wouldn't stop beating a mile a minute. His hands even felt clammy, so he made sure to keep them clasped together behind his back so no one would get the urge to shake hands with him. They'd know in a heartbeat how damn nervous he was.

Juliet and Eve had already arrived and taken a seat in the front row. Aster had as well, though the man himself was strutting toward him.

"He always looks so mad at you," Griffin, who stood right next to him, muttered under his breath.

Bryce couldn't agree more. Considering the weird heart-to-heart they had an hour ago, why did he look so angry?

"Where's Lilac?" Aster asked with a strained breath, blocking his view of the people strolling in.

"I don't know." Bryce wished he did. Her absence was starting to worry him. That she had changed her mind and fled. He'd be making a different speech if that were the case. "She wasn't here when I came downstairs. She was with Becca setting up a table for the social media venture idea."

"Which is void of her or Becca," Aster said, uttering the obvious.

"I'm sure she'll be here any minute." Griffin voiced that with a lot more confidence than Bryce felt.

Why had she disappeared to begin with? So soon to the start time?

Aster cleared his throat. "Did you..." He coughed this time. "Did you speak to her after we chatted? Is that why she's not in attendance?"

He felt Griffin tense next to him. Maybe because he went

rigid himself. He wasn't even sure why his body went into defense mode.

"I haven't seen her since after lunch when her and Becca went to set up the table. I don't know where they disappeared to."

"But Becca's with her?" Aster asked. The agitation he'd been displaying toward him turned to worry for his sister. "Because she better not be alone."

"Becca would never leave her alone. They're together wherever they are." Bryce knew that deep in his bones. Becca would never put Lila in danger. She'd been pushing them together as a couple since Lila returned to town. She adored Lila.

Aster flipped his wrist to check his watch. "There's two minutes until the meeting. They should be here."

"I have to agree," Griffin replied. "Lila might've... changed her mind, but Becca would not bail on a town meeting."

And she wouldn't leave Lila alone either.

"I'll call her." Bryce pulled out his phone.

"No," Aster cut in sharply, "you call Becca. I'll call Lilac."

He listened because he didn't want to argue about something so inconsequential. Who cared who called who? The call went to voicemail. By the look from Aster, so did Lila's.

"Well, we can't start the meeting without Lila." Griffin grimaced. "It won't look good since the subject is about you two. I can't imagine they left the building. Even if Becca stayed with Lila because she decided to back out, she would've convinced her to stay around the area."

A large, nasty feeling settled into the pit of his stomach. "Where's Melody?"

"Duke would've called me if there was an issue. Since

he's not here, that means she's not either. He won't take his eyes off her," Griffin reassured him.

"Where the hell is Lila?" Bryce whispered, his words cracking at the end.

The elevator dinged. He turned around as the doors swished open. Lila stumbled out, losing her balance. She crashed to the floor, the staff she'd been using to carry her flinging across the linoleum.

"Lila! Call an ambulance!" Bryce rushed to her side.

She had a large gash on her chest that had saturated her shirt, but it was the even larger gash in her back near her shoulder that had him jerking off his coat.

He cradled her in his arms with her chest to his, pressing hard on his jacket to stop the bleeding from the wound on her back. She cried out in pain at the touch. Aster joined him on the floor, using his strength as well to push the clothing into her wound.

"Oh my god, Lila. What happened?" he whispered, his hands shaking yet not relieving any pressure from her back.

"Becca..." she whispered against his chest, not even able to lift her head.

"Is she hurt too?"

"Dead..."

His gaze met Aster's. Both of them were wide-eyed and scared to death. Lila's breathing was unsteady, her body getting limper by the second.

"Stay with me, Lila." Bryce squeezed harder on the injury. "Stay awake, sweetheart."

Keep her talking. She couldn't lose consciousness.

"Who did this? Who hurt you? Are they still downstairs?" Maybe a dumb question. There was only one way in the basement and one way out. They blocked the path to freedom if the culprit was still down there.

"Lilac!" Aster shouted. "Answer him. Stay awake."

She didn't lift her head, but a heavy sigh released. "Becca..."

"Yes, sweetheart, we'll get to her when we can." Lila said she was dead so there wasn't anything they could do for her. Lila was his concern right now. And apprehending the bastard who dared to hurt her.

"No...Becca..." She still didn't lift her head, but her eyes opened and sought his out. "She....killed Denise."

No.

Not possible.

Becca would never.

Yet, Lila was bleeding out in his arms telling him otherwise. Which meant no one else was stuck downstairs. Becca had hurt her.

And Lila had fought back and won. Barely.

"Where's the damn ambulance?" Aster growled, looking at Griffin who was on the phone while also trying to keep the crowd away from them.

"One minute out," he responded, but didn't give Aster his full attention.

That one minute was the longest of his life. Between him and Aster, they tried to keep Lila awake and talking to them. When it seemed like an hour had passed, the paramedics arrived. So had reinforcements from the police department. Two officers helped push people back into the assembly hall while Griffin followed them outside. Another stood by the elevator to make sure no one used it to go down to the basement. Now a crime scene.

They whisked Lila away in the ambulance and it took all his strength not to argue to be by her side. If anyone had the right, Aster did. Yet, he didn't argue either.

"I'll drive." Griffin clamped a steady hand on his shoulder, guiding him toward his vehicle.

He slid into the passenger seat while Aster hopped in the back. The ride was silent until Aster let loose a string of curse words.

"It took the ambulance forever to get there and now the hospital is too damn far away."

Griffin took a calming breath before responding. "We're a small town, Aster. Our EMTs are all volunteers. Unfortunately, the hospital is a good twenty minutes away. She's in good hands, though."

"What could have made that kind of wound?" Aster's voice cracked. Bryce didn't need to turn around to see him on the verge of tears. He could feel his own rising to the surface. "It was so deep. Like she'd chopped into her."

"I assume they went down there for decorations for the meeting. Right, Bryce? That's where the city keeps that stuff."

He nodded, unable to speak. Nothing but tears would escape if he tried.

"There's a lot of different props down there. It could be anything."

By the time they made it to the hospital, he couldn't hold in the tears any longer. They streamed silently down his face as they made their way to the waiting area. She was being whisked to surgery.

His tears eventually abated. Neither Griffin nor Aster made a comment about it. Aster wouldn't because his own tears appeared. Time passed, and he didn't realize a small crowd had gathered around them until Juliet sat down next to him.

She slid her hand into his and squeezed. "Griffin says you got to her in time. She'll pull through."

He could only pray that would be the outcome.

Eve sat next to Griffin, with Aster on Griffin's other side. Duke was also here along with Chip and Tabitha from the cafe. He couldn't believe he didn't notice anyone walk in.

"Bryce?"

He turned to Juliet. "What do you need from me? You've been in a trance since we walked in. Talk to me."

"I think I need to leave."

She blinked, confused by the request.

He was too. He didn't know where the words came from. But he knew he couldn't wait here with the small chance the doctor wouldn't have good news. He was barely hanging on as it was. He'd lose it if she died.

"No, anything but that."

He frowned. His sister wanted to help. He told her how she could, and she was denying his request. What was he supposed to do with that?

"Come on, man." Duke cleared his throat, suddenly standing in front of him. "Let's find you some new clothes."

Yes, clothes without blood on them would be nice.

He ignored Juliet, stood up, and followed Duke out of the room. He didn't even care where Duke took him, as long as it was far away from everyone else. Duke stopped to talk to a nurse and a few minutes later he was changing in an empty room into scrubs.

Duke held himself back for a good five minutes before he knocked on the door and walked in without waiting for a response. He took a seat on the bed next to him where he'd sat after changing. Bryce couldn't find the will to move.

"I don't know what to say. There are no words that can comfort you at the moment. I know that."

Bryce inhaled and exhaled, then met Duke's caring eyes. "I was mad at her for getting into Gregory's face. She knew it too. We barely talked last night or this morning. There was this huge gap between us, and I knew it was over between us. I knew she'd leave me. But I didn't know it'd be like this."

Duke clamped a hand onto his shoulder. "You don't know that'll be the outcome."

"You know what hurt her, don't you? I zoned out in the waiting area. Please tell me what Becca did to her."

Duke winced but nodded. "We found a bloody axe right next to Becca's body."

An axe. Becca. Sweet, loving Becca used an axe on the woman he loved.

"But Lila got her good with a staff. Stabbed her right through the chest." Duke put pressure on his shoulder. "You know what that tells me. She's a damn fighter. So she's not going to let a little wack from an axe bring her down."

That ridiculous statement produced a snort he couldn't hold in. Duke grinned himself.

"So you guys had a bad moment in your relationship. When she gets out of surgery and recovery, you can apologize for being an ass. She'll forgive you."

"And leave."

Duke shrugged, dropping his hand. "Don't make the same mistake I made with Juliet. I held myself back for so long another guy swooped in. A damn decent guy that makes her happy. I can't even hate Aster for that. Because I haven't seen her look so happy like that in the longest time. That's all I want is for Juliet to be happy, even if it's not with me. If she leaves, she leaves. But make sure it's because you told her how you felt and she rejected you. Not because you kept it to yourself and she didn't want to wait around for you to wake up. Got it, man? Do you hear me?"

"I hear you."

Duke stood up. "Let's go. Because the first thing she should see when she wakes up is you."

Bryce wasn't sure that's what she'd want to see, but Duke was right. He couldn't hold himself back any longer.

They never should've given each other the silent treatment last night, and now he might never get the chance to make it right.

He loved her and he had to tell her.

Even if she still walked away.

22

PAIN RADIATED UP HER SPINE, pulsating right where the axe had hit her.

"Lilac!"

She forced her eyes open, tilting her head to the sound of her sister's voice. Poppy and Zinnia sat by the bed. Poppy grabbed her hand, squeezing as her eyes welled with tears.

"You scared the living shit out of us. Don't do it again."

Zinnia placed a hand on her leg, smiling. "What Poppy said. It's so good to see you awake finally."

"How long—" She swallowed, trying to find her voice. "How long have I been out?"

"Since yesterday. Surgery went well, but everything knocked you out. We got in late last night. We haven't left your side much. Neither has he." Poppy jerked her head toward the other side of the bed.

Lila moved her head, cringing at the slow maneuver. Bryce sat slumped in a chair, eyes closed.

"We left to get breakfast, use the bathroom, stretch our legs. That man has not moved much. When he's awake,"

Poppy said in a quieter voice than she had been using before, "he can't take his eyes off you."

"He's even more handsome in person than the pictures you showed us," Zinnia said.

She had to agree. Pictures didn't do him justice. But right now, he looked tired, even while sleeping.

"You guys didn't have to come, but it's nice to see you."

Poppy scoffed, rolling her eyes, and sharing a look with Zinnia. "Do you hear her? You guys didn't have to come." She scoffed again. "As if we're going to stay away when you were attacked. She nearly chopped your shoulder off."

Yes, the pain felt like that very thing had happened. It made it difficult to breathe because every time a tiny inhale occurred, pain radiated everywhere. Even moving her head caused too much discomfort.

"You'll have a badass scar though."

A low giggle, then a snort escaped, causing a ricocheting bout of torment to rush down her body. Her short laugh turned into a grimace and groan.

Zinnia slapped Poppy's shoulder. "Don't make her laugh. She's in pain."

"Lila…"

At the sound of Bryce's voice, she moved her head in his direction again. Relief poured out of his eyes along with the anguish and guilt, as if he had been the one to hurt her himself.

"We'll go find a nurse to get you some pain meds." Poppy stood up, eyeing Zinnia to make sure she agreed. She didn't hesitate to follow suit. "We'll make sure they get you the good stuff too. The real good stuff."

Another light snort came out, making her groan again.

"Sorry." Poppy winced. "I keep forgetting I shouldn't make you laugh."

Zinnia pushed Poppy to leave, and they were alone a few seconds later.

She didn't even turn her head toward the door when they walked out. She kept it in the same position, directed toward Bryce. One, she didn't want to take her eyes off him. It was good to see his face. Two, it hurt too much to move. She didn't have a choice if she didn't want the ache radiating up and down her body.

"I'm so glad you're okay. It was kind of scary for a moment there."

She could only imagine. The thought of being in a waiting room, anticipating news—whether good or bad—on Bryce's health would put her in a constant state of panic. By the exhaustion in his eyes, he'd been in that very state.

"I'm sorry."

He shook his head. "I'm not sure why you're apologizing, but there's nothing for you to say sorry for. Absolutely nothing." His gaze drew down to her hand and he flinched, as if he wanted to grab her hand but changed his mind at the last second. "This happened because of me. I should be apologizing."

"This happened because Becca didn't want to face the consequences of her actions."

She wiggled her fingers. He took the small gesture as a sign it was okay to hold her hand. The instant warmth from him settled part of her battered soul.

"I don't know why she hid the evidence in that room. I don't think she expected me to find it. When I did, she asked me to keep it a secret. I don't think she would've hurt me if I had agreed."

He was silent for a moment, making her think he wished she had agreed. Would that have been better in the situation? She'd never know now. Becca could've attacked her regardless. It happened and she had to live with her decision.

"Right before she would've delivered the final blow, she said she'd make it appear like I killed Denise out of jealousy. That she'd hurt herself to make it appear like she was defending herself against me. That you'd believe all of it. That I was a killer. Because she's known you longer than I have."

He frowned, leaning closer to the bed. His grip on her hand even strengthened by a small degree. But not enough to cause her any pain.

"I would've never thought Becca was a killer. Not in a million years. But that doesn't mean I would've believed her story about you. I know you." His eyes gathered with unshed tears. "I love you. I'm not sad Becca is gone. I'm pissed I can't unleash some of my anger at her. So don't let anything she said get to you. I would've never believed that about you. Never."

This felt like a pivotal moment. A change in their relationship. They wouldn't be going back to the status quo they'd been living.

"I didn't want to hurt her."

"Don't feel bad you did. Don't let her death ruin you. You did what you had to do." His voice broke, a few tears finding release. "Lila..."

His eyes closed as he heaved a few heavy breaths, trying to regain his composure. She'd never seen him lose his emotions before. This was how she had expected him to react when Denise died. Break down in tears at the loss of life. She remained silent while he gathered himself together. Watching him become so vulnerable in front of her caused her own tears to fall.

His eyes reopened when he heard her sniffle.

"Hey, don't cry." He reached over, wiping the water from her cheeks.

A short laugh escaped. "I can't cry but you can?" She winced as the pain echoed everywhere. "You're not supposed to make me laugh. It hurts."

That garnered a smile out of him. The first one since the moment she laid eyes on him. "I didn't mean to make you laugh. I can't bear to see your tears."

The minor laughing break helped both of them to stop crying.

"I know this is a terrible time to bring it up." Bryce cleared his throat, sliding his hand into his pocket. He withdrew it and opened his palm to reveal the ring she'd been wearing on her finger yesterday. She'd lost it at some point if he was holding it.

The question must've been in her eyes. "They removed everything during surgery. They gave everything of yours to Aster and he handed the ring off to me."

So much had happened with Becca, and all so fast too. She didn't recall losing it during the scuffle. His answer made total sense.

"I wrote my speech for the town hall meeting an hour before it was scheduled to happen. I struggled with my words, trying to come up with something that would sound believable but not the truth. But I decided to go with the truth. Every word I would've uttered would have been sincere. That I love you. That I couldn't wait to spend the rest of my life with you. That I know how fast everything happened between us, but I know it felt right. That you were meant to be with me. That fate finally got it right."

He paused, inhaling again, as if he had to stop the tears from coming again.

She wasn't sure whether they were good or bad ones.

Because his words were frightening her. He kept talking in past tense, as if whatever had been between them was over. That he didn't love her any longer.

"And now none of that is true?"

He looked aghast. "God, no! I feel it now more than ever. The thought of losing you would've been the end of me. I wouldn't have survived it. I love you so damn much, I will follow you to California if you don't want to stay in Sleighville." He held out the ring. "Because I want to make the marriage proposal real this time. Marry me, Lila?"

"You'd move to California? For me? Because Denise wanted you to move out of Sleighville for the longest time and you would never budge." She closed her eyes, not because she couldn't stand to see the heartache in his, but because the pain was becoming too much.

"You don't have to answer now. It was silly of me to bring it up."

His hand disappeared from hers, causing her to jerk open her eyes. He was already standing and rounding the bed. She followed his retreating frame to see Poppy and Zinnia had reappeared with a nurse.

"I'll let you rest." He smiled and left before she could respond.

The nurse asked a few questions, administered some medication that she hoped would be fast acting, then told her the doctor would be by to see her soon. She left.

Her sisters converged on both sides of her. She closed her eyes, not sure who to focus on.

"Did I hear that man propose?" Poppy demanded.

"And without her answering," Zinnia added.

She didn't know what to say because she didn't know how she felt. Making Bryce move away from his hometown felt wrong. He loved this place. He belonged here. Sleighville wouldn't be the same without him as mayor. Giving his statements and speeches when half the time they weren't required. But the town loved it. Loved him. She'd be the enemy if he moved because of her.

"It's not that complicated, Lilac. You're overthinking things in that big head of yours." Poppy brushed her hand over her hair. "Where you live is semantics. It's not the end of things. If you love him like that man clearly loves you, then that's all that matters."

She reopened her eyes. "I hate the cold."

Poppy nodded, her eyes enlarging as if she agreed.

"And I didn't say it to him, but I love him too."

"You don't love the heat either," Zinnia commented.

That was true. She got cranky when it was too hot where they lived. She liked a nice mid-degree temperature, and there wasn't going to be any place where it was like that all year long. Hating the cold wasn't a good enough reason to not move to Sleighville.

"Are you two trying to talk me into him moving by me or me staying here? I'm so confused."

"Hey," Zinnia started, "we're not trying to talk you into anything. But you admitted what we both thought. You love him. So start there. That's all you have to say to him. Because the way he walked out of here, he thinks you don't even care. That was a man running from rejection."

"You want me to go wrangle him back here." Poppy stood, poised to do her bidding.

She chuckled, then groaned. "Damn it, Poppy. Stop making me laugh."

"Sorry. I'm not trying to."

"Leave him be. I can't think with this pain in my back right now."

"Rest." Zinnia placed a hand on her arm and looked at Poppy. "We're leaving so she can close her eyes."

"Fine."

She nearly laughed again at Poppy's pouting, and closed her eyes. The silence was heavenly. It helped to shut out the pain. But it didn't stop her mind from working in overdrive.

All her thoughts centered on Bryce.

Sweet, caring, lovable Bryce.

HE SMILED and waved at people as he left the hospital. The politician part of him was so ingrained into his behavior. But inside he was dying and crying at the loss of the best thing that ever happened to him.

Sure, she hadn't outright rejected him. But her response had been clear. She didn't want him, even if he was willing to follow her. And he would. It'd kill him to move away from the town he loved, from his friends and family, but for her, he would.

When he got to his car, he sat for a moment, wondering what to do. Where to go. He started the car, still unsure, but put the car in drive. He found himself parking at the cemetery twenty-five minutes later.

Not what he had planned, but then again, he hadn't had any destination in his mind when he left. He needed to escape. From everything and everyone.

He made his way to Denise's grave, staring at her headstone for the longest time. The tears still wouldn't release. He didn't feel that emotion bubbling to the surface at all. Not even an inkling. Not like he had back in the hospital with Lila. Back there, he couldn't stop the tears, and damn it, he had tried!

"I don't even hate you. I feel like I should after the way you treated me. I don't just mean during the divorce. I mean, during our marriage. The constant putdowns. Belittling me. Making me feel like less of a man. I want to hate you for it." He sighed. "But I think deep down, I feel sorry for you."

A gust of wind blew in his face, then the air settled. A sign from Denise? A slap in his face? He wouldn't be surprised. She wouldn't have liked to hear him say he felt sorry for her. She'd never been physical with him. He wouldn't have put up with that. But their conversations could get tense at times where he thought she wanted to take a swing at him. And he knew she knew he would've never hit her in return, so she had plenty of opportunities to reach out her hand with a solid smack.

"Lila asked me why I'd move to California for her and I would never do it for you. I think you know the answer to that." He nodded as if she stood right in front of him. "You hurt me. Every single day of our entire marriage. Your words sliced me daily to the bone. You didn't have to hit me physically to hurt me. Your words did that job just the same. The only way I could fight back was by not giving you what you truly wanted. Freedom from Sleighville."

Another gust of wind hit his face, causing him to shiver.

"If that's you, go ahead. Try and hurt me. It's not going to work anymore. I won't allow you to. I love Lila, and if she'll have me, I will leave this town for her. Because I know she would never hurt me the way you did. Relationships need a give and take, and all you ever did was take, take, take. So I never wanted to give, give, give. I won't apologize for that. I deserved better." He gave a merciful laugh. "Honestly, Denise, you deserved better too. We married too young. If we would've waited, we would've known we weren't meant for each other.

"I'm sorry the way things ended with us. I never wanted it to get to that point. As much as it pains me, I forgive you. Because holding in that rage isn't helping me. Lila helped me to see that. I hope you are at peace wherever you are."

Because Bryce couldn't be sure she didn't go to hell. She had treated him like he'd been living in his own hell. It would've been justified, but it didn't mean he wished that kind of agony on her.

More breeze fluttered around him, but this time it wasn't as forceful. As if Denise was accepting his forgiveness and offering a small dose of her own.

He turned to leave, flinching. Melody stood in front of him. He wondered how much she had heard, but not enough to ask.

"How's Lila?" Melody offered a tiny smile. "I hope she's okay. It's horrible what happened. I can't even process that Becca killed Denise."

"Surgery went well. She's awake and alert. In a lot of pain, but she's going to be okay."

"That's so good to hear."

"Is it?"

Melody winced.

"Be honest with me. You're the one who sent the threatening notes to Lila, aren't you?" Bryce knew deep in his gut that Becca had nothing to do with it. She might've killed Denise, but he didn't believe it had been premeditated. Becca had a good heart, even if a rare ugliness had emerged in a heated moment. That left Melody as the culprit.

"Denise was my best friend. I loved her like a sister." Melody's lips drew into a tight line. "But I hated how she treated you. She never deserved you. I would've made you happy. I've loved you for so long, Bryce."

"I never gave you the impression I returned those feelings."

"Well, you might've if Lila hadn't walked into the picture."

"No, Melody," he said through gritted teeth, "I would've never returned those feelings. It had nothing to do with Lila."

She shrunk back and looked contrite. "I would've never actually hurt her. I was angry. I had to let it out somehow."

"If you ever send her something again, you'll regret it. Stay away from her. In fact," Bryce said with a clipped tone, getting into her face, "stay away from me too. I doubt you'll be welcome anywhere soon. You know how rumors spread around town."

He walked around her, leaving her to stew on that. Not that he'd be the one to start the rumors, but it was a small town. Word would get out that she had threatened Lila. No one would take kindly to that.

He felt lighter when he re-entered his car. Not with regards to Lila and where their relationship stood, but about Denise. That closure Lila kept insisting he find, well, he did. The past could be put where it belonged. In the past.

He drove home and took a shower. Then he crawled into bed naked, promptly falling asleep.

Tomorrow would be a new day.

A loud pounding and constant ringing of his doorbell roused him out of a deep sleep. He dragged himself out of bed, fumbling for a pair of sweatpants and a T-shirt, and ambled to the front door.

He groaned when he opened it to see Aster standing on his doorstep. Oddly, he was with Griffin and Duke.

"Where the hell have you been?" Aster snapped.

He gestured aimlessly to where his car was parked in the

driveway, then slammed the door after the three of them walked inside. "I didn't hide where I was."

"I went to visit Lilac and imagine my surprise not seeing you there."

Why the hell was Aster so mad at him? Lila wanted space. He gave her space. Ignoring Aster's irate stare, he walked past them to the kitchen where he grabbed a beer from the fridge. This visit would require more than one.

Politeness was ingrained in him, so he offered all of them one as well. Everyone took a bottle, including Aster, who nearly drained it in one swallow.

"I think what Aster means to say is you left earlier this morning from the hospital and it's now eight o'clock at night and you haven't returned," Griffin said.

"Is this some sort of weird intervention?" Bryce asked, waving at the three of them standing next to each other. "Because I don't need one. I left to give Lila time to relax. I came home and fell asleep. I didn't purposely stay away."

"You proposed," Aster accused him. "This time for real, I understand. So my sister doesn't answer and you decide to be a dick and ignore her?"

Duke stepped up, putting himself between him and Aster before Bryce could step closer to him. "You heard him, Aster. He fell asleep. He didn't leave her side all night long. He had to be exhausted. Give him a break."

Duke and Aster shared a long look before Duke retreated back to his original spot.

Bryce took a long swallow from his beer and jerked a hand at Duke. "What he said. I might not have high hopes she returns the same sentiment, but I wouldn't ignore her. Her wellbeing is my utmost priority. I fell asleep, and your loud banging woke me up. But if my presence causes her undo pain, I'll stay away."

"She wants you there, you idiot." Aster finished his beer and slammed it on the table. "I can tell. She hasn't voiced it, but I can tell it was bugging her that you didn't return."

"I'll go see her soon. Maybe tomorrow. It's getting late now."

"You'll—"

"You talked to Melody," Griffin said, cutting off whatever Aster was about to spout off.

"I saw her at the cemetery."

Duke frowned. "Why'd you go there?"

His eyes cast downward while he took another sip. Maybe he should've kept that part to himself. "Make peace with Denise, I guess. How do you know I talked to her?"

He hadn't imparted that information to anyone. Hell, he hadn't spoken to anyone since her at the cemetery.

Duke smiled. "She admitted it herself. Turned herself into the precinct for sending the threatening letters to Lila."

"You're charging her?" Bryce didn't know what to think about that. The rumors alone would be enough penance, but it didn't make him sad to see her being charged either. She had caused Lila—and him—to fear for her safety.

"Lila doesn't want to press charges, so no," Griffin answered.

So everyone had been to see Lila throughout the day but him. Now he felt like a cad. He hadn't meant to stay away from her. The exhaustion had taken over.

"I don't think she'll be sticking around town for long though," Duke added.

Bryce wouldn't be surprised by her departure either. She wouldn't be well liked around town. He even warned her of that.

"You'd move to California for my sister?"

He turned his full attention to Aster. "I'd move to the ends of the earth for your sister."

"Then don't keep being an ass and wait until tomorrow. Get your ass over there now."

"Again, what Aster is trying to say is she's worried about you," Griffin said. Though Aster snorted at his response. "You don't have to talk about love and relationships or anything. Check in with her. Let her know you're okay."

He set his unfinished beer on the counter and nodded. "Okay. I never meant to make her worry. I'll go change."

He wasn't ready to see her again so soon. Her rejection was still a fresh wound. But if his absence was causing her pain, he'd rectify that problem immediately.

23

ASTER HAD LEFT a few hours ago. Her sisters decided to leave about twenty minutes ago. She'd had more visitors than she cared to have throughout the day. But now that the room was empty and she was alone, she wanted someone else to arrive. The quiet plucked her nerves and she couldn't say why.

A nurse had given her more pain medication right before her sisters left. It had kicked in and now she felt a dull throb instead of the pulsating ache. She'd be spending a few more days in the hospital to monitor for infection and to heal. She had lost a lot of blood. Her body felt so weak. It had taken a nurse and one of her sisters to help her to the bathroom the first two times. By the third trip, she managed with the help of one person. Tomorrow she hoped she could do it on her own.

Which was insane. She hadn't hurt her legs in the fight for survival. Except her entire body felt like it had been beaten with a mallet and needed recovery from head to toe.

The TV was on low, though she didn't pay any attention to it. Her phone had been busted and Poppy said she'd get her a new one tomorrow. Even if she would've had the device to play on, she didn't think she would.

She was tired, yet wide awake.

A light knock sounded on the door. A quick peek at the clock on the wall said it was past visiting hours. Which she figured was why her sisters had left.

"Come in."

The words came out quieter than she had meant it, but the door opened anyway.

Bryce walked in.

He smiled at her, though his steps were tentative as he approached her bed.

"Hi. I hope it's okay I'm here so late."

"Of course." She gestured with her hand toward the chair on that same side since the wound on her left made it hurt to move that arm. She tried not to use it as much.

He took a seat. The chair wasn't as close to the bed as it had been in the morning when he sat in it. She wished he would've moved it closer.

All day she'd hoped he'd return. His abrupt departure had made a tiny hole in her heart. As the day drew on, the hole got larger and larger.

"How are you feeling?"

She wanted to shrug but stopped herself at the last moment. Simple movements like that were a no-no for the time being. Not until the injury healed a lot more.

"It hurts. I mean, it's dull right now because they gave me something for the pain, but it hurts like a son of a bitch."

He had lost his smile, and she understood why. It didn't make her happy about the situation she was in either.

But she wanted to see his brilliant smile. The one that lit up his beautiful brown eyes.

"You look better." His eyes enlarged, the panic clear as

day. "Not that you looked horrible earlier. You have more color in your cheeks. I'm only trying to say—"

"Bryce," she said, cutting off his rambling, "I know what you meant. And I do feel better than this morning. It was jarring remembering the ambulance ride and nothing else until I woke up in this room. I'm feeling much better."

As better as she could be, but she kept that part to herself. He was already looking like he was ready to bolt again.

She patted her right thigh. "Come closer."

He eyed the spot, frowning, then obeyed. She clasped his hand as soon as it was in reach, sliding her fingers within his. That hole that had formed in her heart started to close.

"I didn't think I'd see you again today. You were gone all day."

He looked down at their intertwined hands. "Not intentionally. I made a visit to the cemetery and then went home, showered, and crashed. I didn't wake up until a little bit ago."

She had no idea he had gone to the cemetery. She wondered if anyone else knew and decided not to inform her of it. Not that it was any of her business.

But since he brought it up...

"And how did your visit go?"

He met her gaze, another beautiful smile emerging. "I made that peace you told me I should do with Denise. It felt good to get everything off my chest."

She squeezed his hand, happy to hear that. His eyes did look less troubled in that sense. Though she still saw despair deep in the depths.

"I also ran into Melody."

"I heard she turned herself in. Griffin asked if I wanted to press charges, and I told him no. I want to move on with my life. I don't fear her. Those threats don't feel as dangerous now that I know who the culprit was."

"I'm sorry she did that to you. That all of this happened to you. You're hurt and in a hospital bed because of me."

She pulled on his hand—not too hard, but enough where he leaned in closer. "None of this is your fault. You do not control the actions of others."

She could tell by his wary expression he didn't believe that. At least not yet.

"I hated how you left this morning. And I try not to use the word hate."

He winced. "I thought it was best I leave."

"After you stayed all night long and rarely left my side?"

"I never want to hurt you. This morning, I handled the entire situation in the wrong way. I conducted myself in a very idiotic manner and I apologize profusely for it. You were in pain—still are—and I want you to get better. Not add more turmoil on your plate."

"Bryce," she pulled on his hand, her lips thinning and her brows lowering into a glare, "if you keep talking to me like you're giving one of your smarmy speeches, I will break your hand." She squeezed it hard to get her point across.

He frowned, silent for the longest time as if repeating his own words in his head. Laughter released. "Wow. Yeah, that was the smarmy politician emerging there."

She giggled, then snorted. Thank heavens for such damn good pain meds because it barely made her ache from the laughing movement.

"Lila, I—"

"If you're not about to tell me you love me, don't keep speaking."

He looked like a deer in headlights.

"If anyone was idiotic this morning, it was me. You

opened yourself up to me, and all I did was question you. Then you walked away, and rightly so. I can't ask you to move away from Sleighville."

"You didn't ask. I offered. It's not the same thing." He lifted her hand, pressing a light kiss to the back of it. "I love you, Lila. Marriage doesn't have to be on the table. I rushed things. But I want you in my life. I need you in it. And I don't care where that happens to be."

"Well, I happen to like it here. Sleighville is growing on me. How will you turn the town around in California? How will I get my ideas and plans running and succeeding if I'm not here either?"

His grip on her hand tightened. "Are you saying you want to stay here?"

"I'm saying I love you too. And marriage isn't too soon for me if it isn't for you."

The town might have something to say about it, but she didn't care any longer. Life was too short. Becca had shown her that close-up. She wasn't going to waste a moment of her happiness because of what others might think.

Bryce dug in his pocket, producing the ring that belonged on her finger. "Will you marry me, Lilac Hansley?"

"Yes." Unshed tears appeared as he slid the ring on her finger. "And you better show me the speech you wrote for the town hall meeting. I want to hear every word you were going to tell the town."

"Does that mean we aren't having a special town meeting for the engagement any longer?"

"I don't care what anyone thinks at this point. So no. That speech is for my eyes only."

He smiled, then lowered until his lips brushed hers. "It's honest and real...and a bit of smarminess embedded in it."

A light giggle erupted along with a snort to go with it. "I wouldn't expect anything less."

"You know we have our work cut out for us. Sex scandal rumors, a vicious murder, a horrendous attack, and a—"

"And a partridge in a pear tree," she finished for him, grinning. "We got this. If anything, we'll play on the town's name. I mean, Sleighville." She cocked a brow. "The first thing that entered my mind when I drove through town was horror-esque. I didn't tell you my real thoughts on it."

"We are not turning this holly, jolly town into a horror show. Nope."

"We'll talk more about it later, Mr. Mayor."

He chuckled. "Ms. Hansley, in light of the recent events, we will have to renegotiate your terms working for the city."

"Okay, fine." More laughter filled the air. It felt so good to laugh. She hoped the pain meds worked for a long period of time because all she wanted to do was laugh and tease and have fun with Bryce. "We won't change the slogan for the town from *Welcome to Sleighville, where you'll have a holly, jolly time.* Not if you don't want to. But hear me out. *Welcome to Sleighville...where mayhem meets murder.* It has a good ring to it."

He looked aghast at even the mere suggestion. A deep ruckus of laughter spilled from his lips. She couldn't help but join in.

"I love you."

His lips drowned out her echo of love in return.

EPILOGUE

A LITTLE OVER ONE MONTH LATER

"THANKS, TAYLOR," Duke said, lifting his coffee to take a sip. He tossed a dollar into the tip jar, grabbed the tray filled with the other coffees he ordered, and left Mocha's Merriment.

He'd already had a cup of coffee before he left for his shift, but he liked to support the local shops as much as he could. While Lila and Bryce were working hard on rebuilding their town to a place full of Christmas joy, it was slow going.

Bryce still hadn't hired anyone to replace Becca's position. And while Duke knew Lila hadn't stepped into the role of secretary, she helped Bryce out while also working as an independent PR consultant for the city. She had so much work to do to turn their image around.

The moment she found out Bryce had wanted to pay her out of his own bank account, she blew a gasket he even thought to do something so outrageous—and so generous. Her ire didn't last too long because she knew it had come from a good place. Juliet had the bright idea to pay her what Becca had been paid. Since they had done that, there wasn't any money in the current budget to hire him a secretary. They were making do for the time being. Duke had to admit they were a dynamite duo in work and out of it.

Tourism was still down, but much better than a few months ago before they hired Lila. Her ideas were always brilliant and worked like a charm. In the moment, anyway. Maintaining the crowds in town was the problem. She would have to keep putting on small events to reel people in until something stuck. Something that would change the entire image around. Duke knew it was taking a toll on her.

Bryce fought her all the time about taking it slow. She had been hurt only about a month ago. She had to do things carefully and keep up with physical therapy. It didn't leave her a whole lot of time for everything she wanted to do.

But in the short time she had, she'd done amazing things. Easter had gone wonderfully. The attendance had been off the charts, considering the recent murder and mayhem that had occurred. She'd had most stores set up social media accounts, constantly monitoring that they were doing their part to stay relevant. Harper also pitched in with that project as well. It was too large for one person alone.

Aster had finally left. While he jumped for joy— privately, of course—he could tell Juliet missed him. Not that she had admitted it to anyone. But Duke knew. He saw the sadness in her eyes at his departure.

In the beginning, he had tried to lift her spirits, but she hadn't seemed receptive to anything he attempted to do or say. So he'd given up even trying. He missed their friendship, and he wasn't even sure where he went wrong. No doubt the whole I-hate-Aster thing did it. Though he had never been outspoken about it. His body language had been loud enough on its own.

He made it to Tinsel Lake, not surprised to see Bryce and Lila already there. But he had meant to be first, so it irked him. He made sure to hide his irritation. Lila needed to slow down.

"Don't even say it," Lila said, and glanced at his hands, smiling as she grabbed her coffee cup. "You're the best, Duke."

"Only for the best." He winked, before turning the tray to Bryce, who grabbed his coffee as well.

Lila gulped down what seemed to be half the contents of the hot liquid, then off she went toward the dock where Teddy and a few members of the football team were hanging a sign.

Teddy and his friends were home for the weekend from college to celebrate the fishing opener. Most people in town loved to fish. The fishing contest they had on opening day was a big hit. Lila was going all out with it this year, even more than they had in previous years.

The Christmas decorations around the lake were big and bright, mingled in with singing fish and poles wrapped like presents under the tree. It had a very merry vibe that he enjoyed seeing.

"She needs to slow down."

Bryce nodded, watching her for the longest time, then looked at him. "I keep trying. She's on this crazy mission, and I can't get through to her. Her shoulder is healing well. The cut on her chest is already healed. But I do worry about her."

"Take her on a vacation."

"Actually, I've been talking with Zinnia and Poppy. We're planning a trip to California. Hopefully, it will help slow her down. I know she wants this town to succeed, but I don't want it to be at her health's expense."

Duke agreed. She'd been through so much. She needed to take the time to heal properly and then go all in. Because he had no doubt in his mind she would bring this town back to the glory it used to have.

"You fishing today?"

Bryce jerked his head toward the left where fishing gear sat. "I convinced Lila she had to join the contest. Which means for the next few hours, she will have no choice but to sit and relax with a pole in her hand."

Duke chuckled. "How long do you think that'll last?"

"Oh, she's competitive. She'll play to win. Though I know she'll let someone else take the ultimate prize because she wants people to keep coming back for more."

Duke wished them luck and they parted ways. An hour later, Bryce, as the mayor, gave a riveting speech, and wished everyone good luck on the lake. Some people were in boats. Others fished from the shore. Some even sat on the docks sprinkled around the perimeter of the lake. The event was lively and full of people. Duke, Theo, Griffin, and two other officers patrolled the area, ready for any sort of mishap or problem to arise. Generally, though, not many eventful things happened on the fishing opener other than people squabbling over who had the bigger catch.

There were thirty minutes left until the time would be up. Everyone would have to reel in their catches and find out who had the biggest prize.

"Hey, Chief, you might want to come around to the north side of the lake. We have a problem," Theo's voice crackled through the radio.

Duke cut short the conversation he'd been having with a few folks and decided to check out the issue as well.

He used the four-wheeler he'd brought along, making it to Theo in short order. Not a lot of people had set up camp to fish on this portion of the lake. Which turned out to be a good thing.

Because a dead body was never what they wanted to find and for people to witness.

Ronan stood to the side, near Theo. Duke formulated he had found the body. Or had fished it out if the pole near the body was any indication. Griffin had also arrived.

"Seal this area off. Don't let anyone close," Griffin said in a subdued tone, looking at Theo.

Duke leaned closer, checking out the tattered clothes. The body appeared to have been submerged for a long time, the features indistinguishable to make out who the person could be. But the name tag still pinned to the shirt was clue enough.

"Beth Terden." Duke stood up. "She worked at Noel's Cafe. Abruptly left, leaving Juliet in the lurch. That's around the same time Eve appeared and took her position last summer."

Griffin nodded, remembering. "Apparently, she didn't leave town." He looked at Ronan. "You dragged her out of the water."

He jerked his head once. "My line caught on something. As soon as I saw what it was, I pulled her out. I hope I didn't contaminate anything."

"The water did a good job of that already. It's okay, Ronan. I was only double checking," Griffin said.

Duke looked out at the water to where Bryce sat in a boat with Lila. "Is there any way to keep this information from Lila?"

Laughter burst from Griffin. Even Ronan chuckled, knowing why he'd said it.

Bryce had conveyed her thoughts on turning their town from merry to horror. With another murder on their hands, it wasn't a far-off concept to accept.

"Duke, it's your case. If you want it."

Theo had responded first, but he had seniority. It would be his first murder. Officially. Denise's death didn't count.

"I'll take it."

His first step would be to talk to Juliet. Not something he relished.

They'd grown so far apart, they felt like strangers.

But oh well, he had a job to do.

———

WANT TO SEE HOW GRIFFIN AND EVE MET? READ DASHING THROUGH THE FEAR!

For Griffin & Eve's story, check out
Dashing Through the Fear
A Sleighville Novel, #1

Welcome to Sleighville...where you are sure to have a holly, jolly time.

Running is her only option. He made sure of that. Where better to run to than the last place he'd ever think to look for her. Sleighville. A small, quaint town that celebrates Christmas—every. Single. Day. Just the thought makes her want to puke, but she's out of options. Nothing prepared her for small-town camaraderie. Everyone knowing everyone and everything. Where she lives, where she works, and worst of all...they know something is off. That she's not who she claims to be.

Griffin isn't sure what to make of his new neighbor, but one thing he does know: he can't resist a puzzle. She's skittish, wary, and one of the most beautiful women he's ever met. It's not hard to fall for her, which is bad. He has no doubt she's hiding something—or hiding *from* something. If only she'd let him in, trust him with her secrets. No amount of Christmas cheer is going to sway her his way, but patience and time might. Problem is, he fears he doesn't have much time. She's one step away from running. No doubt not her first time, but he'll do whatever it takes to make sure she stays right where she is. In his town, and in his arms.

FOR DUKE & NOEL'S STORY, CHECK OUT
THE LAST NOEL
A SLEIGHVILLE NOVEL, #3

Welcome to Sleighville...where truth and lies lurk below the surface.

Officer Duke Fisk's life has been one disappointment after another. A cold murder case, married friends while he's the last man standing, and the woman he loves sees him as a brother. When mysterious Noel Lancaster strolls into town giving him sultry looks, he decides it's time for a bit of fun. Just a fling to escape his funk. Except Duke's not built for casual.

Noel Lancaster came to Sleighville for one reason: to find whoever killed her sister. Infiltrating this cheerful town won't be easy when she can't reveal why she's really there. It becomes impossible when she gets involved with Duke—the lead officer on her sister's case.

As Noel digs deeper, dangerous secrets surface along with deadly threats. She knows once Duke learns the truth, he'll hate her forever. But she'll risk everything—her heart and her life—to catch her sister's killer.

Dive into this thrilling holiday romance with a deadly twist, where you'll find merriment and murder all wrapped up with a heart-pounding ending that will leave you breathless.

ABOUT THE AUTHOR

I'm a *USA Today* Bestselling Author that loves to write contemporary romance and romantic suspense novels, although I am partial to romantic suspense. I even dabble in paranormal. Honestly, I love anything that has to do with romance. As long as there's a happy ending, I'm a happy camper. And insta-love...yes, please! I love baseball (Go Twins!) and creating awesome crafts. I graduated with a Bachelor's Degree in Criminal Justice, working in that field for several years before I became a stay-at-home mom. I have a few more amazing stories in the works. If you would like to learn more about me and my books, head to my website by scanning the QR code. Thanks for reading!

Scan me